The Devil in the Details

Sherlock Holmes Bookshop Mysteries

The Incident of the Book in the Nighttime
The Sign of Four Spirits
The Game Is a Footnote
A Three Book Problem
A Curious Incident
There's a Murder Afoot
A Scandal in Scarlet
The Cat of the Baskervilles
Body on Baker Street
Elementary, She Read

Lighthouse Library Mysteries (writing as Eva Gates)

Shot Through the Book
The Stranger in the Library
Death Knells and Wedding Bells
Death by Beach Read
Deadly Ever After
A Death Long Overdue
Read and Buried
Something Read, Something Dead
The Spook in the Stacks
Reading Up a Storm
Booked for Trouble
By Book or by Crook

Ashley Grant Mysteries

Coral Reef Views
Blue Water Hues
White Sand Blues

Year Round Christmas Mysteries

A Slay Ride Together With You
Have Yourself a Deadly Little Christmas
Dying in a Winter Wonderland
Silent Night, Deadly Night
Hark the Herald Angels Slay
We Wish You a Murderous Christmas
Rest Ye Murdered Gentlemen

The Devil in the Details

A SHERLOCK HOLMES BOOKSHOP MYSTERY

Vicki Delany

NEW YORK

Books should be disposed of and recycled according to local requirements. All paper materials used are FSC compliant.

This is a work of fiction. All of the names, characters, organizations, places and events portrayed in this novel are either products of the author's imagination or are used fictitiously. Any resemblance to real or actual events, locales, or persons, living or dead, is entirely coincidental.

Published in the United States by Crooked Lane Books, an imprint of The Quick Brown Fox & Company LLC.

Crooked Lane Books and its logo are trademarks of The Quick Brown Fox & Company LLC.

Library of Congress Catalog-in-Publication data available upon request.

ISBN (hardcover): 979-8-89242-211-6
ISBN (ebook): 979-8-89242-212-3

Cover design by Joe Burleson

Printed in the United States.

www.crookedlanebooks.com

Crooked Lane Books
34 West 27th St., 10th Floor
New York, NY 10001

First Edition: January 2026

The authorized representative in the EU for product safety and compliance is eucomply OÜPärnu mnt 139b-14, 11317 Tallinn, Estonia, hello@eucompliancepartner.com, +33757690241

10 9 8 7 6 5 4 3 2 1

To Nolan and Isla Webb

Chapter One

For reasons unknown to everyone, Sherlock Holmes's birthday is celebrated every year on January 6. For reasons obvious to everyone, Jayne Wilson's birthday is also celebrated every year on January 6. Because that's the date on which she was born.

Which meant that I had two birthday parties to attend in one day.

In the afternoon, the Sherlock Holmes Bookshop and Emporium, of which I am half-owner, full manager, general shop clerk, cat wrangler, and occasional scullery maid, put on a party complete with balloons, streamers, and books on sale. Tea and tea-time sandwiches were served along with an elaborately decorated cake topped by a cutout of the silhouette of the Great Detective as most commonly known: deerstalker hat on head, magnifying glass in hand. The party was well attended. Not only bookshop regulars, but Sherlockians from far and wide came. No one loves a party more than a bunch of Sherlock aficionados. And few people love a sale more, particularly if they happen upon a volume that by chance they'd overlooked earlier.

First party over, old stock cleaned out, used cups, dirty dishes, and the few leftovers returned to Mrs. Hudson's Tea Room, door locked behind the last celebrant, vacuum cleaner put to use, shop cat fed and watered, it was time to get myself ready for the next birthday party.

This time, I wasn't going to be the host. I didn't have to pretend to be enjoying myself, I could really enjoy myself. Even better, I wouldn't have to stay behind to clean up.

Still, I shouldn't complain. The birthday girl herself had put in a great deal of work for the afternoon party, mainly in terms of making the cake and sandwiches, and preparing everything to be perfectly presented.

It had all been flawless, as anything Jayne did always was.

I'm Gemma Doyle, and I own the Sherlock Holmes Bookshop and Emporium, located at 222 Baker Street, West London, Massachusetts. I also own one quarter of Mrs. Hudson's Tea Room, which occupies 220 Baker Street. Jayne Wilson, birthday girl, baker extraordinaire, best friend, owns one half of the restaurant. My great-uncle Arthur Doyle is a silent partner in both businesses. Silent for good reason. Uncle Arthur has a great many life skills, but the efficient running of a business is not among them.

"My friend Rachel's a bartender at the Blue Water Café." Ashleigh, one of my shop clerks, clattered down the seventeen steps from the upper level, pulling on gloves, wrapping a long scarf around her neck, zipping up her coat. All at the same time. "She says it's going to be a big night. Andy's pulling out all the stops."

"I'd expect nothing less."

"Are you going to dress all glam, like?"

"Whatever glam means," I said. The most "glam" thing I owned was the dress I bought the previous autumn at Harrods in London for my sister's wedding. The reason I had to go shopping at Harrods as soon as it opened on the day of the wedding was that my luggage failed to arrive at the same time I did, and I couldn't go to my only sibling's nuptials in my travel-stained (literally in the case of the coffee I'd spilled down my front at the very start of the endless journey) clothes. My mother had taken me on the shopping expedition, my mother who is not known for her restraint in spending on clothes. Particularly when it's someone else's money.

And so tonight I had a very "glam" dress to wear.

"Have fun," Ashleigh said as she slipped out the door. "Take lots of pictures."

I glanced at the clock on the wall behind the sales counter, hanging next to a framed reproduction of Beeton's Christmas Annual, November 1887, the first time Sherlock Holmes appeared in print. Next to which was a shelf containing the glass statue presented to Great-Uncle Arthur for his efforts in promoting the tales beyond England's shores.

Arthur was highly proud of that statue, although honesty forces me to admit, although never to his face, that Sherlock Holmes scarcely needs any promotion anywhere these days. As evidenced by the fact that I can run an entire, and very profitable, business dedicated to nothing but the Great Detective and his creator, and their lives and times.

I had a sudden thought. Maybe Uncle Arthur wasn't as proud of the award as he said he was. Otherwise, why was it here, in the shop, and not at home in his study, which is jammed full of his lifetime of memorabilia?

"A matter to consider another day," I said to the sole remaining shop employee, Moriarty.

If Moriarty were human, he would have curled his upper lip in distain. As it was, he turned and walked away, hips swaying, tail held high. My shop cat is not, to put it mildly, all that fond of me. I've never quite understood why. He gets on well with our customers. He lets young children pat him and elderly ladies fuss over him. He gets along fine with Ashleigh and Gale, my other human employees, and with the staff from the tearoom.

It's only me he doesn't like. Me and Ryan Ashburton, lead detective with the West London police, who also happens to be the man in my life.

I sometimes wonder if Moriarty, the cat, fancies himself an eight-pound version of Moriarty, the master criminal. If so, and if he regards me as some sort of female Sherlock Holmes with curly hair and a tendency to put on weight if I'm not careful, it might account for his distain, if not occasional outright hostility.

"You won't burn down the shop while I'm out, will you?" I said as he settled himself into his bed under the center display table. He did not reply.

I considered checking for concealed pyrotechnic devices before leaving, but I was running short of time. I had to get home, wrap the gift I'd delayed getting until the last minute, "glam" myself up, and head to the restaurant for the party.

It was a few minutes after five, but in early January in Massachusetts it was almost fully dark outside. I bundled myself up, turned out the lights, locked the doors behind me, and walked rapidly down Baker Street in the direction of the harbor.

The windows of most of the restaurants and shops still twinkled with holiday decorations. Illuminated wreaths hung from the tops of lampposts. A strong cold wind blew off the ocean. I wrapped my navy-blue wool and cashmere coat around me, pulled my scarf tighter, and picked up my pace as I approached Harbor Road.

The Devil in the Details

Harbor Road is aptly named. In the summer, the waterside boardwalk is lined with tubs of flowers and crowded with tourists eating ice cream, watching fishing boats unloading and seals playing in the water, visiting the small lighthouse, buying crafts to take home or fresh fish and farm produce for dinner, or finding a seat at the outdoor coffee shops where they can watch other people doing all of those things. Those who don't want to cook for themselves are offered a choice of dining establishments ranging from hot dog stands to full-service bars and restaurants. The boardwalk runs along the small harbor where charter boats bob at anchor and pleasure cruisers tie up for a visit to town. The public pier circles the harbor to the north of the intersection with Baker Street; to the south, jutting over the water, sits the open deck (currently closed for the season) of the Blue Water Café, the setting for this evening's celebration.

Tonight, the boardwalk was mostly empty, flowers in the tubs dug up, awnings pulled down over the cafés and ice cream shops, vendors' booths closed. But the beam of the lighthouse still flashed, as it would throughout the night, and inside the restaurant all the lights were on. Through the wide windows I could see staff laying tables. I wasn't close enough to read the sign on the menu board outside, but I knew what it said. The restaurant would be closed for a private event.

Jayne's birthday party.

This wasn't a particularly memorable birthday, not a year ending in a five or a zero, but Andy Whitehall was making a heck of a big deal out of it.

The birthday party would likely rival their wedding, scheduled for six days from today. Andy initially suggested having the wedding reception at his own restaurant, but Jayne had, wisely, put her foot firmly down. Jayne might be small of stature and soft-spoken, but when Jayne's size-six foot goes down, it stays down.

She knew if Andy's place hosted the reception, he'd spend most of the party on his feet, popping in and out of the kitchen, tasting the food, making adjustments to the seasonings or the garnishes. Yelling at his highly competent staff. Andy would want everything to be perfect for Jayne's wedding, and he still didn't quite understand that his love and attention were all she needed to make the occasion perfect.

* * *

It's my nature to be early anyway, but as the head bridesmaid for Jayne's wedding, I wanted to be at the birthday party before most of the guests arrived. The party wasn't intended to be a pre-wedding reception, but various relatives had come to the Cape ahead of time and had been invited to the dinner. Jayne's brother, Jeff, was in town, and he and his wife would bring Jayne to the restaurant, along with Leslie, their mom.

Me, I was on my own.

Ryan was out of town, some sort of ill-timed police training thing. Fortunately, the training thing would be finished in a few days, so he'd make it home in time for the wedding. Good thing, too, as he was the best man.

Uncle Arthur and I had spent a quiet Christmas morning together in the 1756 saltbox house we share, enjoying mimosas and almond croissants, made by Jayne herself at her bakery, opening presents from each other and our family back in England. Ryan, our friend Donald Morris, Jayne and Andy, and Leslie Wilson joined us later for dinner. Uncle Arthur is the cook in our house, and he made a hearty English roast of beef, served as it should be with Yorkshire pudding, roast potatoes, three veg, and dark rich gravy. Jayne brought homemade fruit tarts for dessert. I'd managed to put together a charcuterie board for pre-dinner snacking while opening more presents.

Before December was over, Uncle Arthur packed a bag, bid the dogs farewell, remembered at the last minute to say goodbye to me, and leapt into a taxi to take him to the airport. I assumed he was headed somewhere hot as he took only one carry-on suitcase. I didn't ask where he was going. He likely didn't know. Uncle Arthur joined the Royal Navy the day he finished school and spent the rest of his life, until compulsory retirement reached him, at sea. Over those years, he'd risen through the ranks from common sailor to master and commander of one of HRH's battleships. The sea still called to Uncle Arthur, and when she beckoned, he answered. He'd been invited to the wedding, and he promised to be back in time. I wasn't holding my breath.

I dressed carefully and studied myself in the mirror. Little I could ever do about my hair—those dratted curls! But I'd added a rare touch of blush to my cheeks, mascara to my lashes, and dark red lipstick to my lips. My dress was navy blue, a wide chiffon skirt with a lacy overskirt, boat neck, elbow-length sleeves, and a thin belt. With some effort, I'd managed to save the overly expensive Harrods dress after it had been in a bar brawl at a top London nightclub (don't ask).

Tonight, as I intended to enjoy a few glasses of the no-doubt excellent wine Andy would order specifically for this party, I'd take a cab home, so I decided to walk to the restaurant. If I did that, I'd have to wear my boots, but I could carry my party shoes in a bag. Snow had started falling while I'd been getting ready, and when I let the dogs in from one last after-dinner romp, they shook a pile of the white stuff onto the mudroom floor.

"I won't be too late," I said to them. "Guard the house."

Violet wagged her stubby tail, which I took to be agreement. Peony sat down and licked ice off his paw.

A cab was pulling up to the house next door to ours as I came down the front step. My neighbor, Mrs. Ramsbatten, was on her front porch waiting for it, and she spotted me as she headed for the car. "Gemma! Are you going to Jayne's party? Would you like a lift? I meant to make the offer earlier, but everything got ahead of me."

"That would be nice," I said.

Mrs. Ramsbatten, all four-foot-eleven of her, might look like the stereotypical elderly neighborhood widow, somewhat confused, always well-meaning, but although her eyesight was failing, and she needed the assistance of a cane to get around, her razor-sharp mind was as alert as ever.

Chapter Two

Our cab pulled up in front of the Blue Water Café. The interior was a blaze of lights. The outdoor deck area on the edge of the pier was closed in winter, but small white lights trimmed the railings, casting a sparkling glow onto the water below. Snow fell softly but steadily, appearing to dance in the glow of the lights. Waves slapped against the pilings holding up the pier and the small boat dock below it. The sea was a vast expanse of black velvet, broken by the few lights from passing ships.

The reception area of the restaurant was full of colorful, sparkling balloons, all bearing messages of some type of birthday greeting. Mrs. Ramsbatten and I handed the hostess our coats and my boot bag, and Andy came running to welcome us. He was so excited, he almost bounced on his toes. Andy was a small man, thin and slightly shorter than me. Most of the time, he was a picture of calm control, but tonight he was a ball of nervous energy. He wore a gray suit and stiffly ironed white shirt with a black tie. He'd made an attempt to slick back his dark blond hair but tufts were escaping already. His warm brown eyes danced with pleasure. "You're here!" He wrapped me in a hug.

"Where else would I be?" I said, once I'd freed myself. English to my core, I don't always care to be almost smothered, even by the closest of friends.

"Mrs. Ramsbatten, welcome, welcome!" Andy cried. "Please, allow me to escort you to a seat."

"That would be lovely, thank you. My, but the place looks nice tonight. Not that it doesn't always look nice," she hastened to add.

And it did look nice. Small electric candles burned on every table, next to a single fresh red rose in a thin glass vase. Silver cutlery shone and glassware sparkled. The bare wood of the tables was exposed, with blue placemats and ironed blue linen napkins set at each place.

A table by the corridor leading to the kitchen and restrooms was piled high with gifts. I took Mrs. Ramsbatten's colorfully wrapped parcel from her and said, "I'll put these with the others."

"I don't know if Jayne will open them tonight," Andy said. "We'll see how it all goes. I'm sorry Ryan couldn't make it."

"So is he," I said. "But he'll be home in time for the wedding." I never apologize for Uncle Arthur's absences. Everyone was used to them by now.

The restaurant began filling up as guests arrived. Waitstaff circled with glasses of wine and trays of small canapés, while the bartenders were busy with individual orders.

"Robbie," I said as a waiter thrust a platter of crab cakes at me. "Didn't expect to see you here. How are you doing?"

He shrugged. "Okay, I guess." When last I'd seen Robbie Ellis, he'd just broken up with Jayne. I never could stand him, and I was nothing but delighted when she ended the relationship and he left town shortly after. He told everyone who asked, and many who didn't, he'd decided small-town life wasn't for him. He was an *artist*; he needed to get away from our provincial town and breathe the free air of the big city in order to fully develop his talent.

That he was back in West London serving canapés came as no surprise to me. His artistic talent was as thin as his personality. I was surprised he was working here, though. Andy had known Jayne when she and Robbie were dating. Andy had long adored Jayne from afar, and it took her longer than it should have to realize it. And to realize she felt the same toward him.

I'd like to be able to claim I had something to do with that, but I hadn't. Jayne always did come to her senses eventually.

As for why Robbie was working here tonight, I assumed kindhearted Andy believed the past was the past. I wasn't so sure about Robbie.

I accepted a crab cake. "You know Andy and Jayne are getting married next week, don't you?"

"Yeah, Gemma, I know. Kinda hard to miss. I'm okay with it." His smile didn't reach his eyes. He'd always liked me as much as I liked him. "I'm here for the winter, like. Things are quiet in the Big Apple in the winter. I'm . . . helping out my mom, like. Just for a couple months."

"Sure you are. How nice of you." I popped the crab cake into my mouth. Absolutely delicious. I turned to grab another, but Robbie and his tray had moved off.

Instead, I nabbed a passing glass of white wine. It was offered to me by another familiar face. "Ashleigh? What are you doing here?"

"Working," she said with a grin. "Surprise! You do glam up nice, Gemma. My friend Rachel told me Andy needed extra staff for tonight. It gets quiet in the restaurant business around here in the winter, and most of the summer help is gone. I don't mind. Bring in some extra cash, plus a chance for a night out with the glitterati of West London."

"And you just happen to have the perfect outfit for it. You never fail to amaze me, Ashleigh."

She grinned at me and moved on. Ashleigh has the largest wardrobe of anyone I've ever known. Her closet must rival that of the Princess of Wales on tour. But, unlike the princess, Ashleigh has a ready-to-go maid's outfit. Whereas the rest of the staff were in regular black skirts or trousers with white shirts and trainers, Ashleigh wore a calf-length black dress with a neat white collar under a knee-length white apron with a lace-trimmed bodice, thick black stockings, sturdy black shoes with black laces. She even had a pert white mobcap on her head and her hair was scraped tightly back.

"Is that Ashleigh?" a woman said to me. "She could be auditioning for a part in Downton Abbey."

I smiled at Irene Talbot, ace reporter (actually the only full-time reporter) for the *West London Star*. "I'm beginning to regret my choice of outfit," she said with a frown. "I fit right in, and not in the way I intended." She wore black trousers and a sleek black satin shirt. Only the red shoes with four-inch heels and the unfastened top three buttons of the shirt distinguished her from the waitstaff. The red glass earrings in her ears and the large red stone nestled in her cleavage threw off reflected lights. Her lipstick matched the color of the shoes and jewelry.

"I think you're safe," I said. "I'd like another one of those crab cakes, but the waiter seems to have disappeared."

"Robbie Ellis. I saw him lurking about in town the other day. He's probably outside having a smoke."

Andy was passing at that moment, and he came to a sudden halt. "Robbie. Are you looking for him? He's in the kitchen."

"I was only joking," Irene said quickly. "It was nice of you to hire him considering . . ."

"Considering what?"

"Nothing."

"You had a crab cake, Gemma. How was it?"

"Super," I said.

His eyes narrowed and he peered at me. "Not too spicy?"

"Moderately spicy, just the way I like it. Is there a problem?"

"No. No." He hesitated. "My new sous-chef, he sometimes likes to do things his own way. I thought he was chopping too many jalapeños to add to the crab and told him so. He started to argue, but I cut him off. I didn't see if he used them all once my back was turned."

"I liked them. Loved them, I should say."

"You need to trust your staff, Andy," Irene said with a smile. "You wouldn't have hired this new guy if you didn't think he was up to the job, would you? I assume he has good references?"

"Yeah, he does. He worked at a seafood place in New York City for a couple years. Has plans to open his own restaurant one day, and he thought the Cape was a better place to try to break in." His eyes lit up and he grabbed his phone out of his pocket, all thoughts of overly spicy crab cakes forgotten. "They're here!" He almost sprinted for the door, and then he turned and said, "Please enjoy yourselves and let our staff know if you need anything."

"Always the host," Irene said with a laugh.

"Which is why this is rapidly becoming known as the best restaurant in West London, if not in the entire Lower Cape," I said. "Andy's going to have to learn to give up some degree of control if he wants a pleasant married life and maybe a family someday."

"Goes for Jayne too. I can't imagine the sort of hours she puts in at that bakery. Change that, I can imagine it and it gives me the shivers. His hours too. Oh, look. Ashleigh's back and this time she has crostini. I love crostini." Irene set off in pursuit.

I was about to join her, but at that moment, applause began to spread through the room, and I looked toward the entrance to see Jayne, blushing and radiant. Her arm was tucked into Andy's and his grin was so broad, the restaurant could have managed without all the candlelight. Jayne looked stunning in a low-cut dress of emerald green that swept her ankles. Tonight, she wore three-inch heels, which still didn't make her reach my height. Her long blond hair was swept up behind her head, held in place by a sparkling clip. Then again, Jayne looked stunning in a hairnet and an apron covered in floury handprints. Her mother, Leslie, and her brother, Jeff, along with Jeff's wife, Christy, followed her. Jayne's father died a number of years ago.

Someone bumped my elbow and I half turned. It was Robbie, clutching an almost empty tray of canapés. His brown eyes were on Jayne, but unlike everyone else in the room, he was not smiling. Instead, as he watched her, something dark moved across his face. He turned to look at Andy and the scowl deepened. His knuckles were turning white where he gripped his tray.

"Careful there," I said in a low voice. "We don't want any food getting spilled."

He started, and then he realized I was talking to him and he turned toward me. His teeth flashed, but the smile contained no warmth. "She looks nice, Jayne."

"Yes."

"Woulda thought she'd want more out of life than marriage to a cook."

"Better a cook than a waiter." I don't often speak without thinking, and instantly I wanted to bite back the words. But it was too late, as it always is. Robbie studied my face for a long time. I did not look away.

"Better get more of these things," he said at last. "People seem to like them." He took a step toward the kitchen, then turned. His words were almost lost in the chatter all around us and cries of "Happy birthday" as Jayne and Andy made their way across the room greeting their guests. "Watch yourself, Doyle. Accidents can happen in restaurants, or so they tell me."

Chapter Three

"Was that Robbie with you?" Jayne said to me.

"The one and only."

"He shouldn't have run off like that before I got a chance to say hi."

"He's working here now," I said. "Part-time job. He's home for the winter to help his mom."

"That's so nice of him. I heard she was having health issues." She smiled at Andy. With her heels on, the two of them were the same height. "And so nice of you to hire him. It can be hard finding work around here in the winter." They moved off to greet other guests.

"So Robbie's back," Leslie Wilson said to me.

"Yup. I don't dare eat another one of those crab cakes."

"What does that mean?"

"Nothing. Nothing. Hi, Jeff. Nice to see you."

Jayne's brother greeted me and then asked his mother, "Can I get you something from the bar, Mom?"

"A beer would be good. I'll save the wine for dinner." She looked around the crowded room. "Someone told me they're calling this the social event of the season. I thought she was joking, but she might not have been. I can't remember the last time I saw everyone so dressed up, outside of a wedding. Did Andy invite everyone in West London?"

"Looks like it."

"I see some people I don't know. Andy's relatives, do you suppose?"

"Probably." I also recognized most of the guests, if not by name, then from them passing through my shop or the tearoom. Leslie was heavily involved in many charities and social groups, and her network of acquaintances would be even larger than mine. "He told me some of the wedding guests decided to make a winter holiday of the occasion and came early."

"I see Pete and Trish Whitehall," Leslie said, referring to Andy's parents. "I'll go over and say hi. When Jeff gets back with my beer, tell him where I got to."

"Will do," I said.

I'm not particularly good at making small talk with people I scarcely know, so I looked around for someone I did know. Mrs. Ramsbatten had found a seat at a table and was deep in conversation with Fiona, who worked at Mrs. Hudson's.

I was delighted to spot Donald Morris, attired for the occasion in his best reproduction nineteenth-century menswear, and I headed toward him. He was talking to a man about his own age—early fifties—wearing a brown tweed sports jacket over a button-down blue shirt. Donald's companion's salt-and-pepper hair (more salt than pepper) was cut short at the back and sides and slightly longer at the front to flip back over his forehead. His gray beard was neatly trimmed. A tiny silver ring ran through the lobe of his right ear.

". . . an intense lifelong interest in spiritualism that was best—" Donald broke off as he saw me approach. "George, have you met Gemma Doyle?"

"I haven't had the pleasure," George said. His deep brown eyes stared into mine as he held out his recently manicured hand. Maybe it's because I'm in love with a cop, but I don't entirely trust men with manicures. I took the hand anyway. His grip was surprisingly limp and cool. "Your friend here is telling me all about Sir Arthur Conan Doyle. Fascinating stuff." His tone contradicted his words, and I smothered a smile. Once someone fell into conversation with Donald, they found themselves trapped in a tsunami of Doyle or Holmes trivia, unable to escape without being overly rude.

"Gemma owns the Sherlock Holmes Bookshop and Emporium," Donald said. George smiled politely, his vacant expression telling me (if not Donald) he was not the least bit interested. He made a valiant effort not to let his eyes wander around the room, seeking someone more interesting to talk to. "It's at 222 Baker Street," Donald continued. "Not entirely the desired address, but number 221 wasn't for sale when Gemma's great-uncle Arthur Doyle was looking to buy. You're clearly wondering if Arthur Doyle is a relation of Sir Arthur. On that, opinions differ. Gemma insists—"

Most people find themselves trapped by Donald's enthusiasm because they're too polite to change the topic or simply walk away. I myself have no such qualms. "How do you know Andy or Jayne, George?" I asked.

His eyes refocused and a genuine smile touched his mouth. "I haven't yet had the honor of meeting the lady, but Andy and I go way back. I own a couple of places in Hyannis, and Andy worked for me at one time. He was too good a cook to stay with me for long, and I lost him to your charming town. I'm giving some thought to opening a place near here." His gesture took in the entire restaurant. "Gonna be hard to compete with this place, though. The setting alone can't be beat. Not in summer anyway, when that deck's open."

"Andy was lucky," I said. "The restaurant here before this one was more of a hot dog and burger shack—"

"I've often wondered," Donald interrupted in an attempt to participate in the conversation, "what Sherlock Holmes would have thought of our modern fast food. I suspect he would have entirely approved. He enjoyed his formal dinners at Mancini's restaurant, but generally he ate whatever he was given. When he bothered to eat at all. Mrs. Hudson, that's his landlady—"

"I know the story," George said, not referring to Sherlock's dining habits. "It was a good hot dog and burger shack. Very popular. It caught fire one winter's night, and the owners didn't want to rebuild, so they sold what was left of the building. Exactly when Andy was looking for a place for his own restaurant. Lucky for Andy."

"And . . ." I waved my arms in the air, taking in the crowd, the atmosphere, the laughter, the clink of glasses, the wonderful scents emanating from the kitchen, and the soft murmur of the sea beyond the windows, rushing to shore. "Here we are today."

"Rumor at the time said the fire might not have been an accident."

"I didn't know that."

George shrugged. "Nothing but a rumor. No charges were ever laid." His gaze left my face as his attention was caught by something happening behind me. I turned my head to see Andy and Jayne chatting with Irene. "Good timing for Andy, though." George lifted his glass in a salute.

* * *

I wasn't entirely sure what George was implying; I wasn't even sure he'd been implying anything, but I took pity on the guy and pointed out to Donald that one of our shop regulars was arriving and searching for someone to talk to. My friend bustled off, likely to ask her if she'd read a good book lately. George muttered apologies and made a beeline for the bar.

"Isn't this a fabulous evening, Gemma," Bunny Leigh said to me. "Reminds me of the time my manager—that's Rupert, you remember meeting him—put on a surprise party for me at . . . goodness, the name escapes me at the moment. In my day, it was the hottest place in L.A."

I hadn't exactly "met" the late Rupert. I had (entirely against my better instincts) once attended a séance at which the gentleman in question put in a (supposed) appearance via a fake medium. Not that there's such a thing as a real medium. I didn't bother to point that out, but I watched Bunny hail a passing waitress, who just happened to be her own daughter. "You look *soooo* adorable, honey," she gushed. "Perfect costume."

"Thanks. Can I get you a drink?" Ashleigh asked.

"A dirty martini would be wonderful, thank you, dear. Why are you carrying that tray?"

"To serve drinks on. I'm working tonight, Bunny."

Bunny's nose crinkled in thought. Once upon a time, the crinkling of that perfect little nose would have had teenage girls in fits of ecstasy. Bunny had been a major pop star in her youth, but her fame, along with her youth, soon faded and now she lived in West London, always planning the never-to-happen comeback. "You're working here? But you work at Gemma's store. Gale's here as a guest, as are the women from the tearoom."

"I was invited," Ashleigh said. "But when I heard Andy needed staff, I decided this would be fun. Make a few bucks too. I won't work at the wedding, promise."

"If you're short of money, honey . . ." Bunny said, a touch reluctantly.

"I'm good. Thanks, Mom. One dirty martini coming right up."

Bunny blinked in confusion. She'd been discovered almost the day she stepped off the bus from Lincoln, Nebraska, and had shot straight to the top of the pop charts. She'd lost most of her money in the following years, a combination of bad luck, bad men, bad financial advice. She still had a small income, enough to get by on, if she lived modestly, which she did. The idea of working for a living was a nebulous concept to Bunny Leigh.

"May I offer you some crab cakes, Miss Leigh?" Robbie held out his platter and gave Bunny a little dip of the head.

"Thank you." She took one. And then she took another. Robbie turned to me. He did not bow, nor did he smile. I wondered if someone had opened a window as a chill washed over me.

"No, thanks," I said.

"You should be proud of your daughter," I said, once Robbie moved on. "She works hard, she's not afraid to get her hands dirty, and she's learning the ropes at the shop. I have absolutely no doubt one day she'll have that bookstore empire she's dreaming of."

"I suppose." Bunny soon lost interest in me and her gaze wandered around the room. "Good heavens, who is that adorable man over there? The one at the bar, talking to Irene Talbot?"

"His name's George. Didn't get his last name. He's a restaurant owner."

"A new man in West London. A handsome one to boot, and not a sign of a pack of kids begging to go to the beach. He's not even wearing a wedding ring." She abandoned me in flash.

"Where'd Bunny go?" Ashleigh appeared at my side, her tray bearing a full martini glass with a single olive on a toothpick.

"I'll take that," I said, as I did so. "Thanks."

I carried the drink across the room. Jayne was standing next to her tower of gifts, momentarily alone.

"I know you're rather fond of a dirty martini." I handed her the glass.

She accepted it with a smile. "The perfect bridesmaid. I didn't even have to say I could use a drink and, poof, here it is."

"Where'd Andy get to?"

"Some trouble in the kitchen." She took a sip. "Yum. This is nice. And that, Gemma, is why I insisted on not having my wedding reception here. Andy promised he'd leave everything tonight to his staff, but I knew he wouldn't be able to keep that promise."

"His attention to detail is what makes this restaurant such a success."

Her smiled died and she frowned. "I know that. I do. But . . . other chefs manage to let other people take over sometimes. Many of the best chefs in the world have several restaurants. They can't be in all of them, all the time, so they hire the best people they can and trust them to get on with it. I mean . . . I just wish . . . I . . ."

I put my hand on her arm. "Andy can do that too. And he will. He had a great time in England in the fall, didn't he? He scarcely thought about the restaurant the entire time he was away."

She smiled at me. "He did keep thinking up new ways to cook fish when he was at that fancy fishing lodge, but other than that, you're right."

"As I usually am. Tonight's so very special to him, Jayne. That makes him nervous and overly protective. Cut him some slack."

"He's not too happy with Martin, his new sous-chef. The guy came with great references, but Andy's worried he's the sort to do things his own way when Andy's not looking. Some imagination is fine and Andy's always open to suggestions, but he fears this guy's fiddling with his cherished recipes."

"Tonight, none of that is your problem. Relax and enjoy yourself. Everyone here is here because they love you."

"That's a nice thought, but not entirely true. I don't even know some of these people."

"And once you get to know them, they will love you."

"To know me is to love me," she said with a laugh.

"I have no idea what you two are talking about, but I have to agree with it." Andy slipped his arm around Jayne's shoulders. "We're ready, if you are."

"Ready," she said.

"Ready for what?" I asked.

"The three best words in the English language," Jayne said. "Time for dinner."

Chapter Four

Andy stepped forward and clapped his hands. The room fell quiet as everyone turned toward him and all conversation stopped. From the kitchen came the clatter of serving dishes. Glasses clinked as the bartender put them on a waiter's tray. I was standing next to Jayne, watching Andy. I half turned to give my friend a smile, but the smile died on my face.

Robbie Ellis stood by the swinging doors to the kitchen. His eyes were fixed on Jayne, his face a picture of outright longing.

"Ladies and gentlemen, and you too, Dad." Everyone laughed politely, Andy's father most of all. "Please take your seats for dinner."

Robbie's attention left Jayne to focus on Andy, and his expression changed to one of pure rage. He caught me looking, gave me a glare, before he abruptly turned around and disappeared into the kitchen, barely avoiding colliding with Ashleigh, her tray covered with baskets filled with bread rolls.

"Careful there," she said, "I might have had something hot."

Robbie snarled at her and disappeared.

"You okay, Gemma?" Jayne asked.

"Yeah. Fine. I'm looking forward to dinner."

"Unassigned seating." Jayne indicated the big round table in the center of the room. "Except for Andy and me with our families. Talk to you later." She walked away and I looked around the room, searching for suitable table companions as everyone else did the same. I decided to join Mrs. Ramsbatten. "May I?" I asked.

"Of course, you may, dear." She indicated the vacant chair next to her and I sat down. I picked up the single printed page resting on top of my napkin. We would not be offered the full restaurant menu tonight, but a choice of soup or salad to begin, then either the fish, steak and frites, or pesto pasta, followed by birthday cake.

Bunny brought George to our table, and he didn't look as though he found that to be a hardship. Donald was next to sit down with a flurry of his tails.

The lady on the other side of Mrs. Ramsbatten was in her late seventies, perhaps her well-preserved eighties. I looked for signs that she'd had work done on her face but didn't see them. Either it had been exceptionally well done or her genes were that good. Probably the latter. She wore a glittering brown and silver pantsuit perfectly suited to her age and dignity, and her heavy gray hair was tied into a neat chignon. Diamonds glistened from her ears and throat. A silver cigarette case lay on the table next to her napkin and cutlery. You don't often see cigarette cases these days.

A young woman I hadn't yet met plopped herself down next to the elderly lady. She was in her early twenties, dressed in a tight, sparkly pink dress revealing razor sharp collarbones and the outline of her breastbone. Rows of silver hoops ran up both ears. Her black hair, so black it had to be dyed, was cut very short. The aura of tobacco smoke hung around her like a cloud.

One chair remained unoccupied.

"Please, allow me to begin the introductions." Mrs. Ramsbatten held out her arm toward me and dipped her hand. "Gemma, Jayne's closest friend and bridesmaid. Also my next-door neighbor." She continued around the table. "Bunny, a . . . retired singer. And . . . I don't believe I caught your name, sir?"

"I'm George Friedman. I own a couple of restaurants around the Cape. I gave Andy his start in the cooking business. Not that Andy needed much help."

Mrs. Ramsbatten continued, "Next to our new friend George, we have Donald, dear friend and noted scholar." Donald beamed at being so regarded. "To my right, Audrey Whitehall, Andy's great-aunt." The older lady gave us a smile, revealing a mouthful of tobacco-stained teeth. "And her granddaughter, Madison."

The young woman in the pink dress lifted one hand and offered us the sort of wave the late queen specialized in. "Honorary granddaughter. Audrey and my grandma have been fast friends for a long, long time."

"Madison and I live in Los Angeles, and we're here for the wedding," Audrey explained. "I haven't been back to Massachusetts for far too long, not since my own parents died, so I decided to give myself a treat and come early for Andy's wedding. A nice vacation, as well as a long walk down memory lane. Heavens, I hardly recognize the place, so much has changed. Fortunately, the view out to sea has not. I have no children of my own, so dear Madison agreed to be my companion. She's always so thoughtful that way."

Madison downed the last of her wine and looked around for a waiter.

"Audrey Whitehall?" Bunny said with a considerable amount of awe. "From L.A.? Are you, possibly, *the* Audrey Whitehall?"

Audrey dipped her head modestly.

"I'm Bunny Leigh. After your time, I guess."

"I know the name. Toward the end of my time, as you put it."

I searched frantically through my memory banks for that name. Audrey's bone structure was excellent, her skin still flawless beneath the lines laid down by time. Her eyes were wide and an unusual shade of deep blue, and her lips plump. She lived in California so she might have been an actress, but if so, that was long before I started paying attention to what was popular in movies or on TV. Not that I do, even now.

My memory banks came up empty.

Clearly, I was not the only one having trouble placing her. Everyone else at the table, with the exception of Madison, was looking blank, and trying to hide it.

"Audrey Whitehall was *the* gossip columnist of note in Hollywood from the fifties to around the mid-nineties," Bunny said. "She knew absolutely everyone. And she knew everything there was to know about them. More than a few major stars lived in fear of her, didn't they, Audrey?" Bunny laughed.

Clearly pleased at being recognized, Audrey smiled. "Ah, yes, the good old days."

"That must have been something," George said as he helped himself to a bread roll, warm and fragrant. "Hollywood in the fifties. Wow!"

"Now but a mere shadow of its former self," Audrey said.

"Did you know Basil Rathbone?" Donald asked as he accepted the breadbasket. "In my mind, still the greatest portrayal of Sherlock Holmes on screen. Although I will admit Jeremy Brett did an excellent job and—"

"Basil Rathbone," Audrey said sharply, "was long before even my time."

Madison laughed. "You can't pretend to be offended, Audrey. All those old-time actors blend into each other."

Audrey didn't appear to be entirely pleased with the phrase "old-time," but she let it go.

The waiters begin serving our first courses. I'd selected the curried squash soup. Perfect for a cold winter's night. Not that it was cold in here, far from it, but a good meal should be as much about atmosphere as taste.

"What do you do, Madison?" Bunny asked politely after we'd all been served.

"Me?" The girl speared a lettuce leaf. "I look after Audrey."

I glanced quickly at Audrey. She didn't look as though she needed a full-time caregiver.

"When I'm not doing that, I'm an influencer," Madison said.

"A what?" Donald asked.

"An influencer. You know, I'm all over the socials. I have almost a hundred thousand followers on Insta and more joining each day. People like my style, and so they want to be like me."

"Is that a job?"

"A totally useless and unnecessary job, one with the potential to influence a lot of people and thus make a good deal of money." Audrey had taken a single sip of her soup before laying her spoon to one side and dabbing her lips. The breadbasket was offered to me, and I passed it on without taking anything. "Not that Madison has yet made any money out of this endeavor," Audrey continued. "But give her time. In some ways, she's following in my footsteps. Aren't you, dear?" She patted the younger woman's hand. Madison shrugged it off. "I could end a young actress's career with a single word. It was harder to end an actor's career, but not impossible. These days, everyone spreads their dirty laundry in public without a qualm. And no one much cares. People seem to have lost the ability to be shocked. What I wouldn't give to get my hands on a truly juicy scandal. One last time."

"Do you still have contacts in L.A.?" Bunny asked. "I was in talks for a major motion picture bio of my life story about a year ago, but the option sorta . . . fizzled. I'm hoping to get it back on track, and then I have some ideas for a comeback album."

Audrey was saved from answering by the arrival of a new guest.

A woman put her hands on the back of the empty chair at our table. "Do you mind if I join you? I'm a gatecrasher, but it looks like there's a seat free. Lucky me." Without waiting for our permission, she pulled out the chair and sat. Her face momentarily twisted in a slight wince, which she tried to hide with a smile. "Thanks. I'm Tina Armstrong. Nice to meet you all."

"A gatecrasher?" I said.

"Just joking. My invitation must have gotten lost in the mail." Her words were slightly slurred, her actions unsteady. Not her first stop of the night. "I'm a friend of Andy's from way back." She was around my age and stunningly beautiful. High sharp cheekbones in a thin pale face, small chin, huge hazel eyes under thick black lashes. Light brown hair, expertly highlighted, fell in a stylish, uncombed mess to her shoulders. Her only flaw was a small but noticeable scar running from the corner of her right eye down her cheek to curl around and disappear behind the bottom of her ear. Her body was tense, her smile forced, and she, probably unconsciously, stroked the line of the scar.

She waved her arm in the air, and Robbie came over. His eyes widened as he saw her, clearly impressed by her looks. He started to smile, but the smile died when she failed to return it. "Still at it, I see," she said with a dismissive sniff. "I'll have a glass of pinot noir. That soup looks good. I'll have that, and then whatever's going for the main course."

Not pleased at being so easily dismissed, his face tightened, but he contained his anger and walked away.

From the moment she sat down, Tina's eyes began darting around the room, and they soon found what they were looking for. I half turned to see Andy slowly getting to his feet.

Tina's smile became even more forced as Andy approached. Before he reached our table, she jumped up with a squeal as fake as her long, light pink fingernails. She staggered slightly and almost fell into him. She saved herself by throwing her arms around him. "Andy! So great to see you!"

He returned her hug with a brief, barely polite one of his own before pulling away. "Tina. It's been a while." His expression was flat, the tone verging on chilly.

"I know! Way too long! My mom told me you're getting married. Congratulations! I can't wait to meet the lucky girl!"

George asked Bunny about her comeback album, and Donald asked Madison what her favorite TV or movie interpretation of Sherlock Holmes was. "You mean, like Henry Cavell in that Millie Bobbie Brown movie? I liked that one." She finished her glass of wine and searched for a waiter to bring her another.

When Tina introduced herself, I saw a flicker of interest pass across Audrey's face. Now the older woman ignored the conversation swirling around the table as she watched Tina and Andy

I was also watching Tina and Andy. I wouldn't have thought it possible for anyone to use so many exclamation marks in a sentence. Tina was more than simply excited at seeing Andy. She was extremely nervous.

One didn't have to be Sherlock Holmes to deduce that Andy was not thrilled to see her.

"You don't mind me popping in like this, I hope," Tina trilled. "I wanted to have dinner here tonight, I've heard so much about what a great success you've made of this place. But when I tried to make a reservation, the web page said you were closed for a private event. I decided to have a walk on the pier anyway, even though it's freezing out tonight, and I was passing, like, and I looked in and saw an empty seat. Wasn't that lucky!"

"Very lucky," Andy said, clearly meaning it was anything but.

Tina was tall and slim, dressed in a close-fitting knee-length navy-blue dress accented by a thin white belt, long silver earrings with a tiny pearl embedded at the ends, and a matching silver necklace with a single pearl. Her shoes were navy pumps with two-inch heels. Her makeup was subdued but recently applied. Not the sort of outfit one wore on a dark winter's night for a walk along the icy, windswept pier.

She covered another wince as she dropped back into her chair. Ashleigh put a glass of wine in front of her. Tina's hand shook as she picked it up. The large ring on her right hand didn't match her up-to-date outfit. Old-fashioned, verging on ostentatious, likely a family heirloom. Art Deco, featuring a square green stone, large enough to cover the first joint of her finger, set into a base of white gold. The stone was unlikely to be a genuine emerald, and the ring probably not excessively valuable, but it would have some sentimental value. An inheritance from a great-grandmother, perhaps.

Andy appeared to be struggling with a decision. He reached it and let out a long breath. "Okay, Tina. You're here now. One of my friends had to bail at the last minute when he had car trouble, so you might as well enjoy the dinner."

"Great! Thanks. I can't wait to meet your newest girlfriend."

Mrs. Ramsbatten caught my eye, and her mouth formed a round "O." Not the politest of ways to refer to Andy's bride-to-be.

"After dinner, maybe," Andy said. He made to return to his own seat and then stopped and gave me a look. Conversation and laughter swirled all around us. Candlelight glowed, cutlery clinked, waitstaff slipped between the tables, bringing more drinks, clearing away soup bowls and salad plates.

"Gemma stocks the Enola Holmes books in her store, if you'd like to read them," Donald was telling Madison.

"I don't read," she replied.

Donald made a sound as though he were choking. I ignored him as I received the message Andy was attempting to send me. Tina was not welcome here, but short of throwing her out, he didn't know what he could do. Other than ask me to keep an eye on her.

I gave him a nod. His face relaxed as he returned it, and then he went back to his seat.

When I refocused my attention on the table, Audrey was watching Tina, a sly smile playing on her red lips. Mrs. Ramsbatten once again went around the table, introducing the new arrival to everyone. Tina fiddled with her wine glass, drank a lot of it very quickly, and couldn't have looked less interested if she tried. The only sign of interest she showed was when Mrs. Ramsbatten said Audrey's name.

"Nice necklace, Tina," Madison said. "Did you buy it locally?"

Tina's hand grabbed the pearl. "This old thing? I hardly remember where I got it."

A tiny patch of glue was stuck to the side of the chain. The necklace was so new, the price tag had only just been torn off.

"Too bad," Madison said. "I'm an influencer, and I like to seek out cute little shops when I travel. The sort of places that sell locally made, organic, all-natural products. Your ring's interesting."

Tina rubbed her finger. "A present. From a friend. It's not worth much, but I like the old-world charm."

"Do you know anyone in the movie or music business, Madison?" Bunny asked.

"I might be able to get your band a gig at one of my restaurants," George said. "We're always looking for good acts."

Bunny was forced to admit she didn't actually have a backup band at the moment. But if George could find her a pianist—and a piano—she'd be willing to sing.

"Tina," Audrey said. "I didn't catch your last name."

"Armstrong."

"Tina Armstrong." Her tongue lingered over the name. "A good name. Unpretentious, yet not instantly forgettable, implying friendship and strength. You have a . . . presence about you, Tina, not to mention, if I may, Hollywood-friendly looks. Did you act at one point?"

"I did. For a while." Tina touched her scar. "It wasn't for me. I gave it up. I didn't much like Los Angeles." Her laugh was more like a choke. "I was homesick the whole time for Cape Cod. So here I am, back again!"

A silence fell over the table as the staff began serving the main course. I'd ordered the stuffed sole. I always have the sole at the Blue Water Café. Some people find it odd that I always have the same thing. Why risk trying something new and being disappointed, I reply. I also always have the clam chowder as a starter, but that hadn't been on offer tonight so I had to satisfy myself with the squash soup. It was so good, I might have it another time.

"I try to keep my hand in, when I can," Audrey said once we were served and digging in. She spoke loudly, addressing the whole table. "The internet has ruined my profession. My former profession."

"Profession?" Tina asked.

Audrey smiled at her. "As I explained before you arrived, I was a publicist for the movie industry, of a sort."

Madison laughed. "That's one way of putting it."

"No need for my specific skill set any longer," Audrey said. "Every scrap of dirt on anyone is out there the minute it happens. Heaven knows the stars themselves spread the gossip, trying to get ahead of the story, as they call it. Although not always. Some things remain buried deep."

"Yeah, Audrey, tell us about the good old days," Madison mumbled as she dug into the pile of small, crispy fries next to her steak.

Audrey's lips twitched, but she pretended not to hear the comment. "Perhaps there's simply too much information around now. Everything is available to everyone at any time. I made a point, as soon as it became *a thing*, of familiarizing myself with the world wide web. It's become somewhat of a hobby for me in my retirement. Learning things, I mean." Her eyes lingered on Tina, twirling pasta on her fork. And twirling. And twirling. "For example, I know that you, Gemma Doyle, own the Sherlock Holmes Bookshop and Emporium. I know you live with your uncle Arthur, renowned seaman, honored several times by the late queen for his service to your country."

"Great-Uncle Arthur," I said.

"My mistake. I know you are in a committed relationship with a West London policeman. I know you have some reputation for making it your business to know things others do not."

Donald's eyes lit up and his ears almost stood to attention. "A quote! Do you know the Canon that well, Audrey?"

"I might have heard the phrase somewhere, and it appealed to me. It might have even been applied to me, at one time." She continued watching me as she spoke to Donald.

"Cannons? Is he an artillery expert?" George asked Bunny. "Wouldn't have thought it to look at him."

"He means the Sherlock Holmes books. They're kinda obsessed with that stuff around here."

"My life is an open book," I said. "I have no secrets."

"Mr. Morris," Audrey said, "your dedication to Sherlock Holmes is to be admired."

Donald beamed. "Thank you so much. Perhaps after dinner, we can have a glass of brandy and discuss—"

"Admired by those who care for that sort of nonsense. I do not. Mr. Friedman, you invited the once-famous Bunny Leigh to sing at one of your restaurants. I must say, I wouldn't think her type of out-of-date pop music would suit the sort of so-called fine dining establishments you run. Or I should say are attempting to run. Some financial difficulties, I understand."

Bunny blinked, unsure as to whether she should feel insulted. George's eyes widened, but before he could think up a clever reply to what was an amazingly personal question, Madison raised her voice. "Waiter! This steak is, like, way underdone."

Robbie was closest and he hurried over. "Everything okay here?"

"No, it is not okay," she said. "Take this away. I can't eat this. I'll get *E. coli* or something."

Andy was beside our table before Robbie had reached for the offending plate. "Is something wrong?"

"Like, yeah. I asked for my steak to be well done." She poked at it with her fork. She did have a point, the meat in the center was a light pink. "I can't take chances. I have a very delicate stomach."

Audrey snorted. "Like a horse."

"Robbie," Andy said. "Ask the chef to prepare another plate."

"Never mind," Madison said. "I've lost my appetite."

Robbie took the plate and looked at Andy. Andy grabbed it out of his hand and jerked his head toward the kitchen. Robbie scurried off, glad to be away from the drama. Madison stood up. "I'm going out for a smoke. Audrey, ready for a ciggy?"

"Not right now, dear. My steak is perfectly done." Hers was so rare, red juices leaked from it. "No need to ruin a good piece of meat by overcooking it, as though one has to throw it on an open fire and leave it there until it burns." She tossed a small piece of meat into her mouth.

Bearing the unwanted meal, Andy headed for the kitchen, his expression furious. I got to my feet and looked toward the table where Jayne was sitting with her mom and Andy's parents.

She was watching Andy, and she did not look happy. She caught my eye and threw me a silent request to check up on him. I nodded and followed him.

The swinging doors were still swinging as I reached them, and I pushed my way through.

Chapter Five

A kitchen is not my natural habitat. Not even in my own house. On the rare occasion I visit the heart of a restaurant, I'm always impressed. Knives flashing, pots of water boiling, burners glowing red, fire leaping from gas elements. Everyone working calmly and professionally, shouting orders, dodging laden plates, hot soup, open flame. Most of the main courses had been served and the staff was stacking pots and pans, wiping down counters, organizing dessert plates. A huge, elaborately decorated cake stood on a far counter, waiting to be presented.

The kitchen was small, almost tiny, for the number of people and the amount of activity. I've been in home kitchens twice the size. Twice the size and barely used.

Andy stood in the center of the space, gripping the plate bearing the unwanted steak in his hands. A young man dressed in the chef's uniform of gray-checked trousers and white jacket faced him. His looks were what might be called "ruggedly handsome": a fashionable degree of dark stubble on his chin, prominent cheekbones, large eyes under black lashes, thick dark hair tied back into a knot and stuffed under a hairnet. He was taller than Andy, slightly more than my height of five-foot-eight, thin and wiry.

"The lady at table five asked for her steak to be well done. And she got this." Andy shoved the plate toward the chef.

"I don't do well done," he replied. "That's no way to treat a piece of meat of that quality."

"You'll do what the guest wants." Andy threw the plate into the sink, food and all.

"That was a waste, don't you think?" the chef said. "I could have heated it up again. Made it even worse."

The other staff had stopped what they were doing. People shifted uncomfortably from one foot to another. All except one: Robbie had tucked himself into a corner, where he watched the two men with a smirk.

"It's okay," I said. "Madison's that sort. If it hadn't been the steak, it would have been something else for her to make a fuss over."

Andy spoke to me without turning to face me. "That's not exactly unusual in a restaurant, Gemma. Is it, Martin? We accommodate their whims and their fusses. That's our business. Right?"

Martin shrugged.

"Right?" Andy repeated.

They faced each other. No one else said a word. Ashleigh took a half step forward, thought better of it, and stepped back.

We all waited for one of them to be first to back down.

If Martin quit, I didn't know what Andy would do. His wedding was due to be celebrated in less than one week. He and Jayne were going to a Caribbean resort for their honeymoon. Andy would have to leave his restaurant in the care of someone.

"Yeah, okay," Martin said. "The customer's always right, right? It woulda broke my heart to ruin that steak, but . . ."

Andy's shoulders relaxed. "Don't let it happen again. Not in my place. You get your own place someday, you can do whatever you want."

"And I will," Martin said. "Want me to fix her another?"

"No," I said. "She's happy to have had her moment as the center of attention. She's gone out for a cigarette."

Andy addressed his watching staff. "What! You people think the night's over? Nowhere near it. Robbie, people need drinks. Get to it. Ashleigh, top up water glasses. Someone get that coffee on, now!"

He pushed his way past me and stalked out of the kitchen.

"Cheerio!" I called. "By the way, I had the sole and it was great."

"Thanks," Martin said.

"Careful everyone," Robbie said. "Little Martie's hand's been slapped and he'll be looking for someone to take it out on."

"Shut it," Martin snarled. "I've had about enough of you."

In the hallway, I almost bumped into Andy and his mother.

"—doing here?" Trish Whitehall whispered, clearly agitated.

"Not now, Mom, please. Let it go. I can't throw her out, can I?"

"No, but I can."

"Do not do that. Please, Mom."

He walked away.

"Problem?" I asked Trish.

"Oh, Gemma. I didn't see you there for a moment. That woman who came in late. She sat at your table. She's . . . I'm not happy to see her here. Not tonight, of all nights."

"You mean Tina? I noticed some, shall we say, tension between her and Andy."

"They were together for a long time, in a relationship I mean. Before he met dear Jayne."

I assumed that was the case. People rarely react so strongly—whether positively or negatively—to someone unless they once had romantic feelings for the person.

"And?" This was obviously none of my business, but I'm the curious sort. The thought crossed my mind that I might have made a highly successful gossip columnist, if I'd been born fifty years earlier.

"We never liked her, Pete and I. But we knew better than to interfere. They started dating in high school. They graduated: Andy went to New York to culinary school, and she went to theater school. She wanted to be an actress. They continued dating for another couple of years while Andy was at school and then in his first restaurant jobs. Over that time, when he came home for a visit, we could tell he was increasingly disturbed."

"Disturbed in what way?"

"Not happy. You know how unremittingly cheerful he is?" Trish glanced over my shoulder toward the kitchen. "Other than in his work, if things go wrong."

"I do."

"He wouldn't talk to us about it. At first, Pete and I were worried he was failing his courses, and then he wasn't doing well at his job, but he said he was loving living in New York, immersed in the food scene and learning the restaurant business. Matters came to a head when he and Tina came home for the Christmas holidays. Separately. Andy had broken up with Tina, and she was not happy about it."

"Why? I mean, why break up with her? Did something happen between them?"

"Several somethings happened, Gemma. Or should I say several someones."

"That doesn't sound good. How was her career going? Did she finish theater school?"

"She did. She got a few small parts in plays off Broadway. She was starting to talk about moving to Hollywood and she wanted Andy to come with her, but that wasn't the issue."

"What was the issue?"

"Some of this we only know from Angie, you understand. That Christmas, Andy confided in his youngest sister that Tina had been . . . seeing other men in New York."

"Definitely not good."

"No. When Andy found out and confronted her she told him she didn't have any feelings for those men, but she hoped they would be able to get her good auditions and even some roles, if she was . . . uh . . . dating them. That's even worse, isn't it?"

"Yeah. That might be worse. Is it possible she was being coerced? Some young women don't know how to refuse."

"She never claimed so. When Andy finally told her he knew what was going on, she tried to laugh it off. Saying it was how the game was played, and it wasn't her fault if men wanted to help her in her career, now was it."

Trish and I had stepped out of the way of the kitchen door. Waiters were bringing the last of the used dishes back. Few were not scraped down to the pattern on the plates. I thought of my sole and hoped it wouldn't be cleared away before I could get back to it.

"Obviously, they broke up and stayed that way," I said. "That had to have been some time ago." I met Andy not long after I moved to West London, around seven years ago. He'd been in love with an oblivious Jayne even back then. I'd never heard of this Tina until less than an hour ago. "Does it matter if she's here tonight?"

"I don't know, dear. I saw my son's face when he noticed her, and it didn't leave me with a good feeling. You're right that they broke up, but it wasn't pleasant, and it wasn't easy. Not for Andy. Of course, he didn't tell his father and me the details, but one hears things in a town like West London. No, I'm not happy to see her here. I fear she has an ulterior motive. Tina always had an ulterior motive. Doesn't help that she appears to have had a couple of drinks earlier. Stoking her courage, likely."

"I'll take a guess her acting career didn't reach the heights she wanted. It's immaterial that I don't recognize her, but no one else seems to either." No one had openly recognized her, but Audrey had shown a spark of interest, which made me wonder if she'd met Tina previously or had heard about her. Hollywood is, so they say, a small town, and Audrey admitted she tried to keep herself appraised of as much of the gossip as she could.

A smile touched the edges of Trish's mouth. "Last I heard, Tina's taken an apartment in West London and is studying for her real estate license. Times are tough these days for a great many people."

"She's still very beautiful."

"Perhaps, but that beauty is all on the surface."

"That scar isn't an old one and she has a limp she tries to hide. Can I assume she didn't have them when she and Andy were together?"

"I've never seen the scar before, Gemma, and she didn't limp the last time I saw her. I heard she'd been in a serious car accident in Los Angeles a year or two ago. I don't know if that had anything to do with her decision to return to West London." Trish gave me a weak smile. "Fortunately, my dear son found a woman whose soul truly matches her looks. I might have told you too much, Gemma. Please don't share this with Jayne. I don't want her to be concerned."

"I won't, but there's nothing for her to be concerned about. Andy's the least shallow person I know, and he loves Jayne beyond measure."

"He's very lucky in that. As long as we're on the topic, I couldn't help but notice Detective Ashburton isn't with you this evening."

"He's away. For work. Should be back the day after tomorrow. He'll be ready to do his duty as best man."

Andy's mom patted my arm. "I'm glad to hear it." From the main room came the tinkling sound of a spoon being tapped against a glass, then Andy's father bellowing, "Seats everyone. Let's have a toast!"

"I was on my way outside for a smoke," Andy's mum said. "No time now. Pete doesn't approve of me smoking, and if I miss Andy's toast to Jayne, I'll hear about it. Let's take our seats." She bustled off.

I slipped back into my own chair. All the other plates at my table had been cleared away, but to my infinite relief, mine had not.

"I told him to leave it," Mrs. Ramsbatten said.

I picked up my knife and fork. "Thanks."

Madison had returned, the scent of tobacco hanging heavily around her. Tina watched me through those gorgeous eyes. She'd seen me following Andy and was clearly wondering what he and I were to each other. I gave her a steady look, and she flushed and turned away.

Waitstaff began placing champagne flutes in front of the guests. "Everything okay back there?" I asked Ashleigh.

"All good. Robbie tried to get in a dig at Martin, but no one was on his side, so it fizzled out. Martin made a crack that when he has his own restaurant, people won't come there because they want to eat what they want to eat, but because they want to eat what he wants to cook for them."

"We all have our dreams," I said. "Not often do they turn out as we initially hoped." I'd once dreamt of owning a chain of mystery bookstores in the south of England in partnership with my ex-and-late husband. In reality, I owned half of one bookstore and a quarter of a tearoom in Cape Cod, and I wouldn't have my life any other way.

I caught Tina's eye across the table. "We grow up, life happens, and we make other dreams, wouldn't you agree?"

"Some people might dream." She held her glass to one side so Robbie could fill it with champagne, but she didn't even look at him. Instead, she said to me, "As for me, no, I don't dream. I do. Some of us make things happen."

"What do you intend to make happen?"

She took a sip of the drink. She didn't answer my question but said, "Andy's looking terribly handsome tonight, don't you think? He's going to make a speech. Isn't that sweet? He's always been so adorably shy." She lifted her glass in a toast—to me or to him, I couldn't tell—and she drank. Perhaps she'd answered my question after all.

Chapter Six

Andy did make a speech, but in true Andy fashion, he kept it short and sweet. He thanked everyone for coming and asked us to toast Jayne.

Everyone lifted their glasses, and cheers and cries of "To Jayne" rang out. I touched my glass to my lips and studied the room. Robbie was standing against the bar, looking between proud Andy and beaming Jayne, his expression alternately envious and furious.

I decided to have a quiet word with Andy. Keeping Robbie around was not a good idea.

Tina finished her champagne in record time and raised her hand to ask for another. Someone else who was having trouble controlling their feelings tonight. I wouldn't have to have a word with Andy about her. He pointedly avoided looking in her direction, and he was clearly not happy she'd come.

Jayne got to her feet, eyes only for Andy. Mrs. Whitehall was right: Jayne was as beautiful inside as she was outside. She adored Andy and he adored her. They were made for each other.

"Thank you so much for coming, everyone," Jayne said. "Thank you to my darling Andy for inviting you all and giving me such a wonderful party. Now, I think there's cake. My mom always said a party without cake is just a meeting. Isn't that right, Mom?"

"It most certainly is," Leslie said to another round of cheers.

At an almost invisible nod from Andy, Robbie and Ashleigh carried the cake ablaze with candles to their table. I braced myself, preparing to get up quickly in case Robbie "accidently" dumped the whole thing onto Andy. But accidents did not happen, and Jayne, blushing and grinning, took an enormous breath, held it for a fraction of a second, and then blew all the candles out in one go.

The room erupted.

When the cheers began dying down, Andy said, "The night is still young, although some of us are not."

"Speak for yourself," his father yelled.

"I am speaking for you, Dad," Andy replied to much laughter.

Pete Whitehall grinned, enjoying being the center of attention. Beside him, his wife watched Tina through narrowed eyes. Was she expecting a scene? In the same way I was keeping my eye on Robbie?

Why did life have to get so complicated? Why couldn't the likes of Robbie and Tina admit they'd lost and slink away to lick their wounds in private?

Another waiter presented Jayne with a big shiny silver knife with a red ribbon tied around the handle, and she began cutting slices of cake. While she did that, Andy announced that the bar would be serving brandy and liqueurs for people to enjoy with their dessert. Guests began getting to their feet. Some went to the bar, some approached Jayne to offer their best wishes, some crossed the room to chat with friends. Men loosened ties and women kicked off too-tight shoes. A few people headed for the doors to the deck, either for a breath of clean, fresh night sea air, or to suck noxious fumes into their lungs.

"Can I get you a drink, Bunny?" George asked.

"A brandy would be nice, thank you."

"I haven't spoken to John Alexander in months," Donald said. "He once told me he's interested in Sir Arthur's spiritual life. I must tell him about that new book coming out soon."

Audrey reached for the cane resting beside her chair and pushed herself to her feet. "A trip to the ladies' room for me. Madison?"

Madison's fingers were rapidly moving under the table. "I'm good, thanks."

"I meant, will you put that thing down, and escort me?" Audrey said sharply.

Madison's head jerked up. "Don't have a fit, Audrey. Jeez." She put her phone on the table and stood up. She made a big deal of taking the older woman's arm and leading her across the room. I didn't think Audrey needed any assistance at all. She seemed to get around perfectly fine. Making a point, I assumed. Particularly if she was paying Madison to be her companion on this holiday.

Tina took her small evening bag (not at all the sort of bag one carried for a night walk on the pier) off the table and tossed the long strap over her shoulder. She left without asking anyone to join her.

"Did you detect some undercurrent of tension swirling around this evening, Gemma?" Mrs. Ramsbatten said when she and I were the only people left at our table.

"Cake?" Ashleigh said.

"Yes, please," we chorused.

Ashleigh put two plates in front of us. Carrot cake, Jayne's favorite, smothered in cream cheese icing. "Mom seems to be enjoying that man's company." She nodded to Bunny and George standing at the bar, laughing and toasting each other with balloon-shaped glasses. "What's he like?"

"Seems nice enough," I said. "He owns a couple of restaurants, but he's not a cook. Just the owner."

"Might have money, then," Ashleigh said.

I thought of Audrey's comment regarding the state of George's businesses. "Or the appearance of it."

"No doubt she told him about her career."

"It might have come up."

Ashleigh looked concerned, so I said, "Don't worry about it. If anyone's after Bunny for her money, they'll find out soon enough she doesn't have any to speak of."

"Yeah, I know that. But it's never easy for her when they openly ask how she ended up living in a one-bedroom apartment in Cape Cod."

"Are you enjoying the evening, Ashleigh?" Mrs. Ramsbatten asked. "Despite working, I mean?"

"I am. Great fun seeing what goes on behind the scenes. After Andy reamed Martin out and you guys left, Martin had a couple of things to say about mixing the personal with the business."

"Meaning?" I asked.

"Meaning Andy can't be a party host and the head chef at the same time. According to Martin, he himself would never mix his roles." Ashleigh laughed. "I didn't mention I'm working here, and at the same time I'm gossiping with the guests about my mom's love life. Speaking of which . . . back to work. When people want cake, they want cake."

"I like her," Mrs. Ramsbatten said as Ashleigh walked away. "She has a sensible head on her shoulders, that girl. Unlike her mother."

Bunny, real name Leigh Saunderson, had not raised Ashleigh. She'd left the baby with her parents in Lincoln and returned to L.A. to pursue her music career. The career soared, taking over Bunny's life, leaving no room for a child growing up in Lincoln, Nebraska, and Ashleigh's grandparents hadn't tried to maintain the bond. Bunny had only recently reconnected with her daughter.

"I get what you mean about undercurrents here tonight," I said. "I've no worries about Andy. He can take care of himself. Chefs are said to be enormously temperamental. I'm more concerned about that Robbie. He has got to go. And someone needs to tell Tina to take a hike. As I believe you Americans say."

"I never say that," Mrs. Ramsbatten replied. "What about Tina and Robbie? Never mind, by tensions swirling, I wasn't referring to them. Madison might be acting as Audrey's companion on this occasion, supposedly because of the close relationship between her own grandmother and Audrey, but they themselves are not at all close. Or even fond of each other. That's my opinion, but I could be wrong."

I doubted that very much.

"George is coming on rather strong to Bunny, but I suppose that's the way of young people these days. When you were away seeing to that nonsense over the steak . . . I mean really, dear, if one's food is not to one's liking, simply send it back. Don't make it all about yourself."

"But it was all about Madison," I said.

"As I suspect was her intent."

"Anything happen while I was away?"

"George told us how he knew Andy. Andy worked at one of his restaurants when he first returned to Cape Cod after learning the ropes in New York." A cloud fell over Mrs. Ramsbatten's timeworn face.

"What's bothering you?" I asked. "What did he say?"

"It wasn't so much his words, but his tone. Implying Andy made a success of himself because he was lucky; always in the right place at the right time. Ready to make a move the moment the time was right. Knowing the right people."

"What of it? Most success in life, for those not born to it, is based on luck and timing and connections as much, if not more, than talent and perseverance."

She didn't look mollified. "By the right people, Gemma, he didn't mean the *right* people. He meant . . . I thought he meant, but I might be reading too much into it. He meant the sort of people Andy would have met in the underbelly of the restaurant world in New York City."

If anyone else said that, I would have discounted their impressions. But not Mrs. Ramsbatten. In her youth, my elderly neighbor worked alongside the legendary Admiral Grace Hopper on the development of COBOL. She and the late Mr. Ramsbatten had been pioneers at Microsoft. Her eyesight might be failing and she had to walk with care, but her mind was as sharp as ever.

I looked up to see Jayne chatting to, of all people, Tina. Jayne was holding a glass of champagne. Tina stood close to her, smiling broadly. She put her hand on Jayne's arm, and I started to stand in case intervention was needed. But it wasn't. When Tina enveloped Jayne in a huge wraparound hug, my friend did not pull away.

"I'm *soooo* thrilled for Andy," Tina said. "He totally deserves to be happy. It simply broke his dear heart when I decided it wasn't time for me to settle down and I had to pursue my career." She turned and walked away, the limp noticeable. Her smile died the second her back was turned, and her eyes filled with tears.

I wasn't the only one who noticed her. Andy's mother was also watching, her face stiff with tension. Tina lifted her hand in a half-salute, and Trish Whitehall's lips tightened further as her eyes darkened. Tina pulled a packet of cigarettes out of her tiny purse and headed for the door leading to the deck.

I got to my feet intending to talk to Jayne, but before I could take two steps, Donald stepped in my way. "Gemma! There you are. Here's someone who's simply dying to meet you."

The man was in his sixties, well dressed, softly rounded but not excessively overweight, clean-shaven, thin hair combed flat. I'm not an expert in men's clothes, and I aways say I never guess, but I took a guess that a bespoke suit of that cut and the quality of the fabric likely cost in the range of a few thousand, and the pink silk tie would have been several hundred. His shoes were Italian leather, if not exactly handmade, then from a very good factory. When he lifted his hand to stroke his chin, the gem in the gold ring on his right pinky finger flashed. A ruby, and a real one.

Despite the quality of his clothes, he showed no signs of an extensive workout routine, manicures, or the use of skin or hair products. He held a tall glass of beer and did not appear to be "dying" to meet me. He smiled politely.

"I was telling Keith here about the birthday party we enjoyed earlier today at the Emporium, and naturally our conversation then moved on to embrace the type of things you stock," Donald said. "Keith's from New York City, but he and his wife recently retired to Chatham. He's related . . . some way, doesn't matter now . . . to Jayne's mom."

"You must be Leslie's brother," I said.

Keith grinned at me. Excellent, and extensive, dental work. "Has she spoken to you about me?"

"No. A simple observation." The resemblance was close enough it wasn't a stretch to determine they were brother and sister. Not only the contours of the face and the similarity in the nose, but his eyes were the same color and shape as Jayne's.

"Gemma has a way of knowing things about people," Donald said. "Isn't that right, Gemma?"

Keith studied my face. I gave him a smile in return. "I hope you don't know too much about me." He didn't appear to be finding this turn of conversation amusing.

"Only what is obvious to anyone who takes the time to observe. You look very much like Leslie."

"I'll take that as a compliment," he said.

"Keith and his lovely wife will be at the wedding," Donald said. "Isn't that nice? Nothing like a wedding to bring families together. Keith's keen to learn more about collecting the works of Sir Arthur. First editions are beyond his price point at this time, so I naturally told him you might have some second editions or not-pristine firsts in stock. Exactly the sort of items to start his collection."

"I, uh . . ." Keith said.

Judging by the way he was dressed and that ring, a first edition was not beyond Keith's budget. He simply wasn't interested in investing in books. Nothing wrong with that.

"I wonder where Audrey got to," Donald said. "With her vast experience in the movie business, she might have met some of the characters who played Holmes or Watson, or even secondary figures, over the years. I wonder if she knew Christopher Plummer. His *Murder by Decree* is an outstanding portrayal of the Great Detective, one of my favorites. Not to mention the movie is truly entertaining, if historically inaccurate. I'll leave you to it, shall I?"

And he was gone.

"I don't—" Keith said.

"Want to collect early Sir Arthur Conan Doyle editions? Not a problem. Donald can get carried away by his enthusiasm sometimes."

Keith let out an enormous sigh of relief. "All I said was I'd read the Holmes stories in my youth and I might want to read them again sometime. If I ever have the time. Now that we've met, I would like to pop into your store. It sounds interesting."

He took his leave of me and went to speak to Leslie. As he moved, he pressed his hand to his lower back and walked with a slight stiffness to his gait.

Jayne had been joined by a group of her friends. The party was thinning out as some of the older people as well as ones with young children or who had to get an early start in the morning were beginning to leave. I was ready to go too. I hadn't had more than a glass of wine with dinner and half my champagne during the toast. I'd enjoy walking home, but as I'd come with Mrs. Ramsbatten, I figured I should check in with her first. I'd talk to Jayne in the morning at work.

Mrs. Ramsbatten was sitting alone at our table. Her eyes were bright with interest as she watched the party swirling around her and she smiled to herself. She twisted the rings hanging loosely on the third finger of her left hand, and I guessed she was remembering parties she and Mr. Ramsbatten attended when they were young and full of optimism over the future of computing.

Ashleigh waylaid me. "Gemma, do you know that waiter? The guy about your age? Robbie?"

"I do. For my sins. What about him?"

"I don't know if I should say anything or not, but he's kinda . . . saying rude things about Jayne."

"What sort of rude things?"

"I overheard him talking to the dishwasher in the kitchen. He said he and Jayne dated for a while, but he dumped her because she was so clingy. He said she was always asking him to buy her things. Things he couldn't afford."

"Robbie's a jerk and a sore loser."

"I know Jayne, and that sure isn't her. I thought you'd want to know, that's all."

"Thanks, Ashleigh. What happened then?"

"My friend Rachel's the supervisor of front of house staff tonight, but she wasn't there. The chef, Martin, told Robbie to get back to work. Said he could gossip on his own time. Robbie told him to mind his own business, although he used stronger words than that."

"I can imagine."

"But Robbie did leave, without saying anything more. Martin told me to remember what I was being paid for, and so I left the kitchen. Far as I'm concerned, that Martin's too full of himself, but that's up to him. At the beginning of the evening, right after we all got our instructions for the night, he asked me out."

"Martin asked you out?"

"Yeah."

"What'd you say?"

"I told him I was here to work, not to meet men. I didn't mean anything rude by it, but I didn't think it was a good time, that's all. I was going to consider it, but after the way he spoke to me just now, I don't think so, even if I don't take any more shifts here. Looks like people are leaving. I'm staying to the end to help clean up, so I'd better get at it. See you tomorrow, Gemma."

"Yeah. Tomorrow." I changed my mind. I needed to talk to Jayne tonight. And not just about Tina.

I leaned over Mrs. Ramsbatten's shoulder. "I'm going to stay to the end in case I'm needed to help clear up."

"Help clear up? Doesn't Andy have staff to tend to those details, Gemma?"

"By clear up, I mean run interference if anyone spends too long at the bar and overstays their welcome."

At that moment, a burst of laughter came from the bar. Bunny was holding court to a group of older men. Her arms were wide, her glowing expression reminiscent of how she must have appeared in her glory days. She waved her brandy glass in the air as she told another joke, this time about a musician even I'd heard of. George checked his watch. An imitation gold Rolex. A good one, but an imitation nonetheless. Audrey had taken a seat at the center table, next to Andy's father, who was struggling to appear interested in what his elderly relative had to say. I didn't see Madison. Tina had not returned from her cigarette break. Leslie Wilson was chatting with Irene Talbot. Jayne's friends had said their goodnights, exchanged hugs and kisses, leaving Jayne and Andy to enjoy a brief quiet moment together. Donald had cornered one of Andy's sisters, and although I wasn't close enough to hear their words, it was obvious by Donald's expression and gestures, he was telling her far more than she ever wanted to know about the Great Detective and his creator. Ashleigh was clearing used cake plates and discarded champagne flutes, but Robbie had disappeared.

"See anything needing intervention, dear?" Mrs. Ramsbatten asked me sweetly.

"Not yet. You know me: always on guard. I can call you a ride if you're ready to leave."

"I might linger a while longer in case my own intervention is needed. I don't care for the way that young male waiter looks at Andy."

"Neither do I. Shout if you need me."

Jayne and Andy were standing next to the table piled high with gifts, underneath two helium balloons spelling out her age. Jayne held a glass of orange juice, and Andy had a beer.

"Brilliant party," I said. "Great job, Andy. I'm sorry to interrupt, but I wonder if I might have a quiet word, Jayne."

"Go ahead," Andy said. "I want to check in the kitchen. My staff need to get on home, never mind me, so I'm going to call last round. Can I get you something?"

"I'm fine, thank you."

He walked away, and Jayne said, "What's up?"

"It's been a fun night. You look as though you enjoyed yourself."

"It was wonderful. Truly wonderful, Gemma. And my wedding's going to be even better." Her words were slightly slurred, and she was none too steady on her feet. Jayne rarely drank, and when she did, it went straight to her head. She smiled at me, all big eyes and love and happiness.

I hesitated, reluctant to pop her balloon. But, I reasoned, she needed to know that no matter what he might say, Robbie did not have her best interests at heart. "Feel like going outside for some air?"

"That would be nice. Did you meet Andy's Great-Aunt Audrey? What a hoot she is. Madison, the young woman who came with her, some sort of companion, I didn't quite get the relationship, she was odd. Like she was doing Audrey this gigantic favor by coming to my party and eating Andy's food and drinking his wine. A heck of a lot of it, I might add." Another round of laughter had us looking toward the bar. Madison had joined the group and was accepting a martini glass complete with olive from the bartender.

Andy clapped his hands and called, "Last round, everyone. I don't need my beauty sleep, but some of you do. Don't say it, Dad."

The main dining area of Andy's restaurant consists of one large room. A hallway runs off it, down the right side of the building, the kitchen on one side and the restrooms and storage areas on the other. The shelves behind the bar, lined with colorful glass bottles, share a wall with the kitchen. The end of the bar intersects the sliding doors leading out to the deck. In the summer, those doors are thrown open and the windows rolled up to let in the cool ocean breezes, the salty scent of the sea, and to provide easy access to the outside dining areas for waitstaff as well as patrons. In the summer, a hostess stand is set up next to the boardwalk to greet people and show those who ask to sit outside directly to the deck area. Tonight, that access was blocked off, and only one of the sliding doors was unlocked.

"Do you need your coat?" I asked Jayne.

"I should be fine for a few minutes if you are. It's getting warm in here."

We passed the line of stools at the bar, the bartender serving last drinks, Bunny telling the men gathered around her about the time she and her band ended up enjoying a night in jail in some small California town. "Of course," she said, "that sort of thing didn't happen often. Not once one of the roadies could tell them *who I was*."

I slid open the door, and Jayne and I stepped out into the fresh, cold night. It was getting late and no one else was out here. The last lingering traces of tobacco hung on the still air.

"It's been a long time," I said, "since I've been in the presence of so many smokers. People at my table were popping up and down all evening, heading outside for a quick puff."

"As was Andy's mom," Jayne said. "Pete's been after her for years to quit, but she says she enjoys the occasional one, so what harm does it do? She's going to die someday."

"A cheerful thought."

"Many years ago, when Andy was just a kid, a fortune teller told her to avoid big ships. I don't know if that's why, but they've never been on a cruise, although Pete says he'd like to go someday."

We leaned against the wooden railing and looked down at the black water rolling onto shore or lapping softly at the pilings. The small dock below the pier bobbed in the light waves. The sky above us was a blaze of stars. A dark shape moved beneath the water, and I said, "Do seals sleep all night?"

"I've never thought to ask one," Jayne said. "They might be up tonight, hoping someone will toss a freshly caught fish out the kitchen window." Her breath formed a little cloud in front of her face. "It's colder out here than I expected. What did you want to talk to me about, and why can't it wait until tomorrow?"

"You won't be in tomorrow. You've taken the day off, or have you forgotten?"

"I haven't forgotten, although I might pop in around lunchtime. Just to check everything's okay. If you need to talk to me, my mom told me about this thing called the telephone. You don't have to be in the same room as someone to talk to them anymore. What will they think of next?"

"I'll make this short, and you can do with the info what you want—"

"Although you'll advise me. Constantly."

"Probably. It—is that gate supposed to be open?"

Jayne turned to see what I was looking at. "What gate? The one to the stairs to the dock? No."

A small dock juts into the water below the pier. A steep narrow set of steps leads up to the restaurant deck so boaters can tie up their craft and pop in for a quick drink or a full meal. The gate to the steps is always kept locked, even when the deck is in use, as protection for temporarily unsupervised children running around the deck while their parents' attention wanders.

No children were at our party tonight, but that gate should be secured. Andy didn't need drunken late-night boaters searching for the American equivalent of a chippie or a kabab stand.

A puff of wind sent the metal gate swinging. I took a step toward it, but Jayne grabbed my arm. "Gemma. Something's in the water. I don't think it's a seal."

Chapter Seven

I looked over the railing in the direction Jayne was pointing. For a moment, I saw nothing, and then an incoming wave lifted a dark shape. I whipped out my phone and turned on the flashlight app. The light wasn't strong, but it was bright enough to give me a glimpse of drifting white arms, tendrils of long hair, a flash of red fabric. An outgoing wave washed over it, and the figure slipped beneath the surface.

I shoved my phone at Jayne as I kicked off my shoes. "Get Andy. Call 911."

"Gemma, no!" Jayne shouted. "That water has got to be freezing."

I'd like to be able to say I dove into the ocean with the grace and speed of an Olympic diving champion, but I had to clamber across the deck railing first. I swung one leg over and then the other. I hesitated, perched at the top. I let as much air out of my lungs as I could, and then I breathed deep. Before I could contemplate the foolishness of my actions, I jumped, throwing myself forward with enough power to sail across the small dock before coming into contact with the water.

Jayne had not been exaggerating: the water was freezing. Icy, salty waves closed over my head as I sank to the depths. My heart stopped, and for the briefest of moments, I hoped it would remember to start again.

Then, thankfully, it did. The cold was like a vice around my chest. The water isn't particularly deep here, but it is well over my head. My lungs screaming, I dropped straight down. My feet hit the rocky bottom, and I kicked up with all the strength I could muster. My head broke the surface and I sucked in air. Above me, I could vaguely hear Jayne shouting and the clamor of voices joining hers.

In the summer, I like to swim off the Cape Cod beaches as often as I can find the time. The summer, of course, is when we're busiest at the Emporium and Mrs. Hudson's, so I don't get the chance to swim as often as I would like. I hadn't been in the water since mid-September, and it was now January. I keep meaning to go to the gym or take up yoga, but somehow my good intentions always come to naught.

Nevertheless, I'm an adequate swimmer, on the surface at any rate. Now, legs kicking, arms windmilling, I treaded water, frantically searching the dark around me, trying to peer over the waves and locate the person floating below the surface of the black water. Suddenly, light was all around me as the lamps on the deck were switched on. A wave dipped, I caught a flash of red, and I headed for it.

Someone—a better diver than me—sliced through the water close to me and came up without touching bottom.

Andy touched my shoulder. I pointed, he nodded in acknowledgement, and together we swam toward the shape bobbing on the waves, about to go down again. It was a person, all right, a woman with long black hair and a red dress. The thin strap of a small purse wrapped around one shoulder. She lay on her belly, face down, the only movement her body following the gentle up and down of the sea.

Andy and I looked at each other across the woman's back. He nodded, and together we struggled to flip her over. She didn't weigh much, and the movement of the water helped us. And then I was looking into the blank, empty, no longer beautiful eyes of Tina Armstrong.

Chapter Eight

"Over here, over here," voices shouted. Andy put one arm around Tina's chest and used the other to propel them both through the water toward the dock. I followed, kicking awkwardly, trying to take some of her weight and help push her forward.

"I've got her, I've got her," a man called.

"Careful there," a woman said.

Light surrounded us, voices called out. In the distance, I could hear a siren, two sirens, approaching.

And then the weight was gone, and Andy and I were treading water.

"Can you get to the ladder?" I asked.

He nodded, and together we swam the few yards to the ladder to the dock. He pushed at me, telling me to go first. I bumped against it as hands and arms reached down. I'd lost contact with my extremities. My hands fumbled for the metal railings, but they couldn't find purchase. My feet felt for the ladder steps, but they found nothing but icy water.

I lifted my arms, and my head slipped under the water. When I came up sputtering and spitting, someone had a powerful grip on my hand. And then more hands were holding my arms, tugging at my sodden dress, and I felt myself being lifted. My feet touched the steps, and I was able to force myself up. Higher and higher I climbed until someone was holding me and something soft and warm was draped over me.

"Get them inside, quick," Jayne said. "I don't know if it's true brandy can warm up a cold victim, but I don't see as it would hurt."

"Don't like brandy," I said. Although I fear it came out more like "d . . . on'l . . . l . . . br . . . tha . . . stuff."

I could hardly hold myself up as I was helped to climb the steps to the deck and guided through the gate. I glanced behind me to see Andy following. Below us on the dock, Irene Talbot was on her knees, crouched over the red dress, giving CPR. Tina's right arm lay flat on the boards of the dock, the green stone sparkling in the lights.

As I reached the sliding doors to the restaurant, medics came out onto the deck.

"She's down on the dock," Jayne said. "These two need help also."

"See to Tina first," I said. "I'm fine." The medics hesitated and gave me doubtful looks. Perhaps I'd said, "S . . . s . . . Tin . . . I . . . I . . . fine. Sorta."

"We've got this," Jayne said.

"Another truck is right behind us," one of the medics said, as she and her partner crossed the deck, heading for the stairs to the dock.

"Get them into the restrooms and out of those clothes," Andy's mother shouted. "This is no time for modesty."

I was bundled away. I was stripped of my clothes, my hands held under warm water, my arms rubbed, my head put under the hand dryer, and then my hair scrubbed furiously with a kitchen towel. Finally, I was wrapped in whatever coats and sweaters could be gathered. Slowly, ever so slowly, I warmed.

"You'll live," Mrs. Ramsbatten said to me, as though she'd had her doubts.

"I doubt that dress will," Irene said.

The dress had been on its second life anyway. First, a full-on, knock-out fight in a crowded A-list London nightclub, then full immersion in the Atlantic Ocean. It had done its duty.

I caught a glimpse of myself in the mirror. I'd rather I hadn't. I now understood the phrase "death warmed over."

"Tina?" I said to Irene.

"Doesn't look good. They've rushed her to the hospital. I've heard paramedics say, 'They're never dead until they're warm and dead,' but . . ." Irene's voice drifted off.

"Are you able to take a seat in the restaurant, dear?" Mrs. Ramsbatten asked. "The police have arrived, and they will have questions. If you like, I can tell them you're overcome by the shock and have to be rushed to bed immediately or I won't be responsible for the consequences."

As though anyone in the WLPD would believe that. "It's okay. I'm fine now." I don't cry often—meaning I never cry—but I felt tears well up in my eyes. My clothes lay in a puddle on the floor; Irene and Mrs. Ramsbatten were, although not quite drenched, mighty wet. Their faces as they studied me for signs of delayed trauma were soft and kind.

"Where's Andy? Is he okay?"

"He will be. Jayne and his mother are with him."

I walked into the dining room, Mrs. Ramsbatten preceding me with the assistance of her cane, Irene not quite supporting me but ready to do so if needed. A chair was provided for me, and I dropped gratefully into it.

"Brandy, Gemma?" Ashleigh asked, "Or we have hot chocolate if you'd prefer?"

"A hot cocoa would be beyond perfect." Moments later, a warm mug was pressed into my hands. I closed my eyes and took a long deep breath, letting the scented steam fill my nose and lungs, and then I took a small sip. Hot and sweet and chocolatey, the delicious warmth spread though my body and I began to think I might actually live.

That matter settled to my satisfaction, I looked to see what was happening around me. On the other side of the sliding doors and floor-to-ceiling windows, blue and red flashing lights broke the night, reflecting off people moving around. The medics had gone and police officers were stringing crime scene tape around the railings and the steps to the dock. A police officer stood at the door to the deck, arms crossed, feet apart, saying nothing, simply watching us all.

The party had been breaking up when Jayne and I went outside, but not one person had left in the interval. Andy's dad paced up and down in front of the bar. Bunny, George, and Madison, along with a few stragglers, perched on stools, facing into the room. Facing me, in fact. Robbie and Ashleigh, along with Martin and the kitchen staff, had taken seats at a table, shot glasses or bottles of beer in front of them. Only the bartender continued working.

Donald was at the next table with his new friend Keith and a woman who was likely Keith's wife. Something, I thought, looked off about Donald. And then I realized what it was: he wore only his shirt, waistcoat, and trousers. I touched the heavy fabric draped across my shoulders. His frock coat. I gave him a smile of thanks, and his worried face relaxed a fraction.

Audrey sat at a table with two of Andy's sisters, her head up, her sharp eyes alert, watching everything. She'd pulled a notebook and pen out of her purse and had it open on the table in front of her. Mrs. Ramsbatten and Irene joined her.

A burst of applause rang out, and I turned my head to see Andy coming into the room. He and Jayne were holding hands, and his mother was with them. Like me, he was dressed in someone else's coat. He gave the room a weak smile. Trish Whitehall's eyes were red, her nose swollen. She and Jayne led Andy to a chair next to mine, as his father brought him a brandy snifter.

Andy's dad then addressed the room. "A toast. To our heroes!"

"Andy and Gemma!" Everyone lifted their glasses. I sort of half-raised my mug. I didn't feel like much of a hero. I'd accomplished nothing by foolishly diving into the winter ocean, other than to endanger Andy and anyone who had to lean over the water to pull us out.

"Any word on Tina?" Andy asked after the cheers died down.

"Not yet," his dad said.

Andy half-turned so he was speaking to the table at the back. "You can all go home. We'll be closed tomorrow, and the day staff can finish cleaning up then. We'll open again day after tomorrow, regular hours."

I knew that wasn't going to happen, but I said nothing. Officer Richter, still not retired although long past his best-before date, cleared his throat, puffed up his chest and said, "Not so fast there, young fellow. The detective has been called. She'll want to talk to you all. Tonight. As for reopening your restaurant, the timing of that will be up to her."

Andy started to get to his feet, but his mum pushed him back down. "I have a business to run here." The force of his statement might have had more effect had not his mother been tucking the coat around him as though she were putting a recalcitrant child to bed.

Richter shrugged. "Not my call. Talk to the detective."

George stepped forward. "Obviously, this has nothing to do with me. Your detective can call me in the morning, if she wants. Bunny, may I offer you a ride?"

Bunny threw a panicked look at Officer Richter.

"I think it best," I said, "if we stay until we're dismissed. After all, at the moment no one knows what has what do to with whom."

"In that case," Bunny said, "as long as we're stuck here waiting our turn to be dragged under the bright lights, I'll have another drink. A martini would be nice, thank you, young lady."

The bartender threw a question to Andy.

"Might as well," Andy said.

"Might as well not," a firm voice said. "The bar is closed. It, and the rest of this establishment, will remain closed until I say it can reopen."

Detective Louise Estrada had arrived.

Chapter Nine

After issuing that order, the first thing the good detective did was look at me and let out a martyred sigh. She didn't actually say, "You again," but such was implied.

I shrugged in response. *Yes, me again.* I've been involved in more police cases than both I and the police would like. I always insist I don't seek out trouble, but trouble seems to enjoy searching for me. Not everyone believes that.

Estrada was an attractive woman: tall, thin, well-muscled, with thick black hair, tonight woven in a sleek French braid, dark watchful eyes, and a flawless olive complexion. She always put me in mind of a racehorse on the verge of leaving the gate.

She and I didn't exactly get on when we first met, and it took some time for her to accept that I did not interfere in police matters without reason and I might even be of help sometimes. That I'm dating her partner, Detective Ryan Ashburton, who seems to be rather fond of me and who does trust me, might have something to do with her (highly reluctant) acceptance of me and my methods.

I stood up, still clutching Donald's frock coat around me, necessary because I had nothing on underneath but my hastily dried knickers and a still damp bra. My dignity and any attempt to appear authoritative were at risk. "You know my methods, Detective," I said. "The first question we must ask is—"

"The first thing I'm going to do, before asking any questions at all, is have a look at the scene. If that's okay with you, Ms. Doyle?"

"Be particularly careful checking the area around the gate to the steps leading to the dock. I have reason to suspect the killer—"

"If there is a killer. From what I've been told, such is still to be determined." Estrada turned to Richter. "Keep an eye on these people. Don't let them talk amongst themselves. Particularly her." Estrada felt no need to mention which *her* she was referring to.

"Not talk!" Madison exclaimed. "Audrey can't live if she can't talk." The joke fell flat. No one so much as tittered, and a few people had the grace to look embarrassed. Audrey glared at Madison, then turned her attention to her notebook and began to write with strong, rapid strokes. I was interested as to what she considered of such importance she had to get it down, right now, despite everything happening around her, but unless I got up, walked over to her table, and leaned over her shoulder to read her scribblings, it was unlikely I'd ever know.

Estrada left to go outside, Richter sliding the door shut behind her. The detective went up to a uniformed officer, and they exchanged a few words. And then, first things first, she studied the gate to the steps leading to the dock.

"Bad time to have the place closed down for a few days," George said to Andy.

"No talking," Richter said.

"We're not talking about anything of concern to you," George replied. "Business is business and—"

"And," Andy said, "this is not the time to bring that up again, George. If you have helpful advice, I'd be happy to hear it tomorrow. If you're going to do nothing but repeat what you said earlier, forget it."

George turned to Bunny. "How was your martini?"

Bunny lifted her almost empty glass. "Excellent. I was somewhat of a connoisseur of cocktails in my wild youth. I always say a good martini is the mark of an excellent restaurant. If a place can't serve a top-notch—"

I didn't hear what a restaurant that failed to meet Bunny's standards was, as Andy leaned over and spoke to me in a voice so low, only he and I could hear. "You know how these things work, Gemma. How long are we likely to be closed?"

"I can't say. Tomorrow for sure, as they'll need to examine the scene in daylight. Maybe longer depending on what the police find out there. Estrada is right; we don't know if Tina was murdered. It might have been an accident."

"Seems highly unlikely, don't you think? The deck railing isn't broken as though she'd fallen through it. I didn't notice anything like that anyway."

"Maybe she went for a swim. Maybe she thought she could balance along the top of the railing and found out she couldn't. I don't know, Andy. You might be able to open the restaurant inside, if the deck is all they need to keep roped off."

"Let's hope," he said. "George had a point. I can't afford to be closed for long."

"I said, no talking." Estrada had returned. "Did you not hear my instructions, Officer Richter?"

His pudgy face turned beet red. "No, ma'am. I mean, yes, ma'am, I heard you. But they said business talk would be okay."

"Nothing Gemma Doyle says is okay with me."

Various of the guests who hadn't met me before gave me curious looks, clearly wondering why I was being singled out. I refrained from giving them a wave.

"Okay," Estrada said. "It's late. Gemma Doyle and Andy Whitehall, I need to talk to you two tonight. As for the rest of you, does anyone here have anything to tell me about why that young woman would have been in the water? She didn't have a coat on when she was pulled out. Why would she have been outside on a night like tonight?"

"She was a heavy smoker," I said. "Sorry, that's a small error on my part. Considering we're all hoping she will make a full recovery, I should say she *is* a heavy smoker."

"How do you know this? Did you go out and smoke with her?"

"Of course not. A matter of observation. Despite her nice party clothes and her excessively applied, drugstore-shelf perfume, the distinctive scent of tobacco hung heavily around her. Not only that, but she had cigarettes and a lighter in her bag. Her phone was in her bag also—when she went outside, at any rate—and she had that purse still on her when Andy and I found her. I trust you recovered it."

Estrada gave me the look I knew so well. "When I need advice on conducting an investigation, Ms. Doyle, I'll ask you."

"Gemma's right," Trish Whitehall said. "About the smoking anyway. I went outside earlier to have a cigarette and Tina was finishing hers."

"If that isn't enough to make you quit, I don't—" Pete Whitehall said.

"Not now, Dad," Andy said.

"Was this shortly before she was seen in the water?" Estrada asked.

"No," Trish said. "I don't remember exactly, but long before that."

"Same with me," Madison said. "I saw her smoking out there. We said hi, but not much more than that. Again, it was earlier. Before cake, I think."

"Officer Richter, take these people's names and contact information," Estrada said. "I, or someone on my team, will be in touch with you in the morning for a statement. But before you go, did Ms. Armstrong say anything to anyone that might indicate she was bothered about something? Did she argue with anyone tonight?"

"She wasn't invited," Trish Whitehall said.

"Not invited? What does that mean?"

"Leave it, Mom," Andy said.

"Mrs. Whitehall?" Estrada prompted.

"She crashed the party. I assume you've been told this is a birthday party for Jayne, my son's fiancée. Tina Armstrong was not invited, and she was not welcome. We should have shown her to the door."

"Any reason she was not welcome?"

Trish's eyes widened as she realized she was saying too much. She closed her mouth and dipped her head. Estrada stared at her, waiting for an answer.

"She's not a friend of our family is all I mean," Trish finally muttered. "This was a private event."

"Wasn't she a former girlfriend of Andy's?" Madison asked. "She said that, didn't she? An old girlfriend back to haunt the new girlfriend's party." She laughed. Her cocktail glass was almost full.

Despite Estrada's orders, the bartender handed Madison another drink when Richter wasn't looking. In return, Madison slipped a twenty-dollar bill across the counter. I decided I had more important things to concentrate on than to report them.

"Tina and Andy were close once, so why should she not come?" Jayne turned her smile on Andy. "She was very pleasant. She wished me a happy birthday and wished us well in our marriage. I thought she was nice."

Andy shifted uncomfortably, and he did not return the smile.

Estrada was watching him in a way I didn't like. "Close? How close?"

"It was a long time ago," Andy said. "We dated in . . . school."

In England, we don't call places of higher education "school," although Americans refer to college and university as such. Tonight, the way Andy pronounced the word implied he was talking about their small-town high school. Not the years he and Tina had been together in New York City pursuing further education and careers. I wasn't about to correct the detective's interpretation.

"She came to the party alone?" Estrada asked.

"Yes," several people said.

"I think Donald here killed her." Keith slapped my friend on the back so hard Donald stumbled forward.

Estrada's eyes narrowed as she turned to them. "Why do you say that, sir?"

"To get me interested in that murder mystery stuff he's so fond of. He was telling me about this store in town that sells Sherlock Holmes things. Nothing better than a real-life murder to stoke interest."

Donald sputtered in indignation.

"I have no evidence—as of yet—that a murder took place." Estrada's voice was chilly. Then again, sometimes it's hard to tell. Chilly is her natural state. "Accidents happen around water, particularly when alcohol is involved. As for you, sir, if you have a serious accusation to make, please do. Otherwise, I do not consider this a matter for jokes."

"My bad. Sorry, pal." Keith didn't look at all sorry.

"It's okay. I think," Donald said.

"How about we go together to this store some time? I'll give you a call, set something up."

"Keith, the detective told you to shut up," his wife shouted.

"Madam," Estrada said. "May I ask what you're writing there?"

Ever since I returned from my brush with death (as I would later embellish the tale to impress Great-Uncle Arthur and my sister, Pippa), Audrey had been scribbling away. She didn't bother to look up as she was addressed. "Just making a few notes, before I forget. Might as well get it down, now, here, while it's all fresh."

"What sort of notes?" Estrada asked sharply. "Are you a journalist?"

"Oh, no. Nothing like that. I'm writing a book. That's to say, I'm thinking of writing a book. Early days yet."

"Audrey was a Hollywood insider," Madison explained. "She's always talking about the stories she could tell."

I considered it odd that Audrey suddenly found inspiration for her insider Hollywood book at a police interrogation in West London, but before I could pry further, Estrada said, "Speaking of journalism, I assume, Ms. Talbot, you will be writing up this incident?"

"Already filed," Irene said. "Mentally, anyway. Let's see what transpires next."

Estrada grimaced, but before she could say more, Officer Stella Johnson opened the door and stepped through. She whispered into Estrada's ear, and the detective nodded. Stella gave me a quick look before going back outside, and I knew what Estrada was going to say before she said it.

"I am sorry," she said. "The hospital called. Ms. Armstrong did not make it."

Someone gasped. A few women started to cry; a man crossed himself and murmured a prayer. Trish Whitehall stared straight ahead, her jaw set, her expression unchanging. Jayne put her arms around Andy's shoulders and whispered, "I am so sorry."

"Her family has been informed," Estrada said. "I need to go to the hospital and speak to them and the attending doctor, but before I do that, I want a word with Gemma Doyle and Andy Whitehall. Everyone else, please give Officer Richter your names and phone numbers and then take your leave. This party is over. You may take your personal items, such as your purses and coats, but nothing else. I assume those," she nodded toward the tower of brightly wrapped gifts, "are yours, Ms. Wilson. They'll have to stay here."

Jayne nodded.

Of all people, Robbie got to his feet and started talking. "It's important you try to remember everything that happened here earlier. Things get forgotten in the turmoil of the moment. Important things. Things the police need to know." He turned to speak to the restaurant employees sharing his table. "Most important for us, the staff. We see things from the shadows, right? People don't pay any attention to us and they say stuff they shouldn't in front of us. We hear things, we see things,

things that seem normal, but on second thought, aren't. Right, everyone?"

Most of the staff murmured agreement and nodded.

Martin snickered and made a show of rolling his eyes, and I was reminded that he and Robbie clashed earlier tonight.

"Who are you?" Estrada asked Robbie.

"Robert Ellis. I was filling in here tonight. Helping out, like, as Jayne and I go way back. Jayne, if Andy has to stay for a while, how about I give you a lift home?"

"That would be—" Jayne began.

"That won't be necessary," I said quickly. "Jayne came with her mother and brother. They can give Mrs. Ramsbatten a lift. They're all going the same way." Jayne gave me a curious look. They were, in fact, going in totally opposite directions, but it was the best excuse I could come up with on the spur of the moment.

The look Robbie gave me, on the other hand, was one of pure poison. I smiled sweetly at him in return.

Martin chuckled. He was seated next to Robbie, and he leaned over and whispered something in the other man's ear. I didn't hear the words, but the anger on Robbie's face deepened. Martin leaned back and crossed his arms over his chest looking very pleased at whatever witticism he'd dispensed, and the reaction he got.

People began standing up. A line formed in front of Officer Richter.

The forensics people had arrived, bringing their powerful lights. They moved around the deck, taking fingerprints and photographs, examining the wood of the railing and the metal of the gate. A woman leaned over the railing and shouted to someone below. Blue and red lights danced cheerfully across the water.

All the usual hubbub and chaos and routine of a suspected crime scene. Ryan would be sorry to have missed it. It can be hard to catch up by reading reports.

Unless this could all be put to bed before Ryan was due to come home. Although that was unlikely. The police would want to be positive Tina's death had been accidental before closing the case.

"Bunny, care to go someplace for a nightcap?" George asked.

"I'm sorry," she said, "but it's getting late and this has all been quite upsetting. Can I take a rain check?"

"Certainly." George whipped out his phone, and Bunny gave him her number. Ashleigh was in line behind her mother and didn't look entirely pleased, although Bunny clearly did. Madison told Richter she and Audrey were staying at the Harbor Inn and would be there until the day after the wedding. Andy told his staff he'd call them in the morning to let them know what was happening. Several muttered that they couldn't afford to be off work, not in winter when business was so slow.

"If I don't have regular shifts here," Martin said, "other places need a chef of my quality."

"What can I say?" Andy said. "It's not up to me."

Finally, only Andy and I remained in the company of the police. Andy's mother had been reluctant to leave, but he reminded her he was an adult, kissed her on the cheek, and told his father to go home. He walked Jayne to the door and they stood together for a long time, holding each other, not speaking. "Talk in the morning," he said when they finally separated.

"Sit," Estrada ordered.

Andy and I sat, and the detective joined us around a hastily cleared table. "For your information, I've contacted Detective

Ashburton. He says he hasn't heard from you tonight, Gemma. On a personal level, I mean."

"I'm hoping this can be cleared up and he can continue with his course."

"You think it will happen that quickly?"

"No. As for me, on a personal level, what happened to Tina is distressing, and I'm deeply sorry for her and for her family. But I didn't know her. I'd never met her before tonight, so my personal feelings are not as involved as they might be."

I thought Estrada might ask Andy what his personal feelings were, but she didn't. She simply asked us to take her through what happened tonight and we did so.

"Why were you and Jayne Wilson outside in the first place?" she asked when we'd finished telling the tale. "Neither of you smoke, and it's a cold night."

"No reason," I said easily. "A quick catch-up and to wish each other a good night. We were standing at the railing, watching the water, and we saw her. Tina. So I jumped in. Which, I will now freely admit, might not have been the wisest course of action."

"Jayne ran inside, yelling for help," Andy said. "Everyone hurried out to see what was going on. I guess I was first to get there. I saw Gemma floundering around in the water and I knew she needed help."

"I wouldn't say floundering. I was attempting to get my bearings."

Estrada asked about earlier in the evening. If we'd noticed Tina arguing with anyone, or anyone behaving at all suspiciously.

"A less suspicious gathering, I can't imagine," I said. "It was a birthday party. A private event. Everyone was on their best behavior."

"Your mother wasn't happy Tina invited herself, Andy," Estrada said.

"My mom never liked Tina," Andy admitted. "Even when we were together. She adores Jayne, that's all. Maybe she thought Tina's presence would be upsetting to Jayne."

"Which it wasn't," I said. "Not in the least. As Jayne said herself."

"Was it upsetting to you, Andy?"

Andy flushed and looked away. Not a wise move on his part. Estrada's eyes flickered, and she sat a little bit straighter. "No, not upsetting," he said. "We had a last-minute cancellation, so a seat was free and we had a meal for her."

Which is not what Estrada had been asking, but she didn't press the point. "You were quick to dismiss that man's offer to drive Jayne home, Gemma. Any reason?"

Louise Estrada's initial dislike and distrust of me had been known to cloud her judgment when I'm around. But I never let myself forget she's highly observant and a good judge of character. "No reason other than Mrs. Ramsbatten needed a lift too, as did Jayne's mother. I've been giving some thought to the accident idea, and I have to say—"

"Is what you have to say based on physical evidence or merely on speculation, Gemma?"

I was rather offended by her tone. I never speculate without data. Well, almost never. "I have taken the available physical evidence, what I saw of it, and considered it in light of events here tonight, general weather conditions, possible state of mind of the victim as observed by me, and—"

Estrada stood up. "Thank you for your time. I'll need to get detailed formal statements from you both tomorrow. Now I have to get to the hospital. It's going to be a long night." Something crossed her face and for a moment she looked almost human. "I hate talking to the family. I really hate it. Worst part of the job."

"You might ask them if Tina was a good swimmer," I suggested.

Chapter Ten

My phone buzzed to announce an incoming text while I chatted with Estrada. Knowing by the sound who it was from, I didn't check it until Andy and I were in his car driving through the dark, quiet streets.

Dark and quiet, that is, once we were away from the Harbor Road boardwalk, small-boat dock, and pier, where bright lights had turned night into day and the few town residents still up stood in the cold watching the activity on the deck of the Blue Water Café.

Ryan: *Not again!*
Me: *Again. Heading home now. Talk in 10?*
Ryan: *I'm here.*

"Ryan?" Andy asked as I put away my phone.

I leaned back in the seat, rested my head on the head rest, and closed my eyes. "Estrada notified him they had a call, and she just happened to mention I was at the scene. He'll want the details."

"First thing I'm doing when I get home is have a hot shower."

“Good idea.” I pulled out my phone and sent another text.

Me: *Talk in 20*

That done, I said, “Are you okay, Andy? Really okay, I mean? About Tina’s death?”

He sighed. “Yeah, I’m okay. This is going to make me sound pretty shallow, but she won’t be my problem anymore.”

“Was she threatening to become a problem?”

“Yeah, Gemma, she was. She called me a couple of times a few months ago, suggested we meet for coffee. She came into the restaurant for a drink at the bar more than once and asked to see me. She wanted me to rethink my marriage to Jayne.”

“And?”

“And after the first coffee meeting, I ignored her calls and told my staff I was too busy to take a break. She told me I was the love of her life and she wanted us to get back together.”

“Tell me you told her that was not going to happen.”

“I did. Firmly and succinctly. Even if Jayne wasn’t in the picture, I don’t want to be with Tina. I have no feelings at all for her. Not anymore.”

“Did you tell her that?”

“Not in so many words. I tried to let her down easily. Maybe I was too easy on her, ’cause she didn’t seem to get the hint.”

Andy pulled up to my house. A light was on in the hallway, the drapes in the front room open, and I could see Violet and Peony peering out the windows. To reach window height, they had to stand on the couch. *So that’s what they get up to when I’m not home.*

Andy stared out the car window into the night. “That stuff happened early in the fall, before we went with you to England in October. The calls and the drop-ins and accidental encounters stopped when I got back, and I figured she'd realized it wasn't on. I don't mean to present myself as some sort of valuable catch, Gemma. I'm just a small-town cook."

"I think you're a valuable catch," I said in total honestly. "A small-town chef who is a genuinely good man."

He turned his head and smiled at me. "Thanks. Not good enough for Tina at one time; she didn't like my lack of ambition. I didn't like some of the things she did in an attempt to further her own ambitions. She wanted me to move to L.A. to make my mark in the restaurant scene there. Way too competitive for me, I told her. But once she gave up her own dreams of fame and fortune and came back to West London . . . I suppose I'd do. So no, I was not happy to see her."

"Did she say anything tonight about you ditching Jayne for her?"

"No. She suggested we have lunch tomorrow, though. Said she had something important to talk to me about. I told her I was busy with pre-wedding plans. I've tried to cut her some slack, Gemma. We were close once. I try to remember that. Things haven't always been easy for her. You know she was in a major car accident less than two years ago?"

"I noticed the scar on her face, about which she is clearly self-conscious, and she has a slight limp she tries to hide. Result of the accident?"

"Yeah. She was pretty banged up. Lots of plastic surgery, reconstruction, physiotherapy, the lot. She spent months in the hospital in California. It put an end to her dreams of an acting career. Not only the scar and the limp, but she was out of the frame for a year, and when she tried to get back, her time had passed. She says she was about to sign for a major role in a big

TV show when the accident happened, but I don't know if that's true or not." Andy shivered, and I suspected it was from more than uncomfortable thoughts. Despite my frock coat and the car's heater on full I was shivering too.

"Get yourself home," I said. "And into that shower." I put my hand on the door, but I hesitated. "One other thing. Get rid of Robbie."

"Robbie? The waiter? Why?"

"You must remember he and Jayne dated at one time, a couple of years ago?"

"Sure, I remember. This is a small town, Gemma. In the off-season anyway. We bump into people we knew from years ago all the time. Friends and enemies. We were just saying the same about me and Tina."

"Robbie means you no good, Andy. He's not full-time at your place, so you don't need to fire him. Don't give him a shift again, okay? Good night."

I got out of the car, waving Andy off. Then I sent another text.

Me: *20 starting now.*

Chapter Eleven

"First things first. Jumping into the sea was darn foolish. For heaven's sake, Gemma, what were you thinking? Or rather not thinking, as you have been known to do."

I'd lit a fire in the fireplace in the den and was curled up on the couch, wrapped in flannel pajamas, a fraying terrycloth robe, and heavy reading socks, with a towel around my hair. I clutched a mug of tea, to which I'd added far more sugar than I'm accustomed to. The portrait of Great-Uncle Arthur's one true love, a Spanish opera singer who died far too young, watched over me. The dogs, quite unperturbed at being chastised for jumping on the couch, rested at my feet, and my iPad was propped on my knees.

On the screen, Ryan shook his head. I took a moment to think how handsome he was with his chiseled cheekbones, close-cropped black hair, expressive blue eyes, and strong jaw thick with five o'clock shadow this late in the night. Or rather, this early in the morning.

"Gemma, are you listening to me?"

"Most definitely hearing, although not listening in the sense of having the intention of never repeating my mistake. What happened happened, and I will freely admit it might not have been the wisest course of action. Although, I must point out, had I been able to reach Tina in time, it would have been not entirely foolish." I smiled at him.

He shook his head and smiled back. "Point taken. I'll be home tomorrow around noon."

"You don't need to cut your course short for me. I'm fine."

"Not cutting it short for you, but because a potential murder happened in my town. Anyway, the last day is usually just a half-day repetition of what we already learned, and then, as you English say, down the pub. I assume you have a theory about what happened. Did you share it with Louise?"

"She didn't want to hear. I readily admit one should not theorize in the absence of data, but I believe I have enough data to form a rough theory."

"And . . . ?"

"If the data, meaning the evidence, changes, I will reconsider, but at this time, I have trouble seeing this as a murder."

"Why?"

"First, Tina was not expected to attend the dinner. Therefore, it could not have been preplanned."

"You didn't know she'd be there. Doesn't mean she didn't tell someone else."

"A fair point. Second, the restaurant was busy. Even the deck was being used, as a good number of smokers were at the event. The deck is visible from the boardwalk, although at that time of night in January, not many people were about and those who were would have their heads down and be hurrying about their business. Regardless, it was too public a place to commit murder."

"You think it was an accident, then?"

"Possible, although unlikely. The railing was not dislodged in any way. No adult would climb to the top of the railing for the view. For one thing, the railing is narrow, it was cold, and Tina was not wearing gloves. The gate to the steps leading to the dock was unlocked, so she might have gone down, but why? To have a quiet moment on the dock and she slipped? Possible."

"Suicide?" Ryan asked.

"Perhaps. I wasn't paying a great deal of attention to her earlier—"

"But you did notice more than anyone else would have."

"Thank you for the compliment. She was chatting, smiling, friendly. I thought her false, but put it down to her being uncomfortable knowing she wasn't entirely welcome. The look on Trish Whitehall's face—" I stopped. I was warm, inside and out. I was comfortable. I was safe. My dogs snoozed at my feet, the man I love was watching me with an expression full of concern, tinged with love, even though it was through a screen. I was forgetting to watch my mouth.

"What look?" Ryan said.

"Nothing."

"Nothing you say is ever nothing. What look, Gemma?"

I avoided answering. "She, Tina, had been in a serious vehicle accident a couple of years ago. That accident ended her dreams of an acting career. By coincidence, a woman, a relative of Andy's, who used to move in Hollywood circles, was seated at our table. Did talking to her remind Tina of her shattered dreams? Did seeing Andy, in love and happy, remind her she was not happy?"

"Are you saying she killed herself?"

"I'm saying the possibility is strong. A sloppy way to go about it to my mind, mostly because of the number of people around. A desperate cry for attention that went wrong? Maybe she didn't intend it to end as it did. I asked Louise to find out from Tina's family if she was a good swimmer. I'll be interested if they can determine if she went in off the deck or the dock, and how much alcohol was in her system. A substantial amount by my estimation; she wasn't entirely sober when she arrived and didn't slow down after that."

"Why does the dock or deck matter?"

"Off the dock would indicate an ill-considered swim. Off the deck, which is much higher, more likely with the intent to do damage. Assuming, of course, she was thinking straight, which is not a given."

"Louise sent me a few preliminary notes a while ago. More coming in now. Give me a sec." He disappeared from the screen as he went to get his phone. I was left facing a standard budget hotel chain room. Generic paintings on the beige walls. Drapes pulled shut. Strong desk lamp.

"Okay. Autopsy still to be done, but the ER doc saw a substantial and very recent bruise on the top of her forehead. Likely caused some internal damage."

"If she hit her head on the way in, that might explain why she couldn't swim to shore."

"Or she was hit before being tossed over the railing. Her parents say Tina was an excellent swimmer. She was on the diving team in high school and she took up surfing when she moved to California. She swam in the ocean here regularly right into the fall, and participated in polar swims several years."

"She went swimming at the North Pole?" Suddenly, I was cold all over, again.

"No. Those are charity events swimming clubs organize, usually held on January first. They go for a dip in the lake or ocean. It's a big thing, usually attracts a considerable crowd of onlookers."

"Perish the thought. Otherwise, that's something worth knowing."

"Why?"

"When I find out why, I'll tell you. Every piece of data is worth knowing. Didn't they teach you that at your course?"

The smile he gave me was as warm as my feet in my reading socks. "Sometimes I think I learn far more from you than any course. Don't tell Louise I said that. What's on for tomorrow?"

"You mean today." The clock on my iPad told me it was two a.m. "Work for me. Jayne's taking the day off, but I suspect that won't last much past the breakfast rush."

"Good night, Gemma."

"Good night, Ryan."

Chapter Twelve

"Jayne in?" I asked Fiona as I placed my usual order for a large tea, with a splash of milk, no sugar, and a blueberry muffin.

"Not physically. She's phoned a few times. Just checking in, she says. My money's on her arriving before two. Jocelyn's betting on noon. Want to get a wager in? It's ten bucks."

"Sure. It's quarter after nine now. I'm in for her showing her face before ten."

Jocelyn opened the sliding door between the Emporium and Mrs. Hudson's, and I carried my breakfast through. The door slid shut behind me, to be opened again in fifteen minutes when the shop was ready for business.

Moriarty emerged from his bed under the center table, yawning and stretching. "I trust you had a better night than I did," I said to him.

The edge of his mouth curled in a sneer, and he headed for the stairs, tail held high. I put my drink and muffin on the counter and climbed the seventeen steps to the first floor, what Americans call the second floor, after him. My first task of the day, like my last, is to check his food and water dishes and clean out the litter box.

For which I get absolutely no thanks.

Activity in the shop was slow, which can be expected on a Wednesday morning in January. At ten to ten, Jayne walked through the tearoom, and I spent some valuable time wondering how to best spend my winnings.

A short while later, she came into the Emporium, hair wrapped in a net, apron over jeans and a T-shirt. "All okay?" she asked.

"All okay. You look ready to work. I thought you were taking the day off."

"Not much point. I intended to enjoy a nice long lie-in the morning after my party, but I slept badly, woke up early, and couldn't settle again." Her pretty face crunched. "Terrible about what happened."

"Yeah. It is."

"Andy was up even before me, and he sent me a text to say he'd gone in to clean up. If the cops will let him. If the restaurant has to stay closed for long, that won't be good. Did Louise have much to say after I left?"

"Not much. I don't know for sure, but they should allow him to open before much longer. They don't have a lot to do inside; all the action, so to speak, happened on the deck, and he's not using that now anyway."

"I can only hope. Police attention is never good at a restaurant. Word's all over town about what happened last night."

I knew that. I'd checked the online sources as soon as I was up. Irene Talbot had filed a report with the paper, but she couldn't say much other than what I already knew: what happened and where. She didn't even mention Tina's name, so likely she hadn't spoken to the family yet. Without having any further information, she chose her words carefully and simply called the death a "drowning," which the police were "investigating." As for the police themselves, they hadn't issued a statement, other than to say what Irene already said. As could have been expected, gossip on the social media pages was rampant. And mostly inaccurate.

"A clerk from the police station called earlier and asked me to present myself later today to make a formal statement," Jayne said. "Did you hear from them?"

"Not yet. Ryan cut his trip short, and he'll be back soon. When you're talking to the police, it's probably best not to mention Andy and his mum weren't all that welcoming to Tina."

"They weren't?"

"She gate-crashed, right?"

"Yes, I know," Jayne said. "That might have been awkward, but they had room for her, and she was a longtime friend of Andy and his family."

"Forget what I said. If you didn't notice their coolness, you won't need to mention it, right?"

"Except you've put the idea in my head."

"Forget me. The police wouldn't let you take your gifts with you last night. Opening them will be something to look forward to."

"Hard to get in the present-opening mood after what happened. I'll be in the kitchen if you need me." She turned to go and then swung back. "Not because I can't leave my business in the highly capable hands of my assistants, but because a kitchen is my happy place. I can forget all the problems of the world when I'm up to my elbows in cake batter or rolling out scones or thumping yeasted dough. Gemma?"

"Yes?"

"This won't affect my wedding, will it? We have less than one week to go."

"I don't see how it should. I've been thinking it over, and I consider it possible Tina's death was either an accident or a suicide. If so, the police will soon come to the same conclusion."

At that moment, the chimes over the door tinkled and the first of the day's customers came in.

* * *

Ashleigh arrived for work shortly before noon. I was not impressed to see her dressed in a gray wool suit with a skirt that fell below her knees, high-necked blouse, shoes of the sort that were once called sensible, and a hat with a small gray feather perched on one side of her head.

"Please, please, tell me you are not Miss Marple," I said.

"Harriett Vane. Miss Marple is older. This is the best I could do on the spur of the moment. Like it?"

"I hope you're not planning to play detective."

"Nah. I leave that stuff up to you. That guy Donald cornered yesterday, Keith something, is coming in later. I wanted to make an impression, that's all, particularly as he met me in my persona of waitress, and that is not who I am."

I refrained from mentioning that she wasn't Harriet Vane either.

* * *

I ate lunch at my desk, working on the accounts, while Ashleigh minded the shop. I was rolling up my sandwich wrappings and cursing at the email that came in moments before from a prominent gaslight fiction author, canceling next week's scheduled appearance at the store for unstated reasons. I'd ordered a substantial number of her books, and boxes of them were stacked in my office and the storage room, ready to be signed. We'd put up a big flashy display in the shop. Signs advertising the event were in the windows and notices on the website. Several readers told me they were excited about meeting her.

I was heading downstairs to let Ashleigh have her break when a car pulled into the no-parking zone on the street and stayed there. A few minutes later, Detectives Estrada and Ashburton came in.

Moriarty leapt down from his perch at the top of the gaslight shelf and rubbed himself enthusiastically against Estrada's legs, purring loudly. She tried not to look too pleased. Ryan he ignored, as he usually did.

"Who are you supposed to be?" Estrada said to Ashleigh when she tore her attention away from the affections of the cat.

My assistant struck a pose. "Harriet Vane. Like it?"

"I don't want to know, but curiosity compels me to ask. Who is Harriet Vane?"

"Harriet Wimsey née Vane. From the Lord Peter books by Dorothy L. Sayers. A classic of crime fiction. Gemma, when Harriet marries Lord Peter does she become Lady Harriet?"

"No. She would only be Lady First Name if her father was titled. As she married into the title, she would be known as Lady Husband's Name."

"Her personal identity erased," Ashleigh said. "Seems unfair."

"The hierarchy of the British aristocracy is highly unfair. To women in particular, not to mention younger sons."

"Sorry I asked," Estrada said.

Ryan grinned and gave me a private smile before saying, "Gemma, we need to ask you further questions about the events of last night." The store was empty of customers at the moment, but Estrada added, "Can we use your office?"

"Of course."

Preceded by Moriarty, we climbed the steps. I sat behind my desk and waved my visitors to chairs. When they were reasonably comfortable, and Moriarty was watching from the comfort of the top of a box of now-unneeded gaslight fiction books, I said, "Has the autopsy on Tina Armstrong been done yet?"

"They were able to squeeze us in," Ryan said.

"And?"

"No doubt about cause of death—drowning in sea water. She had a substantial amount of alcohol in her system. By what they could determine, and what time we were told she arrived at the restaurant, she'd been drinking earlier. Not enough to completely incapacitate her, but enough to seriously impair her judgment and her reflexes, in the opinion of the pathologist. She appears to have suffered a blow high on her forehead, probably sufficient to render her unconscious, but it didn't kill her."

"Any indication of how the blow was delivered?"

"The pathologist is unable to say if she was struck by someone she was facing or if her head connected with the edge of the dock on the way down."

"Have you—?"

"Hey," Estrada said. "We're the police. We ask the questions here."

"Just trying to help."

Ryan suppressed a chuckle. He didn't suppress it well enough because his partner threw him a stern look.

"Once again, for the benefit of Detective Ashburton, can you go through the events of last night that led you to attempt to rescue Tina Armstong?"

I did so. I remembered nothing new, and nothing I'd seen or heard since had taken on any fresh significance.

"Thank you," she said when I finished. "Any questions, Detective Ashburton?"

"Why were you and Jayne outside?" Ryan asked. "You didn't have coats and it was cold."

"Allow me to follow a train of thought first. The restaurant deck can be accessed from the restaurant itself, the dock below, and the boardwalk."

"I see where you're going," Ryan said. "The gate leading off the boardwalk is secure and it has a solid lock, opened by a code. It was locked when officers arrived last night, and one of the restaurant staff opened it for them. Same for the gate from the public boardwalk to the dock, which is normal for this time of year."

In return for that information, I answered Ryan's question. "I wanted to warn Jayne that Robbie Ellis might be intending to cause trouble for her and Andy."

"You didn't tell me that last night," Estrada said.

"I didn't want to confuse matters at the time. You were impatient to examine the scene again and to get to the hospital."

"Who's Robbie Ellis?"

"A former boyfriend of Jayne's. He was working as a waiter last night. Late thirties, middling height, pudgy around the middle and the face, scruffy goatee. Could be moderately good-looking, if he dropped the sneer, which rarely happens. He was overheard bad-mouthing Jayne. At her own birthday party. I didn't think that was nice." I smoothly threw Robbie under the bus. I didn't think Robbie had anything to do with Tina's death, nor was I suggesting so, but this seemed like a good time to mention my concerns about him.

"I remember him," Ryan said. "Haven't seen him for years."

"He left. He came back. As they so often do. Including, if memory serves, you." No need to remind Ryan he left West London to get away from me. He returned a few years later and found me still here. "Tina had her little crossbody bag on her when she was pulled out. I saw her put her phone in it. Did you recover it?"

"We did," Estrada said. "Obviously totally soaked in salt water. We've been told not to even try to open it for at least forty-eight hours, and even then, it might never come back to life."

"That would appear to negate my idea of an ill-considered evening swim. Who swims with their phone on them?"

Ryan chuckled. "I've known guys to leap in and then remember, halfway down, their phone's still in their pocket. Mighty funny to see the expression on their faces." His own face twisted with the memory. "Or so I've been told."

"Are you talking from personal experience?" I asked.

"Not telling."

Even Estrada smiled at that. She considered it necessary to go through the motions of telling me the police didn't need my interference, but once that was done, she was okay with listening to what I had to say. She managed to choke out, "Do you . . . have any . . . thoughts on the matter?"

"Nothing new. It's been mentioned Tina was a swimmer and a diver, so it's possible she tried a dive from the railing and misjudged the angle with the dark and the amount she'd had to drink. Whether an ill-considered midnight swim or a deliberate attempt at ending it all . . . I can't say."

"What about the unlatched gate?" Ryan asked.

"It remains an interesting part of the puzzle. Could have nothing to do with what happened. Plenty of people were around that night."

"Louise asked Andy about the gate," Ryan said. "Andy said it was secure when he checked the place out prior to the first guests arriving, and he didn't check it after that. The lock isn't really even a lock, just a latch requiring some minor dexterity to open. Enough to keep little kids in and send a message to late-night revelers, but not much more."

"I'm of the opinion her death was by misadventure," I said.

"I disagree," Estrada said. "The open gate. The blow to the head. The intense coldness of the water. Her phone still being on her. We're looking at a murder here."

"I'm not ruling that out," I said, "simply exploring all possibilities. If we want to talk deliberate murder: a strong young man might have been able to catch her unaware and throw her over the railing. But an out-of-shape man or an older woman? No. They would have needed to get her through the gate and then give her a good solid shove down the steps."

"An interesting choice of words there," Ryan said. "What older woman or out-of-shape man are you thinking of?"

"No one in particular. Just speculating."

He studied my face, perhaps looking for clues there.

Estrada stood up. "I trust you'll contact us immediately if you think of anything at all relevant."

"I will," I said.

"We will be in touch." She left, followed by a black shadow.

Ryan also got to his feet, but he lingered after his partner and Moriarty left. I went up to him and he wrapped his arms around me. When we separated, he said, "Your thoughts?"

"I'm not as convinced it's murder as Louise is, but I don't want to rule it out, and she knows more of the finer details about this than I do." I smiled up at him, waiting for him to fill me in on those finer details. He did not.

"Have you spoken to Tina's family to ask if anything, or anyone, was bothering her recently. About her state of mind?"

"We have," Ryan said. "And that is absolutely not something I am going to share with you."

* * *

Estrada and Ryan were focusing on Tina's death being a murder, and that made me waver in my own previous conviction it was death by misadventure.

The number of smokers popping in and out of the deck area that night complicated things considerably. Once again, I mentally ran over the list of those who might have gone out for a cigarette: as well as Tina, among the guests this included Andy's mom, Madison, and Audrey. Anyone else could have gone out for a breath of air or to admire the night. Even to speak in private—Jayne and I had. Of the staff, one of them might have gone onto the deck for any reason. Andy didn't smoke, but he was everywhere that night, all the time, ensuring everything was running smoothly and his guests were having a good time.

In any murder investigation, the first question to be asked is *qui bono*. Who benefits?

I knew nothing at all about Tina and her life. She might have enemies crawling out of the woodwork, for all I knew. But she died at Jayne's party, and that meant a limited circle of suspects, if we needed to be looking for suspects. And some of them were people I did know and whom I cared about.

Theoretically, person or persons unknown could have accessed the restaurant deck directly from the boardwalk or from the dock via the boardwalk. The larger, heavier gate from the boardwalk had been locked, secured by a proper lock with a code, and it did not appear to have been breached. Access to the small dock was also locked at night, and that gate was secure when the police checked. Meaning, other than down the steps from the outdoor restaurant, access to the dock could only have been by boat. Getting a boat, driving it to the dock in the dead of night, tying it up, and lying in wait for the right moment would require a good deal of planning for a not-guaranteed result. The deck might have been packed with smokers when Tina took her break.

If I wanted to consider the possibility that Tina's death had not been an accident or self-inflicted and someone from the restaurant, either staff or guests, followed her outside, *qui bono?*

Decision made, I ran downstairs. I was pleased to see we'd had some customers while I was otherwise occupied, as a few books had been removed from the center table and the stack of World of Sherlock jigsaw puzzles was shorter than it had been. Ashleigh was ringing up CDs containing *Sherlock Holmes: The Definitive Collection* audiobook, narrated by Stephen Fry, for a customer.

"Love your outfit," the customer told her. "You need to stock more Golden Age detective stories: Christie and the like."

"I keep telling the owner that," Ashleigh said, "but she insists we stick to our Sherlock Holmes mandate. I'll convince her someday. Hi, Gemma. Everything okay?"

Ashleigh never tries to pretend she doesn't have any shortage of ideas as to how I should be running my business.

"You okay to watch the shop for a while? I have an errand to run."

"I don't know why you bother to ask, Gemma. You know I'm fine here."

I wasn't entirely sure I liked the sound of that. *Was I so surplus to requirements in my own shop?*

Couldn't be helped now. I usually walk to work, but it was a cold day and I was preoccupied by the events of the previous night, so I'd brought my car. The sporty little red Miata I'm so fond of didn't quite suit the winter weather, but no snow was in the forecast and the streets were well plowed after the last fall. Uncle Arthur's 1977 Triumph Spitfire, even less suited to this climate than my car, spends the winters in our garage.

I prefer not to warn people of an impending visit, thus allowing them time to compose themselves and prepare what to say. But that can lead to a good deal of time wasting because if I don't ask if they're home, they sometimes are not.

The person I was interested in talking to first worked from her home as a bookkeeper, so I decided to take a chance on finding her in.

* * *

Trish Whitehall opened the door with a look of surprise. "Gemma. Is everything okay?" She peered over my shoulder. "Jayne?"

"Everything's fine. When I left her, Jayne was happily scooping dough for oatmeal cookies."

"Best oatmeal cookies I've ever had. And that includes my mother's."

"Can't argue with that, particularly as my own mother never made a biscuit in her life. She's never even owned a baking sheet."

"Is that true? You must have had a severely deprived childhood."

"In matters of home baking only. Can I come in? It won't take long, and there's something I'd like to discuss with you."

She eyed me warily but stepped back, and I entered her house.

The Whitehall home was a standard midcentury bungalow on a huge heavily treed lot. Clean, tidy, but never extensively renovated. A long corridor led to the back of the house, doors opening off it. I slipped off my boots, and Trish showed me into the living room. Soft beige leather couch, numerous red and white cushions, much-loved damask wingback chair, low coffee table. Trish and Pete's wedding picture, baby photos, plenty of pictures of Andy and his three sisters over the years. Souvenirs of trips to Europe and Arizona covered the side tables, and pieces of nice, but inexpensive, art hung on the walls.

I quite deliberately had not told the police, either Ryan or Louise Estrada, what Trish said to me last night about Tina. I also didn't tell them Trish smoked, but they should have been able to figure that out for themselves.

She didn't take a seat or offer one to me. Instead, she lifted her chin and said, "Are you here to accuse me of killing Tina?"

That certainly caught me off guard. "What? I mean, no. I'm not. Why would you think so?"

"It's no secret around town you've often been of help to the police. According to my son, it's more the opposite. The police are occasionally of help to you in solving crimes."

"I wouldn't quite put it that way."

"Why then this unaccustomed visit in the middle of a workday? I don't believe you've ever been to my home before." She was no longer smiling.

"Please, can we sit down?" I, however, did smile.

"Please, make yourself at home."

I took the wingback chair. The fabric on the arms was heavily worn, torn in places, the colors faded. Obviously much used and much loved. The book on the low table next to it was a paperback historical romance, the cover all lurid purple and heaving bosoms and bulging muscles. This was Trish's chair, and she was off-footed having to sit on the couch, where she perched uncomfortably on the edge, ready to leap up at a moment's notice.

I made myself comfortable. Noticeably, Trish did not offer me refreshments. "Tina Armstrong," I said, watching for a reaction.

"What about her?"

"She and Andy were in a relationship for a long time. It ended, as these things do, and they went their separate ways. You were not at all happy to see her last night. No need to be Sherlock Holmes to deduce that. You told me so yourself."

"I didn't know the girl would end up dead."

I decided to back off. I was coming on too hostile and such had not been my intention. "I'm not here to accuse you of anything, Trish. Truly. I have no authority to do so even if I wanted to. I thought we could talk about it. For the record, I didn't tell the police what you told me."

"Why not?"

I shrugged. "You didn't ask me to keep our conversation confidential, but I assumed that was your intention."

She let out a long breath and fell back into the cushions. "Not confidential, no. It was no secret I didn't like her. When she and my son were together, I never said so out loud, but he knew. I wasn't the only one. Pete was no fonder of her than I was. Yes, I was relieved when Tina was out of the picture, and nothing but delighted when Jayne came into it. I adore Jayne."

"That's obvious."

"She's absolutely perfect for Andy." Her face clouded. "You don't think this unpleasantness will delay the wedding, do you?"

"I don't see why it should. I know this is none of my business but humor me. I'm the curious sort. You smoke. Did you nip out for a cigarette over the evening?"

"I did. A couple of times."

"Tina also went out for a cigarette. Did you talk to her then? Smokers have a way of falling into conversation, I believe."

"I saw her there on one occasion, and it was some time before she died. Pete's aunt Audrey was having a cigarette break when I came out, so I joined her. Tina made no attempt to engage me in conversation, and that suited me fine."

"When she went outside that . . . last time, did you see her there?"

"No, I did not. The party was winding down, and I was ready to go. We would have left by then, but Pete wanted one last beer. I was about to offer to help Leslie and Jayne carry the gifts out to the car when the commotion started."

I said nothing. Trish looked at me steadily. I've been wrong before, but I was positive she had nothing to do with Tina's death. If Tina had threatened Andy's happiness, I've not the slightest doubt his mother would have taken whatever steps she thought necessary to ensure that didn't happen. But she didn't need to. Andy was with Jayne now, where he wanted to be, and nothing Tina could say or do would change that. Trish knew it.

She had nothing to gain by Tina's death.

I stood up. "I apologize for barging in on you like this. I'm trying to put together a picture of what went down last night. I've found people sometimes speak more freely and openly to me than they do to the police. Detective Estrada can be . . . intimidating."

Trish gave a genuine laugh. "More like absolutely terrifying."

I smiled back at her. Precisely. Estrada could be so terrifying, potential witnesses were so fearful of incurring her wrath by wasting her time, by saying the wrong thing, by somehow accusing the wrong person, they could clam up around her. No one was ever terrified of me.

Once, I would have confidently told the good detective that. And likely found myself behind bars for my trouble. But over the years since I've known her, Jayne's tried to get me to understand not everyone appreciates hearing my opinion of them.

I have told Ryan, and he replied that sometimes Louise Estrada terrifies potential criminals away from taking up a life of crime.

I left the Whitehall home, firmly crossing Trish off my suspect list.

Not that I had a suspect list. But in the early stages of an investigation, a negative is as good as a positive.

Chapter Thirteen

If I was right, Tina's death had been an accident or suicide. If the police were right and it was murder, then unless someone parachuted onto the deck to throw Tina over, the killer had been at the party. Whereupon the question remained: Who would benefit from her death*? Qui bono?*

And that's where I was stuck. Until I learned more, I couldn't think of anyone who benefited. I simply didn't know enough about Tina and her life to make any assumptions.

Ryan called as I was driving back to Baker Street, and I answered on Bluetooth.

"Free for dinner tonight?" he asked.

"It just so happens that I am. Are you? What about the case?"

"I can take a few hours off, and as I've been away for a couple of days, I've missed you. We're reading through statements and waiting for additional forensic reports to come in. We found more fingerprints on that deck railing and the gate than we know what to do with."

"It's a public place. Even nonsmokers went out for some air. I did. Jayne did. Natural enough for people to gravitate to the edge of the deck to look out to sea."

"Yup. Tina's prints are clear on the railing, but nothing of hers on the gate. Not that we can find anyway. A hodgepodge of smudges on the railing of the steps to the dock and on the ladder from there into the water. Fair enough, considering the number of people scrambling to get down and get you and Andy up."

"Did anyone see a boat tied up to that dock at the time in question?"

"We've asked around. No one did. Absence of evidence, as you know, is not evidence of absence, but at this time of year when most everything on the boardwalk is closed, a boat would have stood out. Although, it was cold and late, and few people were out for a walk. You're thinking someone targeted Tina and went to the trouble to follow her to the restaurant?"

"Not seriously. Seems like a far too difficult and complicated way of going about killing someone." But the idea, like most ideas, was worth considering before dismissing it.

"Agreed. You close at six tonight, right? How about seven at the restaurant at the Harbor Inn? No shop talk."

"Promise."

"Okay if I meet you there?"

"See you then."

* * *

I parked in the alley behind the Emporium and went into the tearoom by the back door. I stuck my head in the kitchen as I passed. The big black industrial mixer was whirling away while Jayne stirred a pot on the stove, and Fiona iced a cake. In season, Mrs. Hudson's offers a proper traditional afternoon tea, complete with fine china cups and plates, linens, silver cutlery, loose-leaf teas, freshly baked scones with local jam and clotted cream, tiny sandwiches, and bite-sized sweets. Over the winter, tea is only on the menu on weekends, and the focus of the restaurant is more on baked goods for breakfast and hearty lunches of soup and sandwiches. Desserts for takeaway as well as dine-in feature on the menu year-round.

"All okay here?" I asked.

"All okay," Jayne answered. "I've just gotten back from the police station, where I gave my statement about last night."

"Jayne forgot," Fiona said. "Detective Estrada had to phone and ask where she was. That woman absolutely terrifies me, and I've done nothing wrong. If I'd been Jayne, I would have fled to Mexico."

"I couldn't go to Mexico," Jayne said. "The cupcakes weren't made yet, and we have a big order for tomorrow. A hundredth birthday party at the retirement home."

"Did Estrada say anything about the direction of their inquiries?"

Jayne didn't bother to look up. "You know her. She asks the questions and shares nothing. Oh, Mom wants to know how you're coming with the place settings for the dinner."

"Place settings?"

Jayne finally did look up. "The little cards with people's names on them? The ones to go on the tables, telling people where to sit at the wedding dinner? The little cards that match the master seating plan you also volunteered to prepare?"

"Oh, right. Those place settings. I'm on it."

"Gemma, if you can't manage those things, please tell me in enough time for me to do it."

"I'm good. Talk to you later."

I ran into the Emporium. The shop was surprisingly busy as people browsed or gathered at the sales counter to pay for their purchases. "Where do you buy little cards?" I used my hands to indicate to Ashleigh the size I wanted. "For place settings at formal dinners?"

"The stationary store, I guess."

"I am so looking forward to that author visit next week." A customer flourished her about-to-be-purchased book. "I've adored all her books, and I can't wait to have this signed."

I winced. "About that . . ."

Once the customers had been served and no one else seemed to need our attention, I said to Ashleigh, "Would you like to earn some extra money?"

"By doing Jayne's seating cards? Sure."

"How'd you know . . . ? Never mind. Leslie and Andy's mom did up a document about who's coming and who's to sit with who. And most importantly, who is not to sit with who. With whom. I'll forward it to you. We need pretty little name cards for every place and a master sheet on some sort of Bristol board to hang on the wall to direct people."

"Shall I sign it with your signature like forged art?"

"Not necessary. They'll be so surprised it got done, they won't ask."

"On it," she said. Then her expression drooped.

"Is something wrong?" I asked. "Problems while I was out?"

"Weeelll, sorta." Ashleigh looked around, and seeing no customers approaching, she said in a low voice, "Bunny has a date tonight. With George, the guy she met at Jayne's party."

"Why is that a problem? He seemed nice enough."

"I don't trust him. It was only when he found out who she was—who she had been—that he started getting interested."

"And?"

"And? I hope he doesn't think Bunny has money. Is that why he asked her out? Supposedly he's taking her to one of his own restaurants. In Hyannis, she said. He's showing off."

"Most men like to show off to women they've recently met. So what if he thinks she has money? If they get closer, he'll soon realize such is not the case, and it will be up to him whether to continue seeing her or not. Although I get your point that she might find it hard to take if he ends up dumping her."

"It's happened before. Everyone she meets thinks because she was a big pop star, she's got to be loaded. Poor Bunny, things didn't quite work out that way. Sometimes when they realize how simply she lives now, rather than understanding and accepting it, people assume she's deliberately slumming it, trying to live like one of the common people, seeking inspiration for a new album."

"You're worrying about nothing, Ashleigh. I agree Bunny's feelings might be hurt if George is only after her for her money and/or connections. But seeing as she has no money to be swindled out of, she can't be swindled out of it. Bunny's a grown woman, and she's been around the block more than a few times. Let her enjoy a nice dinner out at a good restaurant with a man she finds interesting."

Ashleigh gave me a reluctant grin. "I suppose you're right. Maybe I'm so new to this daughter business at my advanced age, I'm acting more like Bunny's mother."

"You care, and that's what matters," I said.

* * *

Risking incurring the wrath of the proprietor of Beach Fine Arts, located across from me at 221 Baker Street and always on the lookout for the slightest infraction of the street's business code, I dared to close the Emporium at quarter to six. I went home, where I had just enough time to let the dogs have a romp in the yard, serve up their dinners, and get myself ready to enjoy a night out. Ryan had only been gone a week, but I'd missed him enormously, and I was greatly looking forward to our date.

Yes, I'd seen him today, but a police investigation doesn't count as a romantic encounter.

I opened my closet and reached for my favorite dress. Then I remembered. It had been drenched in sea water, rolled up into a bundle, stuffed into an evidence bag, and was now in the depths of some police evidence locker. Likely never to be seen again, which was okay with me; if I ever did get it back, it would be in no condition to appear in public.

Instead, I put on a pair of jeans with a crisp white blouse and a cropped dark blue leather jacket, added blue glass earrings and a matching necklace, and called for a ride.

Precisely at seven o'clock, as I was stepping out of the cab, my phone buzzed. I groaned. *Life with a cop.*

Ryan: *Sorry. Something came up. I'll be delayed. Not too long. Hope.*

Me: *Good thing I brought a book.* ♥

My father is a retired officer with the Metropolitan Police; long ago, I learned from my mother not to go anywhere with a cop without bringing along a good book.

I didn't mind, as long as Ryan wasn't delayed for too long. I'd enjoy a glass of wine with my book, and hopefully (always that word), Ryan would show up in time to eat. If not, I never mind dining alone, and the restaurant at the Harbor Inn is excellent.

The veranda is a delight in the summertime, surrounded by well-maintained gardens with a lovely view down the hill to the town and the sea beyond. Tonight, the hostess stand was set up by the indoor room. "Reservation for two for Ashburton. He's been delayed, so I'll relax with a drink while I'm waiting."

She ticked off a line on her tablet and led me into the restaurant. The place was about half full. Flames burned cheerfully in the gas fireplace against the far wall, and candles flickered on tables.

I was about to take my seat when I spotted people I knew and excused myself to the hostess. I put on a friendly smile as I approached their table. "Audrey, Madison. Good evening."

They nodded politely. Menus were closed and set to one side, and they'd been served drinks. They were at a table for four. Two places had been cleared away. Unasked, and probably unwanted, I sat down. "May I join you for a few minutes? My date texted to say he's going to be late."

"Uh . . . please do," Audrey said.

"Might as well," Madison said, barely able to contain her enthusiasm.

"I hope you enjoyed the party last night. Until . . . the end." I caught the waiter's eye. "A glass of white wine, please. A chardonnay would be nice, if you have one."

He nodded and slipped away.

"It was a lovely evening," Audrey said. "My meal was delicious."

"Have you been to the Cape before?" I asked Madison.

"Never. It's okay, I guess. But cold. I can't imagine actually living in this climate." She shuddered. "Me, I'm an Angeleno through and through."

"It was nice of you to accompany your grandmother's friend," I said.

"Free holiday, why not?"

I glanced at Audrey. Her red lips were pressed tightly together. "More than that I hope, dear. A chance for us to get to know each other better, isn't that what you said? You know what young people's lives are like these days, Gemma. Always so busy."

If Madison was able to take two or three weeks away from whatever she did, to come to a place she didn't have much interest in with a woman she didn't show much affection to, her life couldn't be all that busy, I thought but didn't say.

"You yourself are obviously English," Audrey said. "Did you come to America specifically to open your bookstore?"

"My Great-Uncle Arthur bought it. Once he had it, he realized he didn't want to own a bookshop, but he couldn't sell it. So I came over to run it for him."

Madison snorted. "Family responsibilities. They get you every time."

"I like living with Uncle Arthur. On the rare occasion he's home, at any rate. The shop turned out to be the right place at the right time for me."

"Timing," Audrey said, "is everything. As I learned in my early days in Hollywood. I'd gone to California hoping to make it as an actress." She smiled at the memory. "Stars in my eyes, like so many other moderately pretty young girls. I soon realized that although I had a modicum of talent, plenty of others had as much as I, if not more."

Madison ostentatiously smothered a yawn. Audrey pretended not to notice, but something tightened behind her eyes.

"After a few years of tiny parts and being little more than part of the scenery, I decided if I did not want to go home to West London where I would be perceived as a failure, I needed to find another role in Hollywood. Which I am happy to say, I did."

"Tell her about how you snagged a big-money movie producer," Madison said, "and started getting invited to the best parties and the big opening nights. And then how once you got your foot in that door, you got rid of him and moved on."

"Men have used us women for millennia to suit their own needs and their own vanity. Why should we not do the same in return? Although I have to point out Madison is mistaken. My first husband died of a heart attack a mere six months after our wedding."

"Which might have had something to do with the fact that he was, what, forty years older than you?"

"Do you have a problem with enjoying Audrey's hospitality?" I asked Madison. Okay, so Jayne's attempts to get me to be more circumspect don't always work.

She blinked. "What?"

"You're here as her companion, a chance to get to know her better, I believe someone said. Regardless of who's paying for a two-week stay at this hotel, with meals, transportation, and all the rest, you have a funny way of showing your affection."

"What's it to you?" Madison asked.

"Quite a bit, as I'm sitting here enjoying talking to her."

A spark leapt into Audrey's eyes. "Madison speaks her mind. Not everyone appreciates hearing it—all of the time. Reminds me very much of her grandmother, which might be why she and I always got on so well. Although dear Ruth did know when to speak and when to remain quiet."

Indecision crossed Madison's face. Then she took a breath as she decided she didn't want to spar with me. (Or perhaps she didn't want to be told to leave before she'd had her dinner.) She picked up her wine glass, finished the contents in one long swallow, and looked around for the waiter.

"Instead of being nothing more than another in a long line of failed actresses, you made your mark as a gossip columnist," I said. "I bet that was fun."

Audrey laughed. Years dropped from her face. "Oh, yes, my dear. Fun, not to mention highly lucrative. I married four times. Despite what some—" a glare at Madison "—might think, I loved deeply. Just not for long."

I laughed.

The waiter placed a glass in front of me, and I smiled my thanks. Madison tapped the top of her own glass. "Madam?" he asked Audrey.

"Not for me, thank you." When he'd left, she said, "I was at the heart of the Hollywood social scene for almost forty years. I went to all the parties, all the premiers, all the award ceremonies. If by chance I was unavailable or not invited, I had a network of spies everywhere. Waiters at the best restaurants, staff at the exclusive clubs and the in-demand catering companies, gardening and maid services. I would have hired myself out to the CIA, if only they'd paid enough. The stories I could tell." She laughed. "The stories I did tell. But time moved on for me, as it does for everyone. The new stars are not afraid of the studios; bad publicity won't end a career."

"Sounds as though you weren't reluctant to engage in the occasional bit of blackmail?"

Madison snorted. Audrey stared at me, then she laughed again. "My goodness, but you are a blunt young woman.

Blackmail, no. On occasion, I concealed bigger scandals out of sympathy for a wronged woman perhaps, sometimes I covered them up with smaller ones. If I ruined a marriage or two, what of it? The participants were usually better off without each other."

"Last night, you said you're writing a book."

"I might not have the influence I once did, but I still hear things, dear. I still know the right people. Some of the wrong people too. I have many stories I never told, for one reason or another."

"No one cares about what happened in old-time Hollywood, Audrey," Madison said.

Audrey's eyes narrowed. "You have commented upon that more than once, dear. And as I have said to you more than once, some people in the publishing world might disagree. A good number of big stars, people who are still big names, were people I knew in my day. Scandal is scandal, even more so when criminal activity might be involved, and on occasion, the passage of time only increases its newsworthiness. Is that a word: newsworthiness?"

Audrey was clearly enjoying talking to me. If nothing else, I was a fresh audience, a welcome change from the bored, disrespectful Madison. As Audrey chatted on, I began to get the feeling she was being increasingly specific. That she was, in fact, speaking directly to me.

Before I could dig further, my phone buzzed with a text from Ryan. "Sorry," I said, "that's my date."

Ryan: *Here. Are you in restaurant?*
Me: *Yes*

"He's arrived." I picked up my glass and stood up. "I've enjoyed talking to you, Audrey. You've led an interesting life."

She winked at me. "It's not over yet. Still some life in the old girl yet."

"Good luck with your book."

"Luck? Yes, if I learned one thing in all my years in Hollywood, luck is all there is."

"If our food doesn't arrive soon," Madison said, "I might die of starvation."

"You do that, dear," Audrey said. "Save me the cost of your return airfare to L.A."

Madison pushed her chair back. "Very funny. I'm going out for a smoke."

She fell into step beside me as I headed for my table. Ryan came through the doors, looking around. I gave him a wave and a big smile crossed his face. "Cute guy," Madison said. "Good for you. Don't bother rushing to the bookstore to put in an order for Audrey's book. She's been talking for ages about wanting to write one, but my mom says all she ever does is talk about it. Her so-called gossip is all way out of date. I have to say, though, I was surprised last night when she suddenly started writing right there in the restaurant while we were waiting for the cops, and she's been hard at it all day. She didn't even come out for lunch or to go shopping."

Chapter Fourteen

"Gemma," Ashleigh called, "it's time." Ashleigh tells me she dresses according to her mood. Today she must have been in the mood to be a West London shop clerk, as she was dressed in a perfectly normal pair of dark trousers, white shirt, and loose red cardigan. Blue lace-up trainers were on her feet. Earlier, I'd asked if she'd heard from Bunny how the date with George had gone, and she said Bunny hadn't called her and she was afraid to ask.

"Time?" I asked.

"Meeting time. AKA teatime."

I glanced at the clock on the far wall. Thirty-eight minutes past three.

Every afternoon at twenty to four, Jayne and I have a partners' meeting, like the responsible business partners we are. Fortunately, we're partners in a restaurant, so we have our meeting over tea and the remains of the day's baking. As we are also best friends, said meeting is often nothing more than a catch-up session and, over the past few months, wedding preparation. Today, I was looking forward to telling Jayne the work on the place cards for her wedding was well under way.

"You have the comm, Number One," I said.

"*Star Trek*! Where did that come from?"

"I'm a woman of many and varied interests," I said as I sailed out the door to the tearoom.

Truth be told, although I am a woman of many and varied interests, one of them is not *Star Trek*. But Ryan loves the old shows, and last night after dinner he wanted to watch one. And as I love Ryan, I agreed.

Mrs. Hudson's closes at four, and usually by this time of day, only a few customers remain, lingering over their late lunch or midafternoon snack break while last-minute stragglers rush in for a takeout coffee or to take advantage of the end-of-day specials.

"Good timing," Jocelyn said to the man in front of her as I came into the tearoom. "Jayne's about to take her break. Here's Gemma now."

Robbie Ellis turned around. He looked about as pleased to see me as I was to see him.

"What's up?" I asked.

"If it was any business of yours, I'd tell you," he said. "I'm here to see Jayne, not you."

Behind his back, Jocelyn's eyes opened wide and her mouth formed a perfect O.

Before I could reply with a witty yet cutting retort, Jayne came out of the kitchen, rubbing her fingers through her hair before twisting it behind her head to retie the ponytail. "Robbie, hi. Nice to see you."

The smile he gave her lit up his face. "Nice to see you too, Jayne. We didn't get much of a chance to talk at your party, so I thought I'd drop in."

"That's so sweet of you. Isn't he sweet, Gemma?"

"So sweet," I said.

"Gemma and I are about to have our business meeting, and we close at four."

"Skip the meeting. Gemma won't care. Let's go for a drink." He looked at me. "The two of us."

"I'm sorry, but I can't," Jayne said. "Not today. I have a final dress fitting this afternoon, and Gemma's coming with me."

I quickly pulled up a mental image of my calendar. There it was: *5:00 Jayne. Dress.* I'd forgotten to ask Ashleigh to stay late.

"Why don't you drop by tomorrow for lunch and we can catch up then," Jayne said. "It's on me."

"That would be good. I know we're finished and all, Jayne, but I care about you. I hope we can still be friends. I want to be sure you're okay. I mean, what happened the other night at your party was awful. Are you coping?"

She smiled fondly at him. "Friends sounds nice. I am okay, and it's so nice of you to care. That woman who died, Tina, she was a friend of Andy's. I didn't know her."

"I heard she was a former girlfriend. That has to be tough," Robbie said. "For Andy, I mean. I suppose he still had feelings for her."

"Not so you'd notice," I said. "Sorry, Jayne, but something important's come up that I need to discuss with you before we go to fit you for your *wedding dress*. It can't wait."

"Okay. Be right with you. See you tomorrow, Robbie. How about two, after the lunch rush clears out?"

"Yeah. Great. I expect to be in town for the rest of the winter. The art scene in the Big Apple is pretty quiet, so I'm getting some time to work on a few new pieces. Develop some new concepts."

"I'm glad to hear it," Jayne said. "I'd love to see what you're working on now."

"Come around sometime. Anytime. I'm not too far from your place. On McConnell Street, number 1089. It's not much, but only temporary, like."

"Now that that's settled," I said. "We need to get our formal business meeting started, Jayne. Haven't got all day, you know. Neither does Robbie, I'm sure."

He ignored me. "I hope what happened doesn't disturb your wedding plans. Much. Still going ahead with it, are you? Even though Andy's got to be upset about his girlfriend dying."

"Ex-girlfriend," I said. "You know about exes, don't you, Robbie?"

A nerve twitched beside his right eye as he stopped ignoring me. He did not give me the benefit of that smile. He turned back to Jayne. "I'm a shoulder to cry on, if you need one."

"Thank you, Robbie, but I'm fine. No need for a shoulder."

"Do you know something about what happened the other night?" I asked. "If you do, you should tell the police."

"I might. I might not. I see all. I know all." He gave me a wink containing not the slightest trace of good humor before turning back to Jayne. "See you tomorrow, then," he said.

He brushed past me and went out the door.

"Nice to see Robbie back in town," Jayne said as we took our regular seats in the window alcove. "He seems to be doing okay. I was worried about him when he went to New York City. I suppose the art thing didn't work out as he'd hoped."

My friend is smart, well-educated, a good businesswoman, a fabulous baker, a loving daughter, a top-notch friend. But she can be naive at times. Sometimes that's charming. Occasionally, it's dangerous.

I was about to tell her what Robbie had been saying about her at her party, but before I could form the words, she said, "I am seriously worried about this fitting, Gemma."

"Why?"

"What with the shower you had for me, and then Mom's, and the birthday party, and all the lunches and drinks with friends, I've put on weight."

"Not so as I'd notice," I said truthfully.

"Nice of you to say so," she said. "I've been afraid to step on the scales. What if my dress doesn't fit?"

"Here you go." Jocelyn put a plate of sandwiches and another of fruit tarts in front of us. "Any preferences for tea today?"

"English breakfast would be fine," I said.

"Do you think I've put on weight, Jocelyn?" Jayne asked.

"You! Heavens no." Jocelyn put her hands on her own more-than-adequate hips. "I don't know how you do it. Working at this place has added at least twenty pounds to me."

"I'll eat to that," I said, bypassing the sandwiches and going straight for a raspberry tart.

"It's a tough job," Fiona called. "Taste testing all that baking, but someone has to do it."

"Are you taking résumés?" a customer asked as she put her credit card on her table. "Sounds like a job I could do. I'm highly qualified."

Everyone laughed. Jayne most of all.

* * *

As could have been expected, Jayne's dress fitted perfectly. The store clerk wrapped it carefully and Jayne proudly carried it out to her car while I brought the shoes and the undergarments.

Jayne dropped me at the Emporium. She tooted the horn and gave me a cheerful wave, then pulled into the traffic.

I stood on the sidewalk watching her drive away.

I'd deliberately pushed all thoughts of Robbie aside while we had the fitting and once again gushed over the dress. It was the perfect "Jayne" gown: simple, perfectly cut, excellent fabric, absolutely gorgeous. Made even more perfect by the sheer joy Jayne radiated wearing it.

The temperature had risen slightly, giving a cold damp the opportunity to start seeping through my coat. Getting out of the car, I stepped in a puddle and I was not wearing waterproof boots.

I did my best to ignore all that and thought, once again, *Qui bono?*

Did Robbie benefit from the death of Tina?

I had no reason to believe he knew her, although they were both originally from West London. He'd smiled at her, but no more than a young man did to a pretty woman, and she'd been sharply rude in return. But as I now knew, she had other things on her mind that night than being polite to the serving staff and enjoying a nice dinner. Otherwise, they hadn't interacted again. Not in my sight anyway, but even I can't watch everyone all the time.

Could Robbie benefit from the death of Tina in some other way? He was attempting to worm his way back into Jayne's life. All that wanting to be friends, that offer of a "shoulder to cry on," the implications that maybe the wedding should be postponed.

But Tina had not been a friend of Jayne's. Robbie had been watching Jayne carefully at the party; he would have known they were not close. Certainly not such good friends she'd cancel her wedding in mourning.

Had Robbie done something in an attempt to get to Andy? To possibly sabotage his wedding to Jayne? Again, any casual observer would have noticed Andy had not been at all delighted when Tina put in an appearance that night.

Had Robbie hoped a killing at the Blue Water Café would force Andy's business to close? An extended, unexpected closing would put the restaurant in a financially unstable position. If rumors got around the place wasn't safe, that could cause a lot of trouble. That this hadn't happened didn't mean someone didn't think—or hope—it might.

Was it possible Robbie killed Tina, not because he had anything against her, but as a way of causing trouble for Andy? Did Robbie think trouble for Andy meant Jayne would fall back into his arms? Or was he simply that jealous, working for the man who was loved by the woman he wanted for himself?

Did he even want to get back with Jayne, or was he lashing out at what he saw as failure and rejection? It had to hurt, coming back to West London, needing to get by on a part-time waiter job working for a man he saw as a rival.

It was a stretch, for sure, and I had nothing but guesses and assumptions to go on.

Didn't mean I wasn't right.

Andy's mum said something to me that night about "times are tough." I'd taken it as a generic comment: winter is hard for tourist-oriented businesses. Could she have meant more than that? Was Andy in financial difficulties? Robbie only worked casual part-time at the Blue Water Café, but staff talk amongst themselves. If the staff were worried about their jobs, they'd discuss it.

Andy's financial affairs were absolutely none of my business, I told myself. However, Jayne's happiness was.

I'd advised Andy not to hire Robbie again, but I hadn't said why. Perhaps it was time I did. At the same time, I could subtly let him know Great-Uncle Arthur was not without funds, and he was always looking to invest in promising local businesses.

Yes, I can be subtle. Sometimes.

Chapter Fifteen

I sent Andy a quick text asking if he was free for a drink.

> Andy: *Nothing better to do.*
> A second later: Andy: *Sorry about the way that sounded. Drink would be good. Pub?*
> Me: *Sure. Half an hour?*

Fortunately, Ashleigh had been able to stay the extra hour until closing with no notice. She not only stayed, she swept the floor, tidied the shelves, restocked the spaces, counted up the day's cash, took care of Moriarty's needs, switched off the lights, and locked up.

I really did need to give her more credit than I sometimes did. Our businesses had thrived last tourist season and continued to do well over the winter, so far at any rate. I'd given her and Gale, the part-time assistant, generous bonuses at Christmas, but it might be time to give Ashleigh a raise.

As I had almost nothing to do regarding closing the shop, I was at McGillivray's Irish Pub in plenty of time.

McGillivray's is an Irish pub typical of the kind found all over America. Meaning, not Irish in the least, apart from the name.

But it was a warm, welcoming place on a cold, damp day, and I settled myself comfortably in a booth close to the gas fire after hanging my coat and scarf on the hook provided.

"Hey, Gemma," the young waitress said as she put down coasters. "Can I get you something?"

"I'm waiting for—here he is now."

Andy shrugged out of his coat and slipped into a seat opposite me. "Worst possible weather. Freezing rain's started." He asked the waitress to bring him a beer.

"I'll have the same, " I said. "Thanks."

"How did the dress-fitting go?" Andy asked me after she'd slipped away.

"It's perfect, Andy. You're going to love it."

"How can I not," he said, "when I love the woman wearing it?"

"Jayne's a lucky woman," I said in total honesty.

"I don't know about that, but I am a very lucky man indeed."

Two frothy mugs of beer were placed on the table, and Andy and I lifted our glasses. "Cheers."

He drank deeply, then said, "What's on your mind?"

"Does something have to be on my mind for me to ask you out for a drink?" I said with a smile.

"Yes."

"Okay. Something is on my mind. First, what's happening with the restaurant?"

"Looking on the bright side, I've got plenty of time to get caught up on the accounts, pay my bills, check boxes on insurance forms, try out new recipes, all the stuff I normally have trouble finding time to getting around to. On the not so bright side, my income is zero while we're closed, but my expenses are not, and my staff are worried about their jobs, as they have a right to be. Back on the bright side again, I've been told I can have access to the entire inside space tomorrow."

"Oh, that is good news."

"Yeah." He didn't look too thrilled, though. I said nothing, letting the silence stretch out. "Closed for a couple of days isn't too much of a financial hit. Not at this time of year. But I was closed for Jayne's party, and I still had to pay the staff, buy the food and drink, all that. Don't get me wrong, Gemma, I was happy to do it. But the wedding and honeymoon are coming up, I've got bills to catch up on, and I'm not entirely confident I can trust Martin to run the kitchen when I'm not there."

"Why not?"

"He's getting too sure of himself. He's a good cook and a hard worker, and that should be enough. But one of my waitresses, one who's been with me for a long time, said he acts like it's his place when I'm not around. Reprimanding front-of-house staff for things that aren't any of his business, bullying the kitchen staff—on at least one occasion, he threatened to fire a dishwasher—and even sneering at some of the dishes on the menu. If he doesn't like my cooking, I don't know what sort of a job he can do making those dishes."

"Is all this new?" I asked. "He's been with you for a few months, right?"

"I don't know if it's new, but it's coming out now. Like I said, my staff are worried about their jobs. They've been calling me, asking what's going on. And then they say things."

"But you're opening tomorrow?"

"I'm back in business, yes, but I can't open to the public for a couple of days. I had to put a stop to some of my orders because everything was up in the air. It takes time to get things moving again. Some of the part-time staff took other work because they weren't sure about me. With luck, I should be able to open with a limited menu for dinner on Saturday."

"I'll help spread the word," I said. "You know West Londoners will come through to help one of their own."

"I do, thanks."

He'd almost finished his beer, but I'd hardly had any of mine. "Feel like ordering food?" I asked.

"Better not. I want to get some of those accounts I mentioned done tonight." He gave me a tight grin. "Wouldn't it be nice if we could follow our passion in life without having to worry about paying taxes, conforming to health guidelines, dealing with suppliers, managing unruly staff? Or fixing the plumbing in the men's room, which took a heck of a hunk out of my fall profits."

"Are you in trouble, Andy?" I asked. "Financially speaking? If you need help, Uncle Arthur is always looking for an investment opportunity."

His grin widened. "No more trouble than any other independent businessman. I complain, but I love what I do and I'll be okay."

"If you're sure."

"I am. Thanks for your concern." He grinned. "Jayne told me a few stories about goings-on at the Emporium while Arthur was in command when we were in London."

"He tries," I said.

"Speaking of Arthur, is he going to make it home in time for the wedding?"

"Cutting it fine, as usual. He's in Madrid and has a flight booked to arrive in Boston Sunday night. Don't change the subject. I hope you're able to talk to Jayne about any problems you might be having. You are partners now, you know."

"I do. The good thing about her being in the food business too is she understands what can, and often does, go wrong. You know Jayne: never anything but a cheery optimist."

That, I knew, was true. I also knew, as a quarter-owner of a restaurant, it was unlike any other business. The stresses, the hours, the demands. The enormous responsibility involved in the storage and preparation of food that, if mishandled, could actually kill a person.

As a quarter-owner of a restaurant, I was glad I was responsible for a bookshop. At my shop, I never have to worry a customer might collapse from reading a badly written book.

"Is Jayne getting wedding nerves?" Andy asked. "I've heard some brides get overcome."

"She's excited and delighted, but she's still just our Jayne. Practical as ever, but in case not . . . You reminded me she's an optimist. I like to think I'm a realist. I'll ensure everything from her end is on schedule for the wedding."

"Thanks, Gemma. I hate to run, but . . ." Andy dug in his pocket, but before he could pull out his wallet, I said, "Drinks are on me."

He thanked me and left. I sat back with a sigh and cradled my mug.

Andy hadn't told me anything I didn't know or guess. The restaurant business is one of the toughest there is. The turnover is astronomical. Not a lot of places manage to survive their first year. But Andy had been on the harbor for several years. The Blue Water Café had become a West London institution. It was featured in a good number of tourist guidebooks. In the off-season, it was a popular place for locals.

He could potentially be in a great deal of financial trouble if the police ordered him to stay closed much longer, but he hoped to reopen on the weekend.

Andy and the Blue Water Café would survive.

As for Robbie, although telling Andy about his offers of "friendship" to Jayne had been my original intention in suggesting this meeting, I'd changed my mind. Unless things escalated, I wouldn't say anything about it. Andy was generally a calm, considered man. But with the pressures of his impending wedding, as well as the threat to his business, he might not take that news all too calmly and with careful consideration.

Instead, I decided to have a word with Robbie myself, mainly because I now considered it possible Robbie killed Tina in order to disrupt Andy's life, and thus (in his feeble twisted mind) cause Jayne to seek solace with him.

First, I needed to have a peek into what Robbie had been up to over the past couple of years.

I finished my beer, got my coat, and headed for home and my computer.

* * *

In his day, if Sherlock Holmes needed to learn something, he would send a flurry of telegrams racing across Europe and beyond; he'd scour the newspaper notices; he'd order the Baker Street Irregulars to fan out across the alleys and waterways of London.

Seems terribly inefficient to me. If I want to learn something, after giving the dogs their dinner and taking them for a short walk, I put on the kettle, make a cup of tea, curl up on the couch in the den, and open my iPad.

I knew a moderate amount about the life of Robert James Ellis, aka Robbie, from when he and Jayne had been together. He'd been born and raised in West London in a family who'd lived on the Cape for generations. He was what in England we call a "lay-about": shiftless, largely unemployable, and unemployed as often as he could get by while maintaining himself with no income. After barely graduating from high school, he enrolled in a second-rate art college, only to drop out after the first semester. He told everyone who asked, and many who did not, the college had nothing to teach him. He was, in his mind, a true original. Undiscouraged, he attempted to make his living as an artist for a number of years. His style of what he called "brutal realism"—I suppressed a shudder at the image—was not exactly in high demand in a tourist town. Jayne finally managed to talk him into trying something more tourist-friendly. A nice beach at sunset scene, or children splashing in the surf. He gave it a try, and eventually brought several pieces to Beach Fine Arts where Maureen said she'd consider selling them on consignment. As soon as she spotted the dismembered hand, blood dripping from the clawlike fingernails, poking out of the sand close to the holidaying children, she sent Robbie, and his eight-foot-long canvases, packing.

Eventually, he and Jayne broke up and she moved on to the next unsuitable boyfriend before finally, and sensibly, settling on the faithful Andy. Robbie left town, and I hadn't cared enough to ask what happened to him.

I cared now.

According to what little I could find on the internet, Robbie moved to New York City shortly after he broke up with Jayne. I had no trouble locating an out-of-date website attempting to sell ugly pieces of art at exorbitant prices. His bio was unrecognizable, but the photo was of the Robbie I knew, posing next to a huge canvas covered in shades of gray, dark gray, darker gray, and even darker gray. He called himself an "avant-garde" artist. Someone must have supplied Robbie with the words, maybe in mockery, because he was unlikely to know what it meant. He's also unlikely to know that the term avant-garde is decades out of date.

None of the paintings on his web page were marked sold, and the page had last been updated more than a year ago.

I searched for any mention of Robbie's work being shown at galleries and found an instance of a one-man show at a small gallery in Lower Manhattan. Clicking on the URL for the gallery gave me a notice that it was permanently closed; no more information was provided other than the owners' contact details. Judging by the date, the gallery closed only a few weeks after Robbie's show.

I leaned back with a sigh. Was it possible I was beginning to feel sorry for Robbie, of all people? He wanted to be an artist, but he couldn't make it. Much of his failure was down to his own inability to learn or to grow, to experiment, to take advice, to try new things. Maureen McGregor had been willing to give him a chance. But he simply couldn't adapt enough to take it. Other than the dismembered hand, his painting wasn't all that bad. Nothing I considered special, but similar to much of the tourist-market oriented stuff that sold well all over the Cape. Aside from the size of his pieces—if anyone bought one, they would have trouble stuffing it into their overloaded car for the trip home.

I continued digging. Robbie had a good number of friends with social media pages, and his own had absolutely no checks or security features. Between working on his art and begging gallery owners for showings, he did a series of jobs in middle-of-the-road restaurants or with catering companies. I found pictures of him posing with the staff at various events. He seemed to have had a couple of casual girlfriends over the years: wannabe actresses or models he met at his jobs, but nothing that lasted more than a few months.

A recent entry on his own Facebook page showed Robbie at a bar with friends. "BYE NYC!" he'd written. "It's been a blast, but it's home to WL I must go! Big news coming!"

All terribly boring and rather sad.

I was about to give up. I didn't like Robbie, never had. I hadn't approved of him dating Jayne, but not because he was violent toward her or emotionally abusive. On one memorable occasion, Robbie stumbled into my house in time to save me from a demented killer. I could have handled the situation myself, thank you very much, but for a long, long time, he took every opportunity to remind me I owed my life to him.

I simply thought Jayne could do better. Much better. Which, absolutely no thanks to me, she eventually had.

Then I remembered the things he'd said in Ashleigh's hearing at the party, the way he'd looked at Andy, not to mention me, eyes full of rage, and at Jayne, with unrequited longing.

So I continued to dig, checking the gossip pages for some of the private parties Robbie worked at. That reminded me of Audrey and her glory years as a much-feted, and greatly feared, gossip columnist. I waded through pages and pages of pictures of beautiful people, with expensive clothes and expensive jewelry, swilling drinks, admiring art or posing for pictures, arms around each other, false smiles. Waitstaff were generally a blur in the background, but I was able to spot Robbie in a couple of pictures.

My eyes were beginning to water, my vision blurring as I swiped left again and again. The images were running together so much, I almost missed it. I froze, then swiped right. A swanky party, likely a gallery opening. The rich and the famous, the beautiful and the influential. It was a big crowd, guests in the center, staff moving in the background.

I focused in on a young woman holding a serving tray. She was not looking at the camera, and she was not smiling. Her tray was empty, and she was heading toward the back of the room, likely fetching more canapes.

Tina Armstrong.

Robbie was not in that picture, but he'd done other jobs for that catering company.

Did he and Tina know each other?

Entirely possible.

This party had been held three years ago. Tina lived in New York City around that time, before moving to Hollywood. If she was trying to make it as an actress, it was entirely possible she'd be doing waitressing jobs while waiting for her big break. Like all the other actors, singers, dancers, models, artists who gravitated to the Big Apple with stars in their eyes.

I closed in on Tina again. The picture wasn't the best, not blown up this much, and she was half turned away from the camera, but I saw no sign of the scar on her face.

I thought back to the night of Jayne's party. Tina arrived late. She sat at my table. She called for a drink, and Robbie came over. He'd smiled at her, but she ignored him except to place her order after saying something like, "Still at it?" He'd scowled and gone to get her drink. I'd taken her comment to be a simple remark that she was glad the party wasn't over yet, and his

response nothing but his usual surly self. Might it ha
more personal than that?

Might her comment have been a dig at Robbie still try
get by waiting tables?

I glanced at the clock on the iPad. Quarter past ten. No
late for a drop-in visit.

I considered expanding my search and going deeper: i
newspaper files, even to places I wasn't supposed to venture
the internet. Such as police records.

I decided not to take the time. Not tonight.

Time to beard the pussy cat in his den. I had nothing to fear from Robbie Ellis of all people. However, just in case he didn't appreciate me dropping in to ask why he hadn't told the police he knew Tina (and, by the way, stay away from Jayne and Andy), I called Ryan.

It went to straight to voicemail.

I sent him a text: *Are you busy?*

He replied as I was pulling on my coat: *Yeah. Heading for a scene. Bar brawl out of control. One fatality. What's up?*

Me: *It can wait. Love you.*

No reply.

Chapter Sixteen

Number 1089 McConnell Street was a small apartment block on the edge of town. Four stories tall, entrance at the far east end of the building, three tiny balconies on each floor with chipped concrete or rusted railings facing the street. Many of those balconies were crammed with bicycles or children's toys. The cold rain had drizzled to a halt while I'd been at home; the front yard was a mess of dirty melting snow, icy slush, churned-up mud, and boot prints. The building was old, but someone appeared to be trying to maintain it. De-icer had been generously spread across the front walk; the shrubs lining the ground floor windows and balconies were neatly cut back, flower beds dug up and turned over for the winter.

The vestibule was small but brightly lit, the tiles on the floor cracked and covered with muddy prints, human and canine, paint peeling around the door frame. The heat was turned up way too high. I checked the row of admittance buttons, most of which had names next to them.

R. Ellis. Apt 1D.

I pressed the button. It buzzed.

I waited. It was entirely possible my quarry was not at home. I had no worries about Robbie being able to prepare himself for a visit from me, so I would have called him, if I had his number.

One of the disadvantages of the cell phone era: not many people have numbers listed in the phone book, in print or online. Sherlock Holmes would have sent a telegram announcing his pending arrival. I didn't know of any telegram services in West London.

I pressed the bell again. Again, it buzzed, and again, no voice came through.

"Can I help you?" A woman walked through the front door.

"Calling my friend," I said. "He doesn't seem to be home."

"You're Gemma, right? From the bookstore."

"Yes. I'm sorry I—"

She was in her early sixties, bright blue eyes beneath glasses with heavy purple frames, big smile, curly gray hair, timeworn face. "No reason you should know me. My friends and I like to have afternoon tea at Mrs. Hudson's on special occasions. Birthdays and the like. I've seen you there, and absolutely everyone knows who you are. You're looking for Robbie?"

"Yes."

"Can't help you, I'm afraid. I don't know him except to say hello to as we're collecting the mail. More like advertising materials these days than mail. Nice enough young man. He's a famous artist, did you know that?"

"Uh . . . no, I didn't."

"West London boy done good. Come back to work on a series of paintings showing the underbelly of the tourist industry. He's living here to absorb the atmosphere." Her face twisted in something like disapproval. "I wouldn't call this building the underbelly. It's small and the plumbing sometimes makes the most dreadful noise, but they do their best to maintain it. You know what it's like in places that get so many tourists. No one wants to rent to salesclerks like me." She smiled at me. "Not that I'm complaining. Good night."

"Night. I haven't been to Robbie's apartment yet. He's in number 1D?"

"Yes. I have 2D, directly above him. Nice to have the corner unit; it lets in a bit more light, particularly on dark days such as these ones. He sometimes plays his music too late and too loudly, but it doesn't often bother me. I work late shift at the supermarket, and I like to unwind and watch some TV before going to bed."

"Would the flats beginning with a one be on the ground floor?"

"Yes, and so on up. Six apartments on each floor. Not many of us, so it's nice we all get on."

"You must have a good view."

"Not one of the best, I'm afraid. The higher floors overlook the parking lot down the hill. Still, it's better than looking out onto the street." She pressed her fob against the reader on the wall. It buzzed, the door lock responded, and she opened the door. "Good night, Gemma."

"Night."

The door swung shut behind her. I made no attempt to put my foot in it, or to otherwise gain access. I had no excuse for barging in where I did not belong, and I suspected my supermarket night-clerk friend was an observant woman.

Instead, I left the building.

But I didn't give up and return to my car. I set off across the cold wet grass. The remains of melted snow and frozen rain instantly soaked into my shoes and from there my socks. Foolishly, I'd worn trainers tonight, thinking I'd be inside the whole time.

From what the woman told me, easy enough to determine which apartment was Robbie's. Ground floor, corner unit, rear of the building. From there, he couldn't have seen my highly distinctive Miata drive up. He hadn't answered the bell when I rang, but a camera was mounted high on the wall, facing down at the panel to show whoever was standing in front of it. He might have seen me and decided not to respond.

I rarely take no for an answer.

I did not intend to break in. If there were signs Robbie was at home, I'd knock on the window and let him know I had no intention of leaving without speaking to him. If he was not at home, I'd come back on another occasion.

I passed three apartments. The drapes were closed on them all, and the flickering blue light of a TV showed from behind two. The third was dark.

As I rounded the building, a light went on in the window on the second floor, the apartment at the corner. My new friend preparing for an evening of watching telly.

Somewhere in the distance, a dog barked. The occasional car drove down the street and continued on its way. Otherwise, all was quiet. Cloud cover was heavy, letting through not a trace of moon or stars, but lights shone from the streetlamps above the sidewalk, and over the parking area at the back, as well as spilling from windows. This building was part of a pair, sharing the parking area. A scattering of cars filled the lot, most of them not the newest models, some in a state of considerable disrepair. One was covered by a tarp, indicating the owners likely wintered away from the Cape. The engine idled on another, headlights on, waiting for its owner to return. A meal delivery, I assumed.

I stepped around the corner. The downstairs flats had tiny outdoor patios, matching the position of the balconies above, enclosed by a rough concrete wall about two feet high.

In the flat closest to me, the front room was dark, but a light burned further back in what was likely the kitchen. The drapes were open. Shabby couch, thrift-store table holding a pizza box and several cans of beer, huge flat-screen TV, light flickering. The walls were painted an unimaginative beige, matching the heavily worn carpet. No art was on the walls, no photos on the tabletops. The only color came from the TV mounted on the wall. The sound was turned up high, and even through the closed windows and sliding door to the patio, I could hear the squeal of brakes and rapid gunfire.

My phone was in my pocket; I'd left my purse in the car. I prepared to haul myself over the wall to the patio and knock on the sliding door. If Robbie was in the back room with a lady guest, too bad. That might even work to my advantage. He'd be desperate to get rid of me and not want her to know he was interested in another woman.

The sliding door leading to the patio was open just a crack. That would be why I could hear the telly so clearly. Odd on such a cold night. Perhaps Robbie had been showing his date the view and forgot to pull the door shut after him.

I lifted my right leg, swung it over the edge of the cement wall. I was about to pull the other leg up after it when I saw it: amongst the dead leaves, rusting beer cans and rotting chip packets, the dirty puddles on the concrete patio floor, a sprinkling of glass at the base of the door, reflecting the bright lights of the parking lot. The edges of the drapes moved, and I realized they were *outside* the door, pulled by a gust of wind. In the living room, a shape moved; a figure stepped into the light.

It was a man, or perhaps a woman, much the same height as Robbie but substantially thinner. Dressed all in black: black trousers, black winter jacket, black gloves. A black scarf was tied around their mouth and nose, and a knitted black winter hat pulled down over their forehead.

The figure caught sight of me at the exact moment I saw it. He—she? it?—froze. I froze, perched awkwardly on the wall. The weak light behind the person threw a shadow across their face so I couldn't see the details of their eyes.

We stared at each other for a fraction of a moment. Then they moved. The door was wrenched fully open, the figure ran through it. Momentarily trapped by indecision, I made a critical mistake. I didn't allow myself to drop backward to get my footing established on the ground or forward to try to stop the stranger's movement.

They grabbed me by the right arm and pulled hard. I yelled, tried to pull myself free, tottering on top of the low wall as we struggled. I pulled back my other arm in an attempt to get in a punch. Instead, I unbalanced myself. One more sharp yank, and I fell over, crashing onto the hard concrete floor. A sharp stab of pain as my knee hit the surface. The figure vaulted over the wall and ran. I staggered to my feet. To my relief, my knee was sore but still functional. The figure in black ran across the parking lot. They reached the small sedan that had been left running, and jumped in.

I'd assumed the idling car was for a meal delivery. I cursed myself—never assume.

I slithered onto the top of the wall and slid down the other side, taking care to keep my right leg from making hard contact with the ground. The car backed up, barely missing the truck parked behind it. It turned, straightened, and headed for the driveway. Whoever this was, they were no professional. They'd driven into the parking bay front first, not prepared for a rapid exit in the event things went wrong.

I ran across the grass at the side of the building as the car sped past me. It barely slowed at the corner, took a sharp left with a squeal of tires, and tore down the street.

I reached my own car, conveniently parked against the sidewalk near the driveway, facing the direction taken by the other car.

I leapt in and took off after them. I had not taken time to consider what I would do if I caught them. I was lucky they didn't appear to have a gun on them. I was lucky they'd been as surprised to see me as I had been to see them. Perched awkwardly on top of that wall, I'd been in no position to put up any sort of fight in my own defense.

I kept going.

The car I was after was a white Toyota Corolla, about five years old. A good, reliable vehicle, perfect for taking the family on vacation or for the run to the shops. I was in a two-seater Miata. I often had to restrain myself from letting her have her head on the winding oceanside roads of Cape Cod.

I don't leave my phone's virtual assistant on, ready to serve me at any vocal command. That would have been convenient at the moment. Instead, I had to fumble in my pocket with one hand, while trying to steer the car with the other, to turn it on.

"How may I help you?" the computer voice asked pleasantly.

"Call Ryan."

"Do you want the cell number for Ryan Ashburton?"

"Yes!"

"Calling Ryan Ashburton."

The phone rang. Voicemail picked up, and I was asked to leave a message. "Whatever you're doing, drop it. I'm in pursuit of . . . of a housebreaker and possible assailant. Going west on . . ." I glanced around me and pulled up a mental map. Top of a hill, ocean to the east, bright lights of town to the north, an area of small houses, large lots. Intersection with convenience store and petrol station coming up. "McConnell Street, approaching Wyatt Boulevard."

The Toyota tore through the intersection without bothering to so much as slow down to check if anyone was coming. Fortunately, no one was. I also disregarded the stop sign, although I did venture a peek in both directions first. "Okay, we're passing Wyatt. Still going west on McConnell. Toyota Corolla. White. About five years old. Can't read license plate; it's covered in mud. I doubt that's an accident."

"Pip-pip." Ryan's voicemail informed me my time was almost up. "Uh . . . call me," I said.

This was a residential area. Small houses close to the street and low apartment blocks. It was late, but some people were in their living rooms watching telly or out walking their dogs before turning in. The dog walkers stared as we sped past. A man shouted. A car began to pull out of its driveway and managed to stop with a squeal of brakes and inches to spare as the Toyota rushed past.

This, I thought, *might not be the best of ideas.* Someone could be killed. The car ahead of me didn't bother to flick the turn indicators before they took the corner onto the street that led to the main road to Chatham. Water sprayed up from the wheels, soaking a woman standing at the corner waiting for the light to change. If the light facing her had not been red and the woman had been in the intersection, would the driver of the Toyota have noticed her? Would they have cared? It was coming up to eleven, and plenty of traffic was still heading into and out of town. Horns blared as approaching cars gave warning.

I put on my own turn indicator and allowed my car to drift to the side of the road. Once it came to a halt, I sat there for a long time, shaking from more than cold feet.

Chapter Seventeen

My phone rang.

"Are you out of your mind!" Ryan screamed. "Call off the chase now."

"I have. I've stopped. I don't dare continue. He's heading toward the route to Chatham. Possibly going to take the main road to Chatham or circle back to West London."

"Give me that," Louise Estrada said, presumably meaning the phone. "Calls are coming in. A couple of kids street racing. Several near collisions. Might that have something to do with you, Gemma?"

"Possible. Likely even."

"Of all the—"

"I'll handle it, Louise," Ryan said. She mumbled something rude, but she handed the phone back. "Gemma, care to tell me why you were in hot pursuit of person or persons unknown?"

"Someone broke into Robbie's Ellis's flat. I interrupted him—them—whoever—and they tried to get away."

"And you decided it was your business to arrest them?" Estrada said, obviously listening in.

Truth be told, I hadn't decided anything. I'd acted.

"We need to get back to the flat," I said. "You'd better call for backup. I didn't see Robbie, but if he's home, he might need help. I'll meet you there." I rattled off the address and hung up to Ryan's cry of "I don't—!"

I pulled into the next driveway and turned the car around. Then slowly and sedately, I drove back the way I'd come. Red and blue lights filled my rearview mirror, a siren yelled at me, and I was about to pull over when it accelerated and sped past me.

The cruiser reached Robbie's building before I did. By the time I arrived, another was screeching to a halt. I parked on the street outside the building and got out of my car. A uniformed officer was in the brightly lit vestibule surrounded by a cluster of residents. I saw my shop-clerk friend dressed in a long, thick housecoat, fluffy slippers on her feet.

A car pulled up next to mine. Neither Ryan nor Estrada smiled at me.

"Around the back," I said as they joined me on the sidewalk. "First flat on the left side. The door off the ground floor patio's open. That is, it was open when I left. It looks to have been forced. I'll show you—"

"You will show us nothing," Estrada said. "Stay here or I'll have you arrested for interference."

Ryan didn't come to my defense, so I mumbled, "Okay."

An ambulance arrived under lights and sirens. The medics got out, but they didn't rush into the building. They awaited the all-clear.

Ryan and his partner strode across the lawn, shouting orders. "Officer Johnson," Ryan called. "You're with us. Richter, keep everyone where they are. And I do mean everyone."

Ryan, Estrada, and Stella Johnson pulled out their guns, and they walked slowly but purposely around the apartment building. I could have told them not to bother, but I refrained. The culprit was long gone.

Several minutes passed. More people began coming out of the building and the adjacent ones to see what was going on. Nothing was going on. Shots did not ring out. No one cried for help. No one tried to flee the scene. Red and blue lights continued to flash, reflecting off the puddles on the grass and the sidewalk, the faces of the nosy and the curious and those here to do a job. Radios crackled.

Eventually, the medics gathered up their bags and went in the front door. Stella held the door open for them. Estrada came out and walked toward me.

"Detective Ashburton says you can view the scene now," she said. "Be prepared to answer a heck of a lot of questions."

"I am. Is Robbie in there? Is he okay?"

"A white male, late thirties, is dead in the unit you directed us to. Residents of the building tell us that apartment is occupied by one Robert Ellis, which is the name on the mailbox."

I nodded. Robbie. Poor Robbie. I'd never liked him, and he'd never liked me, but I was sorry for his death.

Estrada's dark eyes studied me. "Coincidence you were here in time to almost apprehend the killer, Gemma?"

"Yeah, for once it was. I intended to ask Robbie if he killed Tina Armstrong."

One expressive eyebrow rose. "Didn't see that one coming. Do you . . . still think he did it?" She asked the question almost despite herself.

"I'll have to give it some thought. Falling out among thieves perhaps?"

"If the two incidents are related."

"If," I agreed.

* * *

This time I went in via the main door and down the corridor. A medic stood outside the door to Robbie's apartment talking with Ryan. She gestured, and he nodded. She stuck her head into the apartment and said, "We're good to go."

Robbie would not be taken away. Not yet.

"Go on in," Ryan said. "Shoes off, booties on. Step carefully, don't touch anything."

I slipped out of my wet trainers and into the protective foot coverings, and then I went in. Small entrance hall with closet to the left, bathroom to immediate right. Tiny open kitchen with a table for two on the right next to the bedroom, living room—telly still on, but now quiet—straight ahead. Drapes over the balcony doors at the far end of the room moved gently in the incoming breeze. Robbie lay on his back on the floor just out of sight of the windows, his legs and feet next to the kitchen table, his torso and head partially in the bedroom. His eyes were open, but he saw nothing. The dirty beige carpet beneath him was wet and red, residue of blood spatter on the walls.

The bedroom was a jumble of objects. Half-made bed, clothes on the floor, stacks of cardboard boxes. A tablet sat on a table, screen dark.

Despite what Robbie told Jayne about continuing to work on his art, not a trace of painting supplies or canvases in progress (or even finished) was to be seen.

The only thing on the night table was a framed picture of Jayne. It was the only photograph in the entire flat. I estimated the picture to have been taken about four or five years ago. She smiled at the camera; the wind had caught her long blond hair, her eyes shone with youth and, if not love, traces of affection. The sea was blue and sparkling and calm in the background.

"Yeah," Ryan said following my gaze. "I saw that."

"Poor Robbie."

A knife lay on the floor of the living room, long and sharp, glimmering in the lights.

"Was the man you saw wearing gloves?" Ryan asked.

"He was. Winter coat, some sort of bandana around his lower face, hat pulled down almost to his eyes. Gloves, boots."

Estrada came into the room. "Makes it tough sometimes in winter. In midsummer, everyone would take notice of a person wearing gloves."

I looked at the carpet. Some clumps of mud, but likely not enough prints to be able to identify what shoes had been in here recently.

"What can you tell us about the man you saw?" Ryan asked.

"Was it definitely a man?" Estrada said.

"I can't say. Might have been a woman. Under six feet, more than five seven or eight. Lightly built, meaning not overweight, or from what I could tell, overly bulky." I thought about the way they'd vaulted easily over the balcony wall. "By the way this person moved, almost certainly they are under fifty and in reasonably good physical shape. Although I suppose an older person who works out regularly might have been able to move that fast and clear the wall. Not a police officer or any sort of emergency responder."

"How can you tell that?" Estrada asked.

"He—and I will call this person "he" only because "they" is getting awkward. We really do need to come up with a good singular, gender-neutral pronoun."

"I'll get right on that," Estrada muttered. "In the meantime—"

"He parked face-first in the parking space. Wasted precious seconds having to back out and turn around."

"Good one," Ryan said. His phone rang and he checked it. "Be right back. Gemma, keep looking."

I kept looking, but I didn't see anything more of interest. "Was the door to the hallway locked when you accessed it?" I asked Estrada.

"It was."

Not a surprise, but worth knowing. The killer had obviously come in via the patio after breaking the glass on the sliding door. Unfortunately, it had rained earlier, washing away much of the snow, and people would have been up and down the path to the cars all day. It might not be possible to tell if this person had lingered outside for long, waiting for—what?

"It'll be important to determine if Robbie was drunk," I said. "Judging by the number of cans of beer on the table, that is a possibility."

"Wits dulled. Slow to react," Estrada said.

I stood where I was, conscious of not leaving a trail of my own footprints or knocking anything over. "He's watching telly, beer and pizza. He hears a noise as the glass breaks and the door opens. Or maybe he doesn't hear it because the telly is so loud. Someone steps into the living room. He notices them and stands up, probably confused. Does Robbie recognize this person? Did he have the face coverings on yet?" I took another look at Robbie. His right wrist was cut, but not too deeply. "Not much in the way of defensive wounds, so I will assume, until evidence proves otherwise, he didn't put up any sort of a fight. The killer, again until evidence proves otherwise, came here with the intent to kill. And wasted no time doing so. Therefore, they brought their own knife rather than wander into the kitchen in search of one. That knife looks fairly ordinary, but it might be significant. Did my unexpected appearance cause the killer to panic and leave it behind? Or did they not care if it was found, as it's nothing special?"

"Your *unexpected appearance*," Estrada said calmly. "We only have your word about what happened here."

I smiled at her and held my arms out to my sides. "No blood." I unbuttoned my coat and held it open. "As you can see. Robbie was knifed up close. Look at the spatter on the walls. No way would the killer have been able to avoid getting blood on them. You are welcome to search my car for hastily disposed-of garments."

"Oh, don't worry," she said. "We will."

Ryan rejoined us. "The car you chased appears to have been found," he said. "Abandoned in a big box store lot in West London. Only because we put the word out did anyone check it. Plates were covered in mud, but they're good. Do you know a Rose Jane McMaster of Chatham?"

"No," I said. "I do not."

"Me neither," Estrada said.

"Officers are calling on Ms. McMaster now. At a quick look, she has no record other than a couple of parking offences."

"Car stolen?"

"Most likely."

"Stolen car," I said. "Broken door to gain access. Knife brought. I'd say this is clearly a premeditated killing. Did the neighbors hear anything? Robbie yelling or something like that?"

"We're asking," Ryan said. "So far nothing."

"I don't have my hopes up. That TV was on loud," Estrada said. "Some sort of action movie, all gunshots and yelling and thumping music. I turned the sound off when I came in. This building is old, solid and well built."

"Let's let these people do their jobs," Ryan said. "I still want to know what brought you here tonight, Gemma. We can sit in my car."

Estrada held out her hand. "Keys."

I looked at the hand. "What?"

"Keys to your car. You said I could search it. I intend to do so."

I took the keys out of my pocket and gave them to her. She tried not to smirk. "After I've done that, and presuming I find nothing incriminating, even *if* I find something incriminating, I have a line I want to follow, Detective."

"What?" Ryan asked.

Estrada pointed into the bedroom. "That picture is of Jayne Wilson. I'd say the presence of that photograph in an apartment that otherwise has nothing similar indicates the deceased was, shall we say, very fond of Ms. Wilson. Ms. Wilson is due to be married in a matter of days. Is it a coincidence that a death, which is still under investigation, happened at Ms. Wilson's birthday party? Or that the person who died at the party was a former girlfriend of Ms. Wilson's fiancé, Andy Whitehall?"

"You can't be thinking—" I said.

"I want to talk to Andy Whitehall," Estrada said. "Tonight. His ex-girlfriend died only two days ago. His fiancée's ex-boyfriend died tonight. Coincidence, or did those two individuals somehow threaten his impending marriage?"

"That's—" I said.

Ryan held up a hand. "Do it, Detective. Take a uniform with you. Because I'm good enough friends with Andy to be the best man at his wedding, I can't be involved."

Estrada gave him a nod, gave me a long look, and walked away, tossing my car keys from one hand to the other.

"She can't—"

"She's got a valid point, Gemma," Ryan said. "Let her do what any good detective would do. Now you still haven't told me what brought you here tonight."

Chapter Eighteen

It was late when I finally got home, tired, grumpy, hungry, seriously annoyed. At least, Louise Estrada graciously returned my car keys before heading out to question my best friend's fiancé.

I'd sat in Ryan's car, and as we watched forensics people coming and going, and neighbors peering over balconies or through windows, I outlined the thought process that caused me to be at Robbie's place tonight. I told Ryan I had reason to believe Robbie had been acquainted with Tina Armstrong in New York, and I was curious as to why he never mentioned that. I told him I was worried Robbie would become a pest, or worse, in Jayne's life, and I intended to tell him to back off.

I did not say I thought it possible Robbie killed Tina to cause trouble for Andy. Once Estrada mentioned Andy's name, I didn't want to put any additional focus on my friend.

"If Tina and Robbie knew each other in New York," I said, "that might mean the origins of this case can be found there."

"Except that this picture you dug up on the internet was taken three years ago, and Tina went to California afterward. You're stretching here, Gemma. No need for what-ifs and supposedlies. We know they were in the same place, at the same time, on Tuesday night."

"I am never fond of coincidence. 'The universe is rarely that lazy.'"

"You've said that before. Sherlock Holmes?"

"Brother Mycroft, not in the original Canon but the Cumberbatch TV show. The point is still valid. Unlikely as it sometimes is, coincidences do happen. It might be possible Robbie's death is unrelated to Tina's. I know you and Louise are investigating Tina's death as a murder, but I'm still holding the door open to suicide or misadventure." In the light of the police car behind us, I caught the quick grin flashing across his face. "What?"

"You. That comment is so Gemma."

"Whatever that means. I simply cannot see how anyone could have hit her with such force as to cause injury without being seen by people inside the restaurant. If this person threw her off the deck, again without being observed, they wouldn't have been able to foresee that she'd hit her head and be unable to swim to shore. Granted, it is possible that's exactly what happened; people often act rashly without thinking things through or considering the consequences. I will also admit, I do not know all of the facts. Speaking of which, are you making any progress with Tina's case?"

"Not a great deal. Her family don't know of any issues she had with anyone. She confessed to a girlfriend she wanted to get back with Andy, but reluctantly admitted it didn't look like that was going to happen. She was studying for her realtor's license, and as far as anyone knew, it seemed to be going well. No evidence of any enemies there. Her family tell us she was not happy at having to give up her acting career, but they wouldn't call her seriously depressed. Her doctor says she would have always had some residual pain from the injuries sustained in that car accident, but it wasn't unmanageable or severe. The techies have her phone, but so far, they're still giving it time to dry out before trying to turn it on."

And then he let me go home.

I took the dogs for a walk through the dark, quiet streets. I debated calling Jayne to tell her about Robbie. She would want to know, but it was late. Jayne rose early, unnaturally early by my standards, to get to the tearoom and start on the day's bread and yeasted dough. Time enough later this morning for her to be told of Robbie's death.

Then again, I didn't want her to hear it on the news or even worse, through social media.

Nose to the ground, which isn't far for him to reach, Peony attempted to follow a scent, while Violet, older if not wiser, trotted happily at my side. I watched them and thought. I've found dogs are good at that: letting a person's mind simply wander.

I might have my doubts about the death of Tina Armstrong, but there could be not the slightest doubt Robbie Ellis had been murdered. I'd seen the killer myself. He shoved me aside and ran when he saw me. I'd been exposed, perched on top of a low wall. Why not kill me too? Because he dropped the knife and didn't want to go back for it? Because he, or she, didn't have anything against me?

Because they thought, correctly, I'd put up a fight? I am not inexperienced in taking care of myself, and I would have yelled for someone to call the cops while doing so.

Or because they themselves didn't know how to fight and were afraid of engaging with me and finding out I did?

That line of thought led me nowhere.

I called to the dogs, and we turned around. It was coming up to three-thirty. Jayne would be up soon.

* * *

I crawled into bed but didn't get much sleep. I'd phoned Jayne, deciding it would be best to break the news to her myself, even if that meant waking her up. She'd been shocked and saddened. Her main question to me was, "Why?" and all I could say was I didn't know.

I wrapped the covers around me while the dogs snoozed on the floor. I thought about Robbie, and about Tina, and about who might have wanted them dead.

I came to no conclusions.

The winter sun was doing its best to put in an appearance when I finally gave up on sleep and climbed out of bed. I let the dogs out for their morning romp and was putting the kettle on when Jayne phoned me.

"Andy's been arrested!"

"Arrested or taken in for questioning?"

"Does it matter?"

"It matters a great deal. First, take a deep breath, Jayne. Try and calm down."

She breathed. "I can't calm down. I can't believe this is happening."

"How did you find out? Did he phone you?"

"Yes. He called a minute ago. He was leaving the police station."

"Then he is obviously not under arrest."

The kettle hissed and emitted a stream of steam before switching itself off. I poured hot water into my teapot with one hand and held the phone with the other.

"He was taken to the police station last night and questioned for hours about Robbie's death. The very idea that Andy had anything to do with it is ridiculous. Andy had no reason to kill Robbie and even if he did, Andy's the gentlest man in—"

"I know that, Jayne. You have no need to convince me. Stop and think clearly, and then tell me what you want me to do."

She did not take the time to think clearly. "What do I want you to do? Prove his innocence, of course. Talk to Ryan. Tell him Andy didn't do it."

I took the teapot to the table and sat down. I poured myself a cup. "That Andy was not held means the police have no reason to hold him." That wasn't entirely true. All it meant was the police didn't have sufficient evidence. Yet. Depending on what Andy had to tell her, Louise Estrada might be searching for such evidence. I didn't say so, trying to keep my voice cheerful and upbeat. "Do you want me to talk to him?"

"Yes. Tell him Andy didn't do it. Tell him—"

"I mean Andy. Do you want me to talk to Andy? Ryan will be kept a long way away from this if Andy is . . . a person of interest. They're too close."

Jayne sighed. "Please?"

"Did Andy say where he was going? Home or to the restaurant?"

"To work. When he's upset, he needs to work."

"I'll go there now. I can't say how long I'll be. Ashleigh's off today. Gale isn't due to come until noon. Hang a sign on the Emporium door saying something to the effect of closed for a family emergency."

"Thank you, Gemma."

"No thanks needed," I said.

I finished my tea, checked the weather forecast, and called Violet and Peony to come in. They were covered in mud from the bottoms of their feet to their furry bellies. Violet had managed to get mud on her ears. I toweled them down as they wiggled in delight and then went to have my shower and get dressed. According to the forecast, it would be sunny with increasingly warm temperatures. That should help melt the lingering patches of dirty snow and dry up the puddles of cold rainwater.

My phone rang as I was telling the dogs to guard the house. Louise Estrada. She did not bother with familiarities.

"Where are you?"

"At home. I'm about to go out."

"Wait for me there. I'm on my way."

"Like I said, I'm about to go out. Is it important?"

"If you are not at your house when I get there, I'll have you brought to the station."

"I'll be here."

She arrived no more than ten minutes later. Notably, Ryan was not with her but rather a uniformed officer. He was young, fresh-faced, trying very hard to look stern. I'd seen him at the scene last night but didn't get his name. New to town, perhaps.

"I have some further questions about last night," Estrada said after I'd invited them in. Violet and Peony provided greetings as is traditional when receiving guests. The dogs don't usually know (or care) who's here as a friend and who is not.

I led the way to the kitchen and dropped into a chair at the table. Estrada hesitated and then sat. The uniformed officer stood against the counter, arms crossed, expression stern, watching me as though daring me to make a break for it. The detective got straight to the point; I expected no less. "Have you had any further thoughts about what happened last night? Anything you forgot to mention or later remembered?"

"No. I have thought about it a great deal, but nothing new comes to mind."

"I'm interested in the person you say you chased."

"The person I chased."

"You can't identify this individual by anything more than general size and a guess at their approximate age? No gender. No race. Hair, distinguishing features."

"As I told you, he or she was dressed in loose trousers and a large heavy coat and moved quickly. Their face was concealed by the hat and scarf. They were around my height. Not substantially taller or shorter at any rate, and not excessively large."

Estrada watched me. I shrugged, not knowing what she expected me to say. The officer shifted from one foot to another. Peony sniffed at his boots. He tried to ignore the friendly little fellow.

"This person appears to have killed a man mere moments before encountering you standing in the way of their escape," Estrada said. "Yet they, he, didn't attempt to do the same to you? Have you wondered why not? You were unarmed. By your own admission, you were caught completely off guard and in a difficult physical position."

"I considered that as well. The knife had been left behind. Meaning they likely didn't have a weapon. Perhaps they thought me a more formidable opponent than I am. When fight or flight instincts clash, no one knows which will win out. Sheer panic, usually."

"Has it occurred to you they didn't kill you, or attempt to harm you, because they like you? Or perhaps you're close to someone this person cares about?"

"It has not." So that's what she was after. She wanted me to say Robbie's killer might have been Andy. "I did not get the warm and fuzzies from them, no."

"You and I have known each other for a number of years, Gemma. Sometimes to my intense regret. I know you to be unnaturally observant and almost preternaturally aware of your surroundings. Yet you can't tell me any more about the person you saw last night."

"I might be observant, Louise. But I am human. I can't see what is not visible to the naked eye. It was night. His or her features were almost completely concealed by their clothing and face coverings. They wore baggy winter clothes. They were not particularly large or noticeably small. They didn't run with a limp, and they didn't drag their knuckles on the ground or swing from trees or shout at me in Russian. If they had, I would have told you."

"Would you? Would you tell me if you recognized this person if you wanted for some reason to protect them?"

"The question is moot, as I did not recognize anything about them. Now that's settled, tell me about the car. Did Rose Jane McMaster of Chatham confess to taking her car for a spin last night?"

"Ms. McMaster is a seventy-two-year-old woman, a retired university professor. Of modern European history, I believe. She didn't even know her car wasn't in the driveway until our officers asked her about it."

"A nondescript car, probably not with all the latest in anti-theft gadgets. Parked out in the open in a suburban driveway at night. Easy target."

"The car is being thoroughly gone over, but nothing yet. Once again, those pesky winter gloves." Estrada looked down.

Bored with the conversation, Violet had gone back to the living room for a nap. Peony had abandoned the unresponsive cop and sat at Estrada's feet, still hoping for some playtime. "Does Andy Whitehall have pets?"

"As he would have told you last night, no, he does not. Neither does Jayne. Did you find dog hair in the car?"

"Ms. McMaster has two longhaired dachshunds. She doesn't often clean her car. Complicates the search for evidence considerably."

I jumped out of my chair. "If that's all, Detective, I have a busy day ahead of me. I'll let you know if anything further develops."

Estrada didn't jump, but she did stand up. "You do that, Gemma. You do that."

I showed them to the door and waved a cheery goodbye. Then I closed the door and leaned my back against it with a deep sigh. Estrada was looking to pin this on Andy. Even if Jayne hadn't asked me to, I needed to talk to him.

I decided to walk into town. I needed the air to clear my head, and I needed time to think. Sherlock Holmes had his pipe and time to indulge in a three-pipe problem. I had a fifteen-minute walk. Likely not enough.

The sun was out and it was warm on my face, so that went some way toward improving my mood. As I walked down Blue Water Place to Harbor Road, the ocean stretched out before me, blue and sparkling. Jayne's wedding was to be held at the Cape Cod Yacht Club not far from here. It was less than a week away. We should be finalizing last-minute details, checking in with the club's restaurant, ticking off the guest list one last time, ensuring the flowers were ordered and would be ready when needed. A bride and her best friend should be having fun doing all those things. Not asking the groom if he'd recently committed murder.

As the harbor and the Blue Water Café came in sight, I texted Andy to tell him I needed to talk to him. Now.

He was standing in the vestibule when I arrived. He unlocked the door and let me in. The police tape had been taken down outside; the restaurant put to rights after the party; balloons taken away, tables laid, floor swept. The pile of Jayne's presents was gone.

"I hope the police didn't take the gifts as evidence," I said.

"No. I dropped them off at Jayne's yesterday after meeting you at McGillivray's."

The restaurant was quiet, but the scent of something deeply rich and intensely spicy came from the kitchen.

"You're cooking?" I asked.

"Testing a new recipe. A crab and shrimp curry I've been wanting to finalize for some time. It should be ready right about now. Want to try it?"

"Love to. But might I suggest you need to get some rest." He did not look well. Haggard face, deep circles under his tired eyes, blond hair hanging limp over his forehead. He didn't have his chef's uniform on and drops of orange sauce decorated his T-shirt.

He was, I couldn't help but notice, the right general size to have been the man I saw last night. I shoved the thought away.

"I cook when I'm stressed," he said. "Might as well take all the free time I've suddenly found myself with to try out a few new things. Can I assume Jayne called you?"

"She did. I know you were taken down to the police station last night and questioned about the death of Robbie Ellis. Want to tell me about it?"

He gave me a grin containing not the slightest bit of humor and led the way to the kitchen.

The room was spotless, surfaces scrubbed, floor washed, pots and pans, spices and ingredients put away, everything in its place. Steam rose from a heavy frying pan on the gas stove. Andy picked up a large wooden spoon and gave the curry a stir. My mouth watered.

"You probably know more than I do about what went down, Gemma," he said. "They told me you'd been there. I was home in bed when the cops knocked on my door. Uniforms, not Ryan or Louise. They said the detectives needed to talk to me and they were taking me to the station."

"You were not arrested?"

"No. Just a chat, they said. When I got there, Louise was waiting. Again, just to talk. She wanted to know if I'd seen Robbie that night. I had no idea why she was asking. I told her the restaurant was still closed, so no need for waitstaff. She asked if he and I ever socialized on a personal basis, had I ever been to his apartment. I said no. And then she told me he'd been killed earlier tonight. Murdered." Andy shook his head. "At first, I didn't understand why she was telling me about it. But then she started asking me what I'd been doing tonight and if I knew Robbie had been bothering Jayne."

"He wasn't bothering Jayne," I said. "Although I have to admit I feared it might come to that."

"I told Louise I knew nothing about that. Because I didn't. She then switched to Tina. Was I angry when Tina gate-crashed the party? Did I still have feelings for Tina? Did I fear Tina would somehow sabotage my relationship with Jayne?" Andy stirred the curry. He scooped up a small amount of the gorgeous deep-orange sauce and tasted it. "Almost ready. Hand me one of those bowls."

I did so, and he dished out a small serving. "British people like their curry, right?"

"Chicken tikka masala has been called the national dish of England." I accepted the bowl, and Andy handed me a spoon.

I lifted the bowl to my face and breathed. The scent was powerful, hinting at the strength of the flavors hidden inside. I dipped the edge of the spoon into the curry.

"I want total honesty now," Andy said. "If you wouldn't order this a second time in a restaurant, tell me."

I touched the spoon to my tongue. Flavors exploded in my mouth: hot and spicy, rich and creamy. I dug the spoon further in. The shrimp was firm and infused with flavor, offering just the slightest resistance to my teeth. The shreds of crab were light and flaky, punchy with taste. "Absolute perfection," I said with total honesty. The inside of my mouth burned ever so slightly and exceedingly pleasantly.

Some of the darkness lifted from behind Andy's eyes, and he gave me a genuine grin. "That's what I was hoping you'd say. More?"

"Oh, yeah. Not my usual breakfast, but I can make an exception." I passed the bowl to him and he filled it.

"For serving, I'll sprinkle freshly chopped herbs across the top. Cut some of the heat, add some additional color. I need to experiment a bit more, decide how spicy, or not, to make it." Then his face fell. "If I'm here to make it."

"You will be," I said around another mouthful. "If you want me to help, and I want to help, you have to tell me what you told Estrada—and what you didn't tell her. Robbie died at about ten-thirty. Where were you then?"

"Here. Cooking this curry, as it happens."

"That late?"

"That's not late for me, Gemma. Nights I'm working, I don't normally get home until well after midnight. I thought the curry would benefit from time in the fridge, let the flavors mingle, so I prepared it last night and only reheated it and made some minor adjustments to the seasonings this morning."

"I suppose you were alone here."

"Sadly, yes. I spent a good part of the evening working on my accounts, and then I wanted to give the curry a try. So I stayed. I finished up and was heading home around quarter to eleven."

At a quarter to eleven, Robbie's killer had been driving at great speed west on McConnell Street, pursued by yours truly.

"It'll be nice," he said wistfully, "when I'll be going home to Jayne every night."

"You were here alone. Anyone see you leave?"

"Yes, and I told Louise. Kyle Jackman, the chef at the fish market on the other side of the pier, was passing. We said hi, exchanged a few words. He made a joke about me soon to be a married man. Then we went our separate ways."

"Did Estrada call him?"

"I don't know. She said she was going to."

"Do you have his number?"

"No, I don't."

"The fish market should be open this morning. I'll pop over and talk to him. His place has been in West London forever. He'll make a reliable alibi." I put my empty bowl on the counter. "See, all sorted."

"Thanks, Gemma. Would you like to take a container with you for lunch?"

"Absolutely."

* * *

The fish market serves not only as a place to buy the freshest of fish but also as a restaurant to have it prepared for you. The restaurant wasn't open yet, but the shop was. I asked the young clerk if Kyle was in yet.

"He's popular today," she said. "The police were here earlier."

"And?"

"And I said no. He's not in and not expected to be. He's taking some vacation time. I told the cops that."

"Do you have his number?"

"Yes."

I smiled at her.

"I'm not giving it to you."

"Did you give it to the police?"

"I could hardly say no, now could I?"

"Good enough," I said.

Chapter Nineteen

Still carrying my takeout container, I popped into the tea-room kitchen to tell Jayne Andy had a reliable alibi for the time of Robbie's death. She squealed with delight and wrapped me in a hug. Fiona joined in.

Our joy didn't last for long. A short while later, Andy called Jayne, and an upset Jayne ran into the Emporium to tell me the bad news. Estrada was not able to contact his alibi.

Kyle Jackman was not answering his cell phone. They called the landline at his house to be told he didn't live there anymore. He'd recently separated from his wife and moved out of their home, and she had no idea where he would have gone. And, she informed the police, she didn't care. He'd booked a week's vacation from the fish market, but he hadn't shared his plans with anyone. Staff told the police he was having trouble dealing with the breakup of his marriage.

"Andy wants to postpone the wedding," a tearful Jayne said.

"Gale!" I yelled. "Mind the store."

I hustled Jayne upstairs to my office. I sat her in the visitor's chair, ran to the staff loo for a box of tissues, shoved it into her hands, and let her have a good, long cry. When she finally sobbed to a halt, she looked at me with wet red eyes and blew her nose. "Poor Robbie's dead and all I can think of is my wedding."

"That's okay," I said. "You're worried about Andy."

"What were you doing at Robbie's last night anyway, Gemma?"

Earlier, I'd decided not to tell her about my misgivings regarding Robbie's intentions or that I intended to warn him away. No point now. Instead, I said, "Did you know he knew Tina Armstrong in New York?"

She blew her nose again. "Is that true? He never mentioned it. I'd almost forgotten about Tina. You don't think her and Robbie's deaths are related, do you?"

"I don't see how they cannot be," I said. "But I have not the slightest idea how."

"Andy didn't kill Tina. And he certainly didn't kill Robbie."

"I know that. It would appear it's time I started seriously thinking about who might have done it."

* * *

I encouraged Jayne to take the rest of the day off to be with Andy. "Go for a nice lunch. Take a drive up the coast and stop for a drink at a hugely overpriced place with a spectacular view."

"I don't know about that," she said. "But we're pretty well set in the tearoom for the rest of the day, so—"

"Good. Off you go now."

Before I could shoo her through the sliding door, Donald and the man he'd met at Jayne's party were coming in.

"Uncle Keith," Jayne said, "hi."

"Hello, dear. Nice to see you." He gave her a peck on the cheek. He was nicely dressed in a knee-length camel coat with a jaunty yellow scarf and leather boots. Leather gloves peeked out of his pockets. He smelled strongly of tobacco. I added him to my mental list of smokers who'd been at Jayne's party.

"Keith indicated he had an interest in Sherlock Holmes," Donald said. "Therefore, naturally I suggested we drop in for a visit and later enjoy tea in the tearoom."

"We don't do a proper afternoon tea on weekdays in the winter," Jayne said.

Donald's face drooped in disappointment. Keith's did not. "Not a tea man myself," he said.

"The restaurant's open for lunch and coffee breaks, though," I said. "Soups, sandwiches, lovely fresh baking. Lattes, espressos."

Keith smiled fondly at Jayne.

"Although," I added quickly, "Jayne won't be able to join you. She's leaving for the day. Treating herself to a half-day."

"We still have plenty of time to catch up," Keith said. "Okay, Donald. Let's see what you think's so important."

Donald cleared his throat and straightened his spine. "We will begin with the nonfiction. Come this way."

I should consider hiring Donald to be a tour guide. On our last visit to England, he, Jayne, and I had been given a private tour of Garfield Hall, the grand Yorkshire manor house owned by my mother's cousin, Alistair Denhaugh, the eighth Earl of Ramshaw. Since getting home, my friend showed people around my shop with as much reference, knowledge, and enthusiasm as a volunteer at that Grade Two–listed estate.

Keith gave Jayne an amused smile, me a shrug, and followed.

Jayne jerked her head, indicating she wanted to speak to me. We stepped into the tearoom. "Don't be shy about letting Uncle Keith spend to his heart's content."

"What does that mean?"

"He's the black sheep of my mom's family. Her older brother. He's retired and living comfortably off his investments, or so he says. My mom says everyone in the family suspects those investments weren't entirely on the up and up." She gave me a huge wink, and I was pleased to see she still had some humor in her.

"Meaning?"

"Meaning, no one knows what he does. Or did. Not for sure. He disappeared for a few years, came home and bought his mother and sister new cars, left again, drifted in and out, always with money to throw around. He lives in Chatham now. I haven't been there, but Mom says his house is something to see. Family rumor always said he was connected to organized crime. Mom was never entirely sure; she just thought he kept his business interests to himself."

"Interesting story, anyway. Have fun."

"Fun at what?"

"Your afternoon with Andy."

* * *

Back in the shop, I watched Donald and Keith. Donald was in full lecture mode, pulling out books at random, handing each one to Keith before producing another. Gale hovered behind them. Keith put some of the books back on the shelf, but he handed a few to Gale and her arms were filling up.

"Sir Arthur wrote a great many works of both fiction and nonfiction apart from the Sherlock Holmes ones for which he is best known. Over here we have . . ."

I tuned Donald out.

Did Keith have a mob connection? I didn't see that it mattered regarding my current problem. Surely the mob hadn't put a hit out on Robbie and Tina. Even if they had, I couldn't see this nicely dressed gentleman who is now comfortably retired to a house that is "something to see" getting the contract.

Then again, stranger things have happened.

It most definitely was not Keith who'd been at Robbie's last night. He wasn't all that old, likely in his mid-sixties, but too old to be vaulting over walls and sprinting across icy grass. He moved with a slight stiffness in his gait as though his back was giving him some pain but he was too proud to use a cane. I'd noticed that stiffness at the party, so it was not a result of fleeing from an inconveniently arrived Englishwoman after committing a murder.

"Any interest in Sir Arthur naturally leads one to an exploration of his contemporaries. *The Woman in White* by Wilkie Collins, a close friend of Sir Arthur, is generally considered to be . . ." And another book was added to the pile in Gale's arms.

If it started to look as though the mob, whatever that might mean, was becoming active in West London, I'd focus my attention on Keith. As for now, I had better things to do.

Which at the moment was taking care of my business. Not for the first time, and unlikely to be the last, I envied Sherlock Holmes who could go about solving crimes without worrying about the minor issue of earning a living.

While Gale followed Donald and Keith around the Emporium, staggering under the weight of the ever-growing stack of books in her arms, I served other customers. I half listened to Donald's lecture and learned some things even I didn't know about the Great Detective and his creator.

Finally, Gale dropped the stack on the sales counter with a sigh of relief, and Keith pulled out his wallet. I doubted he'd ever get around to reading all these books, and he hadn't seemed particularly interested in Donald's chatter. Maybe he was merely being polite to a new friend, and nothing's wrong with that.

"And," Donald announced, "as a gift from me, something to use while enjoying your initial exposure to the wonders of the Canon." He proudly put an I-am-Sherlocked mug on the counter. "Now, it's a mite early for teatime, but I think we can make an exception for a nice cuppa and one of Jayne's delicious scones. Do you know, Gemma, in the entire Canon there is not one mention of Holmes and Watson enjoying afternoon tea?"

"I do know that, yes. It was more a woman's thing at the time. A chance to get out of the house, away from supervision by men, to enjoy the company of female friends. You can leave your bags here while you're in the tearoom, if you'd like."

And off they went.

"Is that a record for one sale, Gemma?" Gale asked me.

"It might well be. Are you okay on your own for a while? I have some work to do on the computer. I'll be in my office if anything comes up."

"Sure."

I went upstairs, took my curry out of the small fridge where I'd left it, and popped it into the microwave. When it was fragrant and bubbling, I took it to my desk and prepared to get to work.

Robbie and Tina. It was time I did a deep dive into the both of them. If they did have criminal connections, those connections might well be what brought about their deaths. Whether said deaths were related or not.

Robbie first. This time, I did go places on the internet where I am not supposed to venture.

Robbie's art career in New York had been as dismal a failure as I'd first surmised. It didn't look as though he sold a thing. He'd lived in a run-down area of the city and picked up random work with caterers and restaurants to get by. He had no additional sources of income. No wealthy, and patient, patrons of the arts. No family money or trust funds. No organized crime connections.

All terribly boring. And then—bingo. I read quickly, read again, and sat back with a sigh. Robbie'd managed to get himself into trouble with the police a few times. Bar brawls, unpaid traffic fines, an altercation with a panhandler that turned ugly. Regular low-level stuff. But what caught my attention: a charge of attempted blackmail.

About a year ago, Robbie had been working for the caterers at a big charity function. The rich and famous. Glamorous people, all the major celebrity and political names. A few days after the party, a woman by the name of Christina VanDoosen went to the police. She told them Robbie had taken compromising pictures of her at the party and threatened to put them on the internet.

I looked up Christina VanDoosen. Young, pretty, elegant. She had a few minor roles in major theatrical productions and major roles in minor theatrical productions. According to her official bio, as well as general Broadway gossip, she was on the way up.

Back to the police report. Christina found herself in a compromising situation at the party (the nature of the compromising situation wasn't in the report I had in front of me, but I could guess), and a waiter—one Robert Ellis—had photographed her. He called her the next day, threatening to release the photo unless she paid him a substantial amount of money. Instead, she went to the cops. Wisely, in my opinion.

From what I could tell, the case went no further. Charges were never formally laid, and it never came to court. I assumed

Christina refused to pay Robbie off, and instead told him she was reporting him. She didn't press charges or take the matter further, and the case was tucked away.

She had more nerve than Robbie. If these pictures were that compromising, she would have not wanted them to be shown in court, taking the chance they'd be leaked to the gutter press. But she stood her ground, and Robbie backed down.

Had that failure marked the end of his career as a blackmailer? Perhaps not. Maybe he decided he should have carried through with his threat and tried again when the next opportunity presented itself. I found no more reports of blackmail charges, but I wouldn't, would I? Not if he'd been more successful the next time.

Which raised the question as to whether or not Robbie brought his blackmail habits with him on his return to West London. I didn't know if anyone at Jayne's birthday party was blackmailable, and I couldn't go through the entire invitation list trying to find out.

But it was a definite possibility. Robbie was lucky Christina VanDoosen merely reported him to the police. If she had connections, she might have taken other steps.

Jayne's Uncle Keith was rumored to have "connections." I filed that information away to return to later.

I next turned my attention to Tina. I wasn't so much interested in whether or not Tina Armstrong had a criminal record as to if she had a connection with Robbie, other than what I initially found.

Most of the hits I got for her focused on her accident. She was called an "up-and-coming young actress" seriously hurt in a "tragic accident." As her stay in the hospital dragged on, attention dropped off. By the time she left the hospital and returned to West London, she'd been forgotten. She'd been driving the car with a major star named Julien Best in the passenger seat. Julien Best was so famous, even I'd heard of him. As well as *Star Trek*, Ryan likes action movies, and I'd suffered through at least one of Best's performances.

The actor sustained little more than a few cuts and bruises in the crash. Reading between the lines, some of the commentators said it was better Tina was hurt than the "beloved action hero." It was also mentioned that his "banged-up" face added character to the actor's rugged good looks. If Best's career had been derailed by the accident, he might have been out to get revenge on the person who caused it, but such was not the case. He remained big box office.

Unless I learned otherwise, I'd consider Tina's car accident bore no direct relationship to her untimely death.

Not everything on the internet is freely available even to someone who knows how to look. Not without devoting a considerable amount of time, anyway. But from what I could tell, Tina had never come to the attention of the police in West London, New York, or Los Angeles, other than as a result of the accident. The police report said conditions that night were poor, rain was heavy, the road wet, and Tina swerved to avoid an oncoming car in the wrong lane. The driver of the other car had never been located.

I did find one interesting item about Tina, and I didn't even have to do anything illegal. It was right there on her Instagram page from three years ago. Tina had posted a great deal of content in the years she was trying to make it in New York and Hollywood, hoping to get her name and face out there; I was simply lucky when the picture of interest to me floated to the top. She and Robbie Ellis not only knew each other, they'd once been an item.

The relationship hadn't lasted long. Not longer than ten photos worth. But it had definitely happened. Selfies showed them together, laughing, kissing, posing with big smiles and arms around each other. The background of one of the shots was almost certainly Central Park. Pictures of her with Robbie abruptly ended around the time she went to L.A., and she made no mention of him again.

She and Robbie hadn't exactly had a joyous reunion when they saw each other at the party; rather the opposite, but that might not be significant. It was entirely possible they'd run into each other on an earlier occasion, now they were both back in West London. If their relationship ended on a sour note, they wouldn't have been all that joyous at any time.

I leaned back in my chair, steepled my fingers, closed my eyes, and thought.

Did it matter that Tina and Robbie knew each other? I couldn't see why. Everyone at the party knew at least someone else, staff or guests. West London in the winter is a small town.

Was it possible Robbie had been blackmailing Tina and they'd fought and she died? Try as I might, I couldn't see it. She was studying for her real estate license, not running for political office.

I refused to believe the two deaths were not related, but I had to consider that "not related" in this case didn't mean they happened for the same reason.

Had Robbie seen who killed Tina? Had Robbie threatened to go to the police with the evidence unless the killer paid up?

I felt my excitement rising. I might be onto something. That scenario was entirely possible. As a waiter in a restaurant Robbie could go anywhere, watch everything, and no one would pay him the slightest amount of notice. He had a history of blackmail, and although the instance I knew about hadn't gone anywhere, he might have taken the opportunity to try again. He was on the down and out, not a whole lot of promise on the horizon. The Robbie I knew was shiftless and lazy. Blackmail might have seemed like an easy way to make some extra money.

I reached for my phone and punched buttons.

"I hope you're calling to confess," Louise Estrada said.

"Sadly for you, no. I have a question. If you don't mind."

She sighed. "Go ahead."

"Robbie's phone. Do you have it?"

"No. We can't locate it. Not on him, not in his car, and not in his apartment. We have searched. We've called, and it appears to be turned off, perhaps destroyed."

"I consider that to be significant, don't you?"

"I do. The killer didn't take the time to pick up the knife, but they did grab the phone."

"Which means the killer believes something incriminating is on it."

"Or they intend to sell it. We don't believe this is a robbery gone wrong, but we have not dismissed the idea."

"I suppose that could be the case."

"You once told me the theory of Occam's Razor. Do you remember?"

"I do."

"The simplest solution is usually the most likely."

"Is anything significant about the knife?"

"Not that it's any of your business, but as long as you're on the phone, no. It did not match the other kitchen utensils found at the scene, and there weren't many. A cooking knife, not particularly expensive, but not dirt cheap either. A type sold in most housewares and hardware stores as well as the online outlets.

Not that we had much doubt, but it has been confirmed Ellis was killed by the knife found at the scene. One solid strike to the center of the chest."

I'm not one to refuse to admit when I've been wrong. I initially believed Tina had not been murdered, despite what the police thought, but if Robbie died because he'd been blackmailing Tina's killer, then Tina had been murdered.

Which line of thought took me absolutely nowhere new.

The person I confronted at Robbie's apartment last night had been fit enough to pull me off the wall, vault over it, and run. Not an Olympic-class feat of athletic endeavor, but it did exclude a substantial number of people who'd been at Jayne's party.

But this still didn't mean Tina's killer was the same person who killed Robbie. The first killer might have found a second person to do it, either paid or otherwise.

Unlikely to be paid, I thought. It had not been a professional hit man. Not if they'd parked face-first on their way to a contract killing.

Questions. Questions. In searching for answers, I'd found nothing but more questions.

I rubbed the back of my neck. I rolled my shoulders. I glanced out the window, and to my considerable surprise, I saw that the midwinter daylight had come to an end.

I checked the time. Ten to six. I'd been here for hours. My lovely curry sat on my desk, cold and congealed and forgotten.

I ran down the stairs. To my surprise, Ashleigh was behind the counter, ringing up a copy of *Sherlock Holmes and the Telegram from Hell* by Nicholas Meyer for Mrs. Ramsbatten.

"What are you doing here?" I asked. "Where's Gale?"

"She was scheduled to leave at four. Doctor's appointment. She phoned me, said you were so wrapped up in whatever you were doing, you didn't hear her calling, and she was afraid to disturb you." She handed a bag to her customer. "Have a nice evening, Mrs. R."

"You too, dear." Mrs. Ramsbatten turned to me. "You need to give this young lady a raise, Gemma. She's worth her weight in gold, this one. I can't believe I forgot my sister's birthday is next week. If I don't get this in the mail first thing tomorrow, it will arrive late and I'll never hear the end of it. I'd love to stop and chat, but I must be off. I'm having dinner at the Harbor Inn with that lovely woman I met at Jayne's party. Audrey. I'm looking forward to hearing her stories of inside Hollywood. Nothing like a bit of gossip to liven up an old lady's evening."

She left. Ashleigh grinned at me.

"Thank you for coming in," I said. "I appreciate it. Mrs. Ramsbatten has a point. Tomorrow we'll have your regular quarterly performance meeting."

"We have a regular quarterly performance meeting?"

"We do starting tomorrow."

Chapter Twenty

Even in January, the Emporium stays open until nine on a Friday night. Off-season, we rarely get busy, so I thanked Ashleigh for coming in on the spur of the moment and told her she could leave. "Any plans for tonight?" I asked her.

"I'm meeting a couple of friends for a drink in town, maybe go for dinner after. Bunny's seeing George again." She pulled a face.

"They must have had a good date the other night then."

"He had to cancel, supposedly some press of business, but he rescheduled so she was okay with that. She's all bubbly and giggly about it. Nothing serious, she says, but he's good company. She loved his restaurant. The staff fussed over them, and he bought a really expensive bottle of wine and all that stuff. He even sent flowers this morning. A big bouquet of red roses, of all the stereotypical rubbish." The face pulled down even more.

"Some gestures are stereotypical because they have a history of working. Why are you upset about this? Doesn't Bunny deserve to enjoy herself?"

Ashleigh shrugged. "Yeah, I suppose."

"Has he said anything to her about investing in his restaurants or using her contacts, assuming she has any left, to promote his businesses?"

"Not in so many words."

"Discreetly?"

Ashleigh winced. "No. Not that she's told me."

"I'm your employer, not your mother or your spiritual advisor, Ashleigh, but I suggest you let it go until and if he does express any ulterior motives."

"I suppose you're right, Gemma."

"As I usually am."

She cracked a grin. "Not always. Maybe I'm just . . . I've found my mom after so long. I don't want to lose her again."

"Judging by what I've observed of your and Bunny's relationship, you are not going to lose each other again. She's thrilled you're in her life. Nothing's going to change that. But at the same time, time is not going to stop. For either of you. Life continues."

"Okay, Gemma. You win. For now." She touched her index fingers to her cheeks and pulled her mouth up into a hideous grin. "See, me being happy for her."

"I see."

Ashleigh left, and I passed the time by tidying the shelves. Keith, with the assistance of Donald, had made a substantial dent in my stock. A few people walked by, but no one stopped or even slowed down to admire the display in the windows. Which reminded me I'd forgotten to take down the advertising for the visit of the bestselling writer. I plucked the glass stand with her picture off the main display table and stuffed it under the counter.

Chimes tinkled and Madison came in. She carried a bag from a woman's wear shop further up Baker Street. "This town," she proclaimed, "is a massive bore."

As if to prove her right, Moriarty didn't bother to rouse himself from his bed under the center table to greet her.

"Nice to see you, Madison," I said cheerily. "Are you looking for a good book to pass the long, lonely hours? If so, you've come to the right place."

"I was doing some shopping—" she held up the bag in evidence—"and saw this store. Audrey said you own it." She glanced around. "Never been all that crazy about Sherlock Holmes myself. Although Cumberbatch is cute. Is that—"

A life-sized cardboard cutout of Benedict Cumberbatch as Holmes and Martin Freeman as Dr. Watson occupies a corner of the shop next to the games, puzzles, socks, scarves, and other assorted merchandise (just about anything and everything) to do with the Great Detective. Madison stepped forward and peered at the image. She gasped. "It's signed. Goodness, where did you get this?"

"Benedict dropped in one day, just a casual hi, and he kindly signed it for me." I put on my very poshest English accent, and I made it sound as though the actor and I are fast friends. In truth, it took some string-pulling and calling up of old acquaintances on the part of Great-Uncle Arthur to arrange the visit as a way of placating me for the near-disasters that struck the Emporium on his watch.

"You know him? Cumberbatch? Wow, that's so cool."

"If you're a fan, we have some books on the making of the *Sherlock* TV show."

"Great!"

I led the way to the movie and TV tie-in section and produced a hardcover copy of *The Sherlock Files: The Official Companion to the Hit Television Series.* Madison grabbed it and eagerly flipped through the pages. "Could you have him sign this for me?"

I put on my sorry-to-disappoint-you face. "I can't promise. I don't know when we'll next have the opportunity to get together." *As if.*

"Yeah, I guess. Him being so busy and all."

Obviously, I had risen considerably in Madison's estimation, even if it was only because of one movie star. Maybe I'd get her started on a lifelong love of Sherlock.

Unlikely.

"This isn't a boring town," I said as I rang up the purchase. "Not at all. It's busy in the summer, always plenty happening. Concerts, boat races, food festivals, art and craft shows, whale-watching. Life on the water or down at the beach. Something for almost anyone. It gets to be too much sometimes. A few months of downtime does us all some good. You should come back during the summer."

"If you say so. But for now, *booooring*! I'm here in a tourist town in the off-season with my grandmother's best friend for the wedding of two people I'd never even heard of before. It's cold, everything's closed, no swimming, no sailing." She pretend-shuddered.

I was finished with Madison. I'd tried to make nice, but she couldn't be bothered to hide her distain.

"What's a good place for dinner?" she asked. "Someplace with a well-stocked bar where a woman on her own isn't looked upon as a freak. And please, don't say the Blue Water Café. Everyone I ask suggests I go there, but when I tried to make a reservation, it says they're closed. Big surprise—not. Not after what happened there the other night."

"What about the Harbor Inn where you're staying?"

"*Pleeeze.* Audrey and some lady even older than her who she met at the party are having dinner there tonight. If I go in, she'll call me over, insist I join them, and I'll be stuck listening to them talk about the best arthritis medicine and the latest in hip replacement procedures. Not to mention cataract surgery." This time her shiver was real.

Mrs. Ramsbatten had lived a fascinating life, a true pioneer in the most important technological development in her lifetime. Audrey had listened in on the gossip of the rich and famous. I doubted they'd spend the night talking about their medication routines. I handed Madison the bag containing her book and was about to send her on her way when one word of my thought process lit itself up in lights.

Gossip.

Two more words: *Rich. Famous.*

Had Audrey herself not been above a touch of blackmail?

"I hope the death at Jayne's party didn't upset Audrey too much."

Madison laughed. "Anything but. She's spent almost all the time since in her room writing up a storm. She brought her iPad with her on this trip, but the next morning, she woke me up real early, like, to order me to go out and buy her an extendable keyboard. It's too hard for her, she said, to write more than a sentence or two poking on the iPad screen itself."

At the party, after the police and ambulance had been called, Audrey was writing so intently in her notebook, she barely paid any attention to the activity happening around her. "Do you know what she's working on?"

"The book she's been talking about for years. Talking is all she's ever done, according to my mom anyway. Until now. All of a sudden, right there in that restaurant, Audrey began scribbling away. It'd be okay, I guess, if she was a mystery writer and suddenly had an inspiration 'cause of what happened to that girl. But her book, a memoir about a lifetime listening to gossip? Weird."

"McGillivray's Pub's a nice place. Good food, friendly atmosphere. They often have live music on a Friday night. Even in winter." I gave her directions and wished her a good evening.

I followed Madison to the door and put up the "Back in 10 minutes" sign.

I'd be a lot longer than ten minutes, but I didn't expect many more customers tonight anyway.

"Guard the shop," I told Moriarty. He yawned in response.

* * *

I drove to the Harbor Inn. I decided not to pretend to be here for dinner and to "accidentally" run into Mrs. Ramsbatten and Audrey. Sometimes the best thing to do is simply say what one wants to say.

I spotted my quarry the moment I walked into the restaurant. The place wasn't busy, and they'd been given a table for four in front of the fireplace. Fake logs burned cheerfully. A bottle of wine rested in a cooler next to them, and they'd been served their appetizers. Caesar salad for Mrs. Ramsbatten and tiny crab cakes with spicy dip for Audrey. Seeing those crab cakes reminded me I hadn't had dinner. I hadn't even had lunch as I never did get back to Andy's curry.

"Hi," I said.

They both turned to me and smiled.

"Gemma, dear," Mrs. Ramsbatten said. "How nice to see you. You know Audrey, of course, Andy's aunt."

"Cousin, actually," Audrey said, "but a relation nonetheless."

"Would you like to—" Mrs. Ramsbatten began.

"Thanks." I sat.

Audrey blinked, but good manners won out and she said, "Would you like a glass of wine? This is an excellent California chardonnay. One of my favorites, so I was delighted to see it on the menu here."

"No, thanks," I said. "I'll get straight to the point. I hear you're writing a book about your days in Hollywood."

Her eyes narrowed and she studied my face. Mrs. Ramsbatten looked at each of us in turn, curious as to what I was getting at.

"I am," Audrey said. "It's been on my mind for a long time, and this little sojourn gave me the time and space to get my ideas down."

"How interesting it will be," Mrs. Ramsbatten said. "Do you have a publisher yet?"

"Not yet, but I have an agent. She's been after me for years to get the book finished. She's thrilled I'm working on it again. I never dared tell her I hadn't even started."

"Something happened Tuesday night to inspire you," I said. "Not just inspired enough to start thinking but to start writing. Right there in a public place while the medics tended to a drowning victim and the cops asked questions."

Audrey lifted her glass of wine. She took a sip and studied me through lashes thick with mascara. Her makeup was heavy but expertly applied. Her gray hair, liberally highlighted with lighter streaks, was tied into a chignon. The glistening red polish on her left thumb was badly chipped. She had been busy, I thought: a woman like Audrey wouldn't normally allow that to remain unattended to. "You own a bookstore. When my book comes out, would you like me to do a signing?"

"Great idea. Your book won't fall within the mandate of my shop, but I love to make exceptions for local authors, and as you're related to Andy, we'll consider you to be local. We can discuss the details closer to the time. At the moment, I'm asking what happened regarding the death of Tina Armstrong that got you so inspired."

Audrey twirled the stem of her wine glass between her fingers and turned to Mrs. Ramsbatten. "Is this young lady always this impertinent?"

As Audrey and I talked, Mrs. Ramsbatten had sipped her wine, nibbled on her salad, and listened to every word. She put on her best Bronx accent. "You ain't seen nothin' yet, doll."

"I see." Audrey took a long drink and then put her glass down. "I'd never met Tina Armstrong before Tuesday, but I knew of her. As I believe I said the other night, I am largely retired, more because the world of gossip has moved on and left me behind than because I wanted to. Never mind that now. I maintain my circle of contacts and keep my ear to the ground. Tina was a minor actress trying to get herself known, as so many of them were and still are. For her, time was quickly passing. She had to have known if she was going to make it, it had to be soon. She was talented and attractive in that all-American girl-next-door way, but no more talented and no more attractive than hundreds, thousands, of girls who wash up on the shores of Hollywood with their dreams and ambitions. What she did have, which many of them do not, was a way of getting to know people. The people who matter." She smiled. "It's unfortunate I didn't meet her sooner. Reminds me of myself in many ways. Talent and ambition help, but when it comes down to it, Hollywood and

Broadway are all about who you know. Tina got herself invited to some of the best parties, and there she met people."

"People like Julien Best. Way out of her league, professionally speaking."

"And so you get straight to the point."

"She has a way of doing that." Mrs. Ramsbatten's eyes danced.

"I have what used to be known in the newspaper business as a scoop," Audrey said. "I am not about to let my scoop slip, not in front of people I barely know, and in a public place. Let us simply say the true details of the accident involving Julien Best and Tina Armstrong are not entirely how they were presented to the public."

"Presented to the public by the police? I've read the reports."

"You are thorough. Even the police can sometimes be circumspect. And if not circumspect, influenced."

"If you knew something, shall we say, gossip-worthy, why didn't you write about it at the time?"

"I also can be influenced."

"You mean blackmailed."

The waiter popped up out of nowhere and lifted the bottle out of the cooler. Audrey nodded to him; he added a few drops to her glass and the rest to Mrs. Ramsbatten's. "Another, I think. Thank you," Audrey said.

"Madam?" he said to me.

"Nothing, thank you."

Mrs. Ramsbatten nibbled on her salad, but Audrey's crab cakes sat untouched. I refrained from asking if I could have one.

"No, not blackmailed," she said at last. "No threats were made, no money or favors requested. I was asked not to report what I knew of the incident. So I did not."

"By Julien Best, I assume."

"His wife, actually. Sandra McCaskill. A powerful person in her own right."

"I don't recognize that name."

"Few would. She doesn't act, doesn't direct. She simply moves the money around. Sandra is one of the people Tina understood she needed to get to know. If Tina hadn't been in that accident and the long stay in the hospital following, she would have become a star, if she had Sandra's help."

"And now her death changed the odds for you. You think the book will be worth enough, you don't have to concern yourself about . . . being influenced not to write it."

"Tina's story—leaving Hollywood after her injury, forgotten by people she thought her friends, only to end up selling real estate in Cape Cod, and then the shock of her premature death—provides the tragic finale to the story. I need to make it a bigger book than it would be otherwise. The book will mostly be about my many years in Hollywood and all the people I knew over those years. Some long-held secrets will be revealed, but few that will do any damage these days. Julien Best, however, is still news. His name, and Tina's story, will guarantee the success of my book. My agent is saying it has bestseller written all over it." She smiled.

"You're prepared to discard what you owe to Sandra, Julien's wife?"

Her face tightened. "I owe her nothing. Promises were made. Promises which did not come to pass. I intend to take this opportunity so conveniently presented to me."

The waiter returned and flourished a bottle. He offered Audrey a taste and she accepted. "Delicious, as expected." She nodded; he filled their glasses, then slipped away.

"Now, please allow me to enjoy my dinner with my new friend in peace."

"I doubt very much you're at all bothered by my being here," I said. "Talking about this stuff is your life blood. But as long as I am here, did you notice a waiter the other night at the party? Late-thirties, middling height, on the pudgy side, short dark hair, goatee?"

"I believe I saw such a person, but I noticed nothing in particular about him. Why do you ask?" She picked up her fork and poked at a crab cake.

"Name of Robbie Ellis. West London native. An artist."

"I don't know any more about art than the average person. Obviously, he is not a very successful one if he's waiting tables in West London."

Noticeably, Audrey referred to Robbie in the present tense. Because she didn't know he was dead or because she was covering up that she knew more than she should?

"He died last night. Murdered."

Mrs. Ramsbatten gasped. "I saw something about that in an online newspaper article. I didn't realize—"

"I heard about it on the radio," Audrey said. "Another murder in your peaceful little town. Positive Cabot Cove you have here. I can be of no help. I didn't even recognize the gentleman's name."

"Does his death have anything to do with Tina?" Mrs. Ramsbatten asked.

"That," I said, "is what I'm trying to find out." I stood up. "Have a nice evening, ladies."

I started to walk away and then abruptly turned around. They were both watching me. "By the way, Madison was in my shop earlier. We had a nice talk about the *Sherlock* TV show. She's a big fan."

"I didn't know that," Audrey said. "No reason I should."

"She seems bored here in West London in the winter. Not much for a single young woman to do. Did you invite her to accompany you to Jayne's wedding or was it her suggestion?"

"Madison is not a blood relative of mine. Her grandmother and I were very close for many years, although my dear friend scarcely recognizes me anymore. Madison's life is not progressing as she might have hoped, so I thought the break would do her good. I might have been mistaken. She is, as you noticed, not having a good time. She is not one to disguise her feelings to make an old woman feel better."

"What did she do last night? Did you have dinner together?"

"No. Leslie Wilson had a few of the people in town for the wedding over to her house for an early dinner. Madison wasn't interested in coming. I don't know what she did."

"Did you see her when you got back here?"

"No, but no reason I should. We are not sharing a room."

Chapter Twenty-One

As I drove back to the Emporium, I called Leslie to ask about last night's dinner guests. Audrey came, she told me, and Keith and his wife, as well as a few people whose names I didn't recognize. They were mostly relatives of hers or Andy's on the elderly side, so dinner had been early and everyone gone by nine. I thanked her for the information and hung up before she could ask why I wanted to know. No clues to be found there, and no suspects to eliminate.

As for Audrey herself, she'd given me a lot to think about. *Qui bono.* Audrey benefited from the death of Tina. Audrey lost no time in grabbing the opportunity she thought she needed to get a story to center her book around. A big enough story to make the book a standout from other Hollywood memoirs.

Had she realized such when she heard Tina had died? Or had she decided to be proactive and create the opportunity herself? The speed with which she started writing made me wonder if the idea had been in the back of her mind all along.

It was possible Audrey killed Tina. Audrey smoked; she might have seen Tina outside alone in the dark and joined her on the deck, the two of them sharing a moment, watching the sea roll in. She wouldn't have been able to lift Tina and toss her over the deck railing, but if she somehow lured Tina to the open gate and the top of the steps, a solid push might have accomplished what was needed.

Not a guaranteed method of killing someone. But Tina had a substantial amount to drink before and at the party, and the ocean was very cold. If Tina managed to make it to shore, her assailant could claim the shove had been an accident. Why they didn't call for help immediately was another matter, but if they acted on impulse, that detail might not have occurred to them.

Regarding Robbie, however, not the slightest trace of recognition, guilt, or even understanding of what I was getting at crossed Audrey's face when I described him or mentioned his name. They had not met, but it might be possible, if he'd seen Audrey kill Tina and decided to blackmail her over it, he sent her an anonymous letter.

Tina died Tuesday night. Robbie died Thursday. Audrey didn't have any connections in West London other than a scattering of distant relatives, certainly no one of the sort that could summon up a private investigator to trace the source of the anonymous letter so quickly. Had Robbie kindly provided his address in the letter?

I didn't think even Robbie could be quite that stupid.

Even if he had, Audrey, elderly, walking with the assistance of a cane, hadn't been the person running from me last night.

Madison?

Possibly, but for what reason? She and Audrey were clearly not at all close. Nowhere near close enough for Madison to murder someone to save Audrey from going to jail.

Had Madison for some reason killed Tina and then Robbie?

My head spun. Too many theories, not enough data.

It was almost nine. Time to close the Emporium for the night. I parked the car and let myself in through the back door. Moriarty popped out from under a shelf. I wondered if he'd been chasing mice. He looked disappointed to see it was only me and disappeared back under the shelf.

My phone rang. Jayne.

Before she'd even said a word, a sob came down the line.

"Jayne, what's happened? Are you okay? Andy?" My first thought was Andy had been arrested and formally charged. Had there been a new development? Had evidence been found to put Andy firmly in the frame for one or both murders?

"He wants to call off the wedding," Jayne sobbed.

"Calm down. Calm down." Maybe my idea that they spend a casual, romantic afternoon together hadn't been the best one. "Are you home? Have you just got in?"

"Yes. Yes. We had a . . . nice day. We went to . . . a nice place for dinner. And then he said—"

More sobs.

"I'm on my way," I said. "Hold tight."

Another journey made in record-breaking time, and I pulled up in front of Jayne's apartment building. I parked under the fifteen-minute maximum sign and ran in. I pressed the buzzer, to be instantly admitted.

Jayne lived in the same sort of midcentury, low-rise apartment block as Robbie had, but hers was larger and nicer with an attractively decorated foyer and freshly painted walls. Her tear-streaked face was waiting for me when I emerged from the stairwell. I wrapped her in a hug. "Don't worry. We'll sort this."

"Come on in," she said.

Moving boxes, both full and empty, were stacked in all the corners. Pictures had been taken down from the walls, ornaments removed from tabletops. Pieces of furniture Jayne didn't want to keep had been thrown away, sold, or donated to charity, leaving the small living room mostly empty.

"Tea?" Jayne sniffled.

"The true Englishwoman's solution to every problem. I have you well trained."

"You do." She cracked a weak smile.

We went into the near-bare kitchen, and she put on the kettle, and took milk out of the fridge, almost as bare as the high Arctic in February.

"First things first," I said. "Did something scare Andy? Did the police call him or pay him a visit again?"

"No. Not that he told me."

"Then why does he want to call off the wedding? I absolutely refuse to believe he's changed his mind about you."

Another weak smile. "It's not that. With this . . . murder case up in the air, he doesn't want to . . . have me commit to him if he might go to jail."

I snorted. "Foolish man. Does he think you're going to say, 'Cheery-O, Andy old chap. Sorry you've found yourself in a pickle. I'm off to find another man.'"

"Maybe he does, Gemma." The kettle came to the boil, and she added the hot water to the teapot in which she'd already placed a ball of tea leaves.

"I trust you told him such is not the case."

"I did. He said he doesn't want me involved if things get . . . unpleasant."

"As though you can cut off your feelings for him like a thread hanging from a hem. He's not thinking straight, Jayne. He'll soon realize how ridiculous this all sounds."

"Maybe, but my wedding is three days away! The dress is hanging in the closet, the minister and church are booked, the yacht club's been paid in full. Some of the out-of-town guests are already here!" She extended her arms, taking in the bare countertops, the empty spaces in the living room, the stack of boxes. "Not to mention that as of next week, I don't have any place to live! The movers are coming while we're on our honeymoon. Our supposed honeymoon. That trip's been paid for too! When we get back, we're moving into a house we've bought and paid for."

It would be somewhat awkward, them owning a house together, if the wedding failed to take place.

It was not going to come to that. "Tea should be ready."

"What?"

"You used Earl Grey. You don't want to let it steep for too long."

"Oh, right." She opened the cupboard doors to reveal two mugs, two bowls, and two plates. She took the mugs down and poured the tea. Fragrant steam rose into the air. She added a splash of milk to mine and handed it to me.

"Cheers," I said. "Do you want me to talk to Andy?"

"No."

"Glad to hear it. I don't want to. He needs to make this decision on his own. When did he drop this bombshell?"

"We had a fun day, Gemma. At least, I thought we were having fun. We drove up the coast to North Truro, poked around the shops, stopped for coffee. We had a walk on the beach but didn't stay long as it was too cold. We went for dinner at a place in Eastham, where Andy knows the chef. He came out of the kitchen to say hi. He mentioned he'd heard about the death at Andy's place and that he'd been closed by the police for the investigation. Andy didn't say much, and for the rest of the meal and the drive back to West London, he was quiet. He pulled up outside, told me he didn't want to stay overnight, and then he said . . ." Jayne swallowed. Fresh tears filled her eyes. "He said the wedding was off."

"Off? Or postponed?"

"Does it matter?"

"Probably not. Not right now."

"I was so shocked, I scarcely even heard the words, Gemma. He doesn't want to marry me!" She wailed and burst into another round of tears.

I put my hands on her shoulders and looked into her lovely face, now red and swollen and blotchy. "He wants to marry you very much, Jayne. He's scared. He's scared he's going to be dragged into something he doesn't want to be. You and I know Andy didn't kill Tina or Robbie. Andy knows it, but Andy also knows miscarriages of justice do happen. He's trying to protect you, if it should come to that."

She sniffled. "I don't want to be protected."

"Precisely. Officially married or not, you're in this for the long haul. Right?"

She nodded.

"My advice, for what it's worth, is to let him have the night to think it over. He said what he said on impulse. He'll regret it by morning."

"And if he doesn't?"

"Then you go and see him in person and tell him he can't get rid of you that easily. Tell him you intend to be in church on Monday, in that excessively expensive dress, with your mother and brother at your side. Tell him if he fails to show up, he'll have Ryan and me to deal with. I also bought a dress I can't afford, and Ryan took his good suit to the cleaners."

"You think?"

"I know. He's scared, Jayne, and he has the right to be. Tell him you intend to be scared along with him."

She gave me a weak smile. "Thanks, Gemma."

I hugged her. "You can also tell Andy, for what it's worth, I've been asking a few questions here and there."

"Are you getting anywhere?"

"Yes," I lied.

Chapter Twenty-Two

When I arrived in the tearoom at quarter after nine the following morning for my regular order, Fiona told me Jayne wanted me to come straight into the kitchen as soon as I could. I accepted a takeout cup of tea and a muffin and went to see what was up.

It was a Saturday and preparations for afternoon tea were well under way: scones browning nicely in the oven, miniature cupcakes on racks waiting to be iced, lovely pale-green macaron shells cooling. Jocelyn was at the stove, one eye on a pot poaching a chicken for sandwiches, the other on a second pot boiling eggs. As well as all that, the regular morning muffins, croissants, Danishes, and breakfast sandwiches filled the display counters.

I didn't have to be Sherlock Holmes to deduce something happened (aside from all that baking) since we talked last night. And that something was good.

Jayne grabbed me and whirled me around. Flour dusted the tip of her nose, a smear of chocolate was on her chin, her skin glowed from within, and her eyes sparkled.

"Let me guess," I said to Jocelyn when I'd freed myself. "The croissants came out perfectly."

"That too," she replied.

"The wedding is on again," Jayne said. "You were right, Gemma."

"As I usually am," I said modestly.

Jocelyn smothered a snort as she took a tray containing rows of gorgeous lightly browned scones out of the oven. I breathed deeply. No nicer scent in all the world than fresh baking.

"Andy called me this morning, first thing," Jayne said. First thing, for Jayne, was the middle of the night for everyone else. "He said he was sorry, and if I still wanted him, he wanted to go ahead with the wedding."

"Sensible man."

"He said he could face anything as long as I was with him. Jocelyn, those muffins should be cool now. Can you take them out front."

"Sure." Jocelyn arranged blueberry muffins on a serving tray and departed with them. The doors swung closed behind her.

Jayne let out a long breath. "One worry out of the way, but only for now. You said you were making progress on the case. The cases. What have you learned?"

I dodged the question and asked one of my own. "What's happening about Andy's alibi? The cook he spoke to Thursday night, around the time of Robbie's death?"

Some of the joy in her face slipped away. "He can't be contacted. His phone's switched off. I'm sorry to say, even that doesn't look good for Andy. As though he made up an alibi that can't be confirmed."

"Kyle Jackman isn't an imaginary figure, Jayne. He lives in West London. He has a job here. He'll show up eventually. Some people like to take themselves out of touch now and again."

"Even though he and his wife are separated, he has two little kids, so that makes the police suspicious about why he turned off his phone."

"I don't know, Jayne. As for the case, as you call it, I have a few lines of inquiry on the go."

"Anything you can tell me?"

"Not yet."

Jocelyn came back, carrying the empty tray. "A man outside wants to talk to you, if you have a moment. He says his name is George Friedman."

"I don't know anyone—" Jayne begin.

"He was at your party," I said. "He owns a couple of restaurants, and Andy worked for him when he was starting out. He's now attempting to charm our Bunny Leigh."

"I guess it'll be okay if he's fine with coming back here. I don't have time to stop work right now. We have more reservations for tea this afternoon than I was expecting."

Jocelyn left, and a moment later she returned with George. I'd been about to take my leave, but I decided to hang around and hear what he had to say. The tearoom kitchen is extremely small, and George, along with Jayne, Jocelyn, and me, filled it. He gave Jayne a big smile and looked around the little room with approval. "Small space, but you use it well."

"Thank you," Jayne said. "I don't want to be rude, but we're very busy."

He looked at me, taking up space while doing absolutely nothing. I sipped my tea and made no attempt to appear to be busy.

"I was passing," he said. "I wanted to take the opportunity to say hi. I was very fond of Andy, still am, and I'm pleased he's done so well for himself. In matters of the heart as well as in business."

Jayne smiled.

"The restaurant world in the Lower Cape is small and well connected. I heard now that the . . . recent unpleasantness . . . is over, the Blue Water Café will be opening for dinner tonight."

"That's right."

"It's a tough business, this one of ours. It's good you have your own place, Jayne. You understand."

"I have good partners." Jayne's eyes flicked toward me.

"You're a partner here?" George asked in something approaching surprise.

"Silent partner," I said.

"Like I said, tough business. Being unexpectedly closed for any length of time can result in a place going under. I'm glad such didn't happen to Andy."

"So are we," Jayne said.

"Have you given any thought as to how you're going to manage after you're married? You and Andy have opposite schedules. Your place is open mornings and afternoons. You close at four. He opens for lunch, doesn't close some days in season until well after midnight. It can be a hard balancing act for a couple."

Jayne blinked.

"They've managed so far," I said.

"And good for them. I'm not a cook myself." He laughed heartily. "My talents in that direction stop at boiling eggs and making toast. Instead, I pay good money to get top people to cook at my restaurants. My late wife was a schoolteacher, so we didn't have the scheduling problems you do. Life takes over sometimes, doesn't it, and enthusiasm dies. It's harder to keep up a punishing routine when you start getting older. As I well know." A hand to his back and a wince to illustrate his point. "And then the kids come with all their demands and more scheduling issues. Assuming you two want kids. None of my business, right, but have you thought about who's going to look after young children?"

Before I could tell him that truly was none of his business, he said, "I'm confident you'll find your own way, Jayne. I have total confidence in Andy. Always did have a good head on his shoulders, that one. I've always made it an important part of my business to do what I can to help promising young chefs get ahead. Part of that mandate, I believe, is warning them about the dangers and pitfalls of the profession."

Jayne just looked confused.

"Thanks for that," I said. "As a silent partner, I am silently telling my head baker to get on with it." I stepped forward, putting myself firmly in George's personal space. "Shall we?"

"Nice talking to you, Jayne," George said.

He and I went into the restaurant together. "Bunny told her daughter she enjoyed having dinner with you at one of your restaurants," I said.

"She's a lot of fun. Great stories to tell. Give my best to Andy next time you see him."

George left.

What, I thought, *was all that about?*

* * *

George's odd visit to Jayne in the kitchen of Mrs. Hudson's had left me with a lot of questions about him. It was time, I thought, to do a deep dive into him, see what I could come up with. Unfortunately, it was a gorgeous winter's day, with a brilliant sun, no wind, and temperatures soaring into the forties, which brought people into town. The shop was busy from the moment I flipped the sign to Open and I didn't get a chance for a break.

* * *

Later that afternoon, Ryan popped into the tearoom for a sandwich and a coffee, which he brought into the Emporium. I hadn't heard from him since Thursday night and wondered if he was still angry at me for giving chase to Robbie's killer.

We have a complicated relationship, Ryan and I. We love each other; we want to be together. It can be difficult for him when I get involved in his cases. Even when I try not to be involved, something always drags me in.

Honesty forces me to admit that "something" is most often my innate curiosity. I sometimes wonder why I risk my relationship over such things. Perhaps I'm trying to prove myself, even if only to myself. I grew up in the shadow of an older, smarter, thinner, prettier sister. She is so highly placed in the British government, no one knows exactly what she does. Am I still trying in some way to compete with Pippa after all these years? Perhaps.

Then again, maybe like Sherlock Holmes, I get involved because the path to do so opens in front of me. In this case, however, my reasoning was simple: I wanted to do everything I could to help clear Andy.

Unfortunately, I wasn't making much progress.

When Ryan came in, I left Ashleigh and Gale to help the customers and led him to the reading nook by the big front window. He handed me the cup of tea he'd picked up for me. Unasked but definitely appreciated.

"Are you making any progress on the Tina Armstrong case?" I asked.

A copy of *Holmes and Moriarty* by Gareth Rubin lay on the wingback chair. Ryan put it on the side table and dropped gratefully into the comfy chair. He took a long sip of his coffee, sighed heavily, and unwrapped his sandwich. A huge stack of roast beef with arugula and spicy mustard on a Jayne-made baguette. It looked delicious. "Progress? No, not much, I'm sorry to say." He spoke as he ate. "We can find no sign of any enemies or any reason anyone would want to get rid of her. She lived a fairly quiet life since coming back to West London. Had a few friends, none of whom can say if she was afraid of anyone or worried about anything other than passing her realtor exams. As for Robbie Ellis, I'm trying to stay out of that one because of the connection to Andy, but we can't help but think the two cases are intertwined, so keeping my distance isn't entirely possible."

I remained quiet, letting him chew and think.

"I can tell you that although Louise first focused her attention on Andy, she's not so sure anymore. Not without concrete evidence to put him at the scene, and she doesn't have that. Doesn't have evidence of anyone having been in Robbie's apartment recently, unfortunately. Except for you. We found your fingerprints on the top of the patio wall and on the cement floor."

"Not a surprise since I was obviously there."

"You must have been the only person in West London not wearing gloves that night. Some clumps of mud got left behind on the carpet, but nowhere near enough to give us a good boot print. A canvass of the neighbors brought up nothing but your name. A woman saw you ringing Robbie's bell and recognized you from this store."

"Yup."

"Do you wonder Louise sometimes suggests we just charge you for every crime that happens in West London and get it over with?"

"Nope."

He smiled at me. I smiled back.

"Are you looking forward to the wedding?" he asked.

"I am. Andy wanted to call it off."

"What? Why?"

"Because he doesn't want Jayne tied up in his troubles if he is charged with murder. He soon changed his mind."

Ryan put his sandwich down and reached out his hand. I put mine in his. "We all need support, and never more than when we're having troubles," I said softly.

We smiled at each other for a long time. Conscious of the shoppers behind us, Gale and Ashleigh's low voices as they helped them, and a disapproving Moriarty glaring at us from the windowsill, we didn't get any closer.

Finally, Ryan cleared his throat and resumed eating his lunch. "In case you had any doubts, the time of Robbie's death has been clearly established as only moments before you say you arrived."

"Before I arrived," I said by rote.

He grinned. "Before then." The grin faded. "It is possible Robbie's death had nothing to do with Tina. He has a police record: minor stuff, but it's there."

"I'm aware of that," I said.

"Can I ask how?"

"No, you cannot."

"Okay. He was clean when he lived in West London originally, far as we know anyway, but he started getting himself into trouble in New York City. Since he's been back in town, there've been a few incidents: a fight in a bar, a speeding ticket in a school zone, a bartender who said he was harassing her. He might have made some enemies, people he had disagreements with, at the very least. He was way behind on his rent, about to be evicted if he didn't pay up."

"Occam's Razor," I said. "Perhaps we're complicating this case, these cases, unnecessarily. Does the bartender have a boyfriend or husband who might have thought it a good idea to warn Robbie off?"

"She has a wife, and she and her wife were at their book club until late that evening." He folded his sandwich papers and got to his feet. I held out my hand and he put the discarded wrappings and empty cup into it. "What's the plan for Monday?" he asked.

"I'm going to Leslie's to help Jayne get ready, and we'll travel together to the church from there. The service is at three."

"I'll meet you at the church, then. I've been hoping to find the time to take Andy and his sisters and some of his friends out for a few drinks. I put it off for too long, and now with this mess, that's not going to happen." He gave me a quick kiss on the top of my head.

On his way out, Ryan passed Bunny coming in. She gave him a wave of her fingers. Two women were browsing the gaslight fiction shelves. One nudged the other and nodded toward Bunny. They put their heads together and giggled. Bunny pretended not to notice, but she lifted her chin, ever so slightly, and a smile crossed her lips.

I should say, her smile broadened. She'd already been smiling. "Good afternoon, my darling." She wrapped Ashleigh in a hug. "And how are you on this beautiful day?"

"I'm fine. I guess."

"Gemma, my other darling, as bright and perky as ever. So nice to see you."

I tossed the trash into the bin behind the sales counter as the two customers cautiously approached Bunny.

"Excuse me, but would you be Bunny Leigh?"

"I am," Bunny said.

"Oh, gosh. I heard you were living in West London. Can I have a photo with you? I owned all your records. The summer I was sixteen, I played them constantly. My dad got so sick of listening to them."

Bunny's smile slipped ever so slightly as she was reminded of how long ago she'd been the highlight of a young teen's summer. "Of course," she said.

The woman and Bunny posed while her friend snapped several pictures. They left happy, unencumbered by any purchases.

"Wasn't that nice?" Bunny said. "I've made that woman's day. Such a privilege."

"What's up?" Ashleigh asked.

"Nothing in particular. I was passing and wanted to see you. Isn't that enough?"

"I suppose it is."

I've seen pictures of Bunny in her glory days, whether in an arena or a small dark bar, lighting up the place, and the fans, with her smile. She was wearing such a smile now. "I had a marvelous time with George last night. As nice as our first date, which is sometimes not the case. He knows how to treat a lady. Being with him in the restaurants he owns almost reminds me of the good old days, the service we got when the head chef or the owner came out of the back to show us to the best table in the house." She sighed happily. "George's restaurants are doing so well, he's wanting to expand, but he's having trouble finding the perfect location. He'd love to open a place in West London, but so far, nothing on the market appeals to him."

Moriarty leapt onto the sales counter and dropped himself down beside Bunny. She stroked him as she chattered on.

Ashleigh gave me a half-wink. The chimes over the door tinkled as a group came in, and Gale called, "Let me know if you need any help."

"Did you know Andy's first cooking job was at one of George's restaurants?" Bunny asked.

"Yes, I did," I said.

"He's very proud of Andy. Tells everyone he gave Andy his start. Not that Andy needed any help, George told me. He's always had luck on his side. Why, the restaurant that used to be on the pier burned down when Andy was searching for a promising location for his own place."

My ears pricked up. "George said that, did he?"

"The earlier restaurant had been struggling, and the fire was the end of the line for them. Rumors circulated in the Cape Cod restaurant world that Andy set fire to the place himself, hoping to be able to take it over at a fire-sale price." She laughed lightly. "Look at me. I made a pun. George put a stop to those rumors. Andy was in the right place at the right time, ready to put in a good offer, that's all. George made sure everyone knew it."

It seemed to me George was no longer doing much of a job of quashing that rumor. If ever he had. He told me at the party, but I hadn't taken any notice. Now he was repeating it to Bunny. "Stuff and nonsense. That fire happened years ago. First time I heard about it was at Jayne's party and from George himself."

"Andy did buy the place, didn't he? And turn it into such a successful restaurant."

"Bunny, do not repeat that rumor, please."

"I don't gossip, Gemma."

"Mom," Ashleigh said. "You are gossiping, right here, right now."

"I'm not gossiping. I'm telling you what my new friend told me about a mutual acquaintance of ours."

"Other people call that gossiping."

Bunny sniffed. "If you insist."

"Andy doesn't need the dregs of that old story coming up again," I said. "He didn't ever need it, but particularly not now in light of the recent death at the Café and the murder of one of his waiters almost immediately after."

"Oh, yes. George told me about that. I hadn't even realized the man who died had been working at Jayne's party. Nothing but a coincidence, he assured me."

To how many other people, I wondered, *was George attempting to subtly point out the connection?*

Bunny changed the subject. "I've always thought the restaurant business would be so interesting. So much fun!"

Ashleigh's eyes widened. She threw me a frightened look.

Here it comes.

"If George does expand into West London, he'll be offering people shares in the business. I told him I might be interested, but he insisted he wouldn't want to take advantage of our friendship."

I bet he did.

"You can't afford to invest in a restaurant, Mom," Ashleigh said. "Even if you could, you know nothing about the business, and restaurants have an extremely high rate of failure."

Bunny scratched behind Moriarity's ears. Moriarty purred.

"Sometimes, sweetheart, investments involve more than money. It would be so exciting to get the band together one last time. I'm thinking I could invite special guests to the opening. I still keep in touch with dear Bruce."

"Bruce?" Gale asked.

"Springsteen. Such a help to me when I was starting out." Bunny's face fell. "Although it has been a while. I'm sure he'd come if I asked. We were," wink, "very good friends at one time. I'll drop him a line today. For old times' sake."

Gale's mouth hung open.

"Aren't you getting ahead of yourself?" Ashleigh said. "Talking about a grand opening when a minute ago you told us George hadn't even found a location yet."

"I'm thinking more of the grand reopening of the Blue Water Café. With all the ideas George has, it's sure to be a huge success."

"This is the first I've heard of any reopening, grand or otherwise," I said. "The Café's opening tonight, business as usual. What do George's ideas have to do with anything?"

"As you two keep telling me, the restaurant business is a difficult one. George's thinking is when he and Andy combine forces, they'll make the Blue Water Café into something very special. A true landmark destination. He wants to drop the café part of the name for one thing—sounds like a coffee shop, not a fine dining establishment. Now I must run, dears. I need a new dress. I can't wear the same old thing if I go out with George again." Big wink. "And you can guarantee I will, if I have anything to say about it."

She bustled off.

Moriarty jumped off the counter.

"Does she really know Springsteen?" Gale asked.

"Unlikely well enough he'll come to a restaurant just because she asks," I said.

Ashleigh groaned and dropped her forehead to the counter. She lifted it and pounded it against the surface three more times.

"Yup," I said. "Looks like you were right. He wants her for her connections, if not for what money he thinks she can dig up."

"She does know people who are well off," Ashleigh said. "Not everyone in her band squandered it all, and some of her old friends are still doing pretty good. Don't get your hopes up though, Gale. That's the first time she's mentioned Springsteen. If she goes to her friends asking them to invest, and it doesn't turn out well . . ."

But I was thinking along other lines. So good old George was repeating the unfounded rumor that Andy committed a crime to get his restaurant open. George was looking for a prime spot in West London for his own place. If the Blue Water Café had to close, if it began to struggle because the owner was in jail or occupied with defending himself against a murder charge, if business dropped off because of lingering whispers of murder, would good old George be ready to step in? To buy it at fire-sale prices?

Could he force Andy to relinquish control of his own business under the pretext of them being partners?

Most important, what might George have done to put that train in motion?

Chapter Twenty-Three

"Andy's in the clear!" Jayne burst into the Emporium shortly before closing at six, still in her apron and hairnet. Despite having turned on the ovens in the tearoom kitchen at four this morning, she was still hard at work, trying to get extra prep done and the freezer filled before she left for her honeymoon.

She threw her arms into the air. "His alibi came through." She did a little dance. Moriarty wandered over to see what the excitement was, and she swept him up. She planted kisses all over his face. Moriarty likes Jayne just fine, but he didn't seem all that pleased at being held so tightly and he squirmed in her arms. She put him down.

I flipped the sign on the door to Closed. "What happened?"

"Kyle turned his phone on at last. He and his wife are getting divorced, and I gather it's not going to be pleasant. He had a few days off work and wanted to get away. He rented a little beach cabin up by Provincetown. He turned his phone off because he didn't want to talk to his wife's lawyer, and he was afraid if they called, he'd answer and start yelling. Which wouldn't have done him any good, so better turn the thing off. When he finally switched it back on, he had exactly zero messages from the lawyer, several from Andy, and whole lot from the WLPD."

"He alibied Andy then?"

"He headed straight to the police station. Gave his statement, and Detective Estrada phoned Andy a few minutes ago to say that as far as she's concerned, the alibi is solid."

"That is good, Jayne. I don't suppose she came right out and said he was in the clear?"

The smile drooped a fraction. "No, but she isn't going to commit to anything, is she?"

"She is not. For now, that's good enough for me. Is Andy ready to open tonight?"

"Ready and raring to go, and already open. They opened at five, and the reservation book is almost full for the next couple of days. It helped that Irene spread the word so widely."

"Feel like joining me for dinner tonight?"

"Why?"

"My thoughts on this business are starting to coalesce. I'd like to talk to Andy, if he can find a minute. I'm also hungry."

She grinned at me. "Give me half an hour to finish up what I've got in the oven."

"I'll try and get us a reservation."

"Mention my name." She gave me a broad wink. "I have influence."

Jayne skipped happily away, and I called Ryan.

"Dinner with Jayne and me tonight? I thought we could go to the Café, offer our support to Andy. My treat."

"Sounds good, Gemma, but I'll have to say no. I have something on tonight, not because I don't want to be seen offering any support to Andy. Did you hear his alibi came forward?"

"He told Jayne, and Jayne told me."

"Louise is happy with it. Helps she knows Kyle from the boxing club and—"

"Louise boxes?"

"You didn't know that?"

"Obviously an oversight on my part." I summoned up a mental image of the detective: tall, slim, extremely fit, high-energy. In a serious case of gender stereotyping, without thinking about it, I assumed she ran and worked out at an ordinary gym. I'd not make that error again.

"She knows Kyle and knows him to be reliable," Ryan said, "but alibis can be faked or innocently misinterpreted. Unfortunately, until we wrap this up, Andy will still be in the corner of our eye."

"How close are you to wrapping this up?"

"Not as close as I might like, and that's all I'm saying. Main reason I can't have dinner with you, much as I'd like to, is my dad's receiving an honor tonight from his service club, and I told him some time ago I'd take Mom."

"You'd get a better dinner at the Café."

He groaned. "Don't I know it? Speaking of wrapping this up, have you come up with anything?"

"Since I last saw you a couple of hours ago? Perhaps, and too early to say for sure. I'll fill you in tomorrow. Have fun tonight. Give your dad my congratulations." I hung up before he could ask what was too early for me to say.

Instead of trying to make a reservation online and risk being told nothing was available, I called the Blue Water Café. When I told the young woman who answered I wanted a table for Jayne and me, she said they'd squeeze me in. If we came soon.

Chapter Twenty-Four

The place was hopping. The queue spilled out the door, and the hostess was telling those who arrived without reservations how long they'd have to wait until a table came free. We edged ourselves past the envious would-be diners. The hostess recognized us and we were immediately shown to our table. For the briefest of moments, I wondered what it must be like to be a celebrity. To always be whisked past the waiting hoi polloi, escorted to the best seats, served the best the venue had to offer, wined and dined. No wonder Bunny missed it sometimes.

Not one of the best seats in the house by far, we were given a small table for two in the back of the main room close to the corridor leading to the washrooms, office, and kitchen.

"Can I tell Andy you're here?" the hostess asked as she arranged menus in front of us.

"Go ahead," Jayne said. "Thanks."

The hostess slipped away.

"I'm thrilled so many people came tonight," Jayne said. "It'll mean the world to Andy to see how much support he has in the community."

"Hey, Jayne, Gemma." A smiling waitress flipped our water glasses over and filled them. She'd worked for Andy as long as I've been coming here. "Nice to see you. Can I get you something to drink?"

After we ordered, I said, "It must have been a big relief to you when Andy opened again so quickly."

"Gosh, yes. I don't know what I'd have done if I lost my job here. It's a long time until the season starts up again."

"Did you know Robbie Ellis? The part-time waiter who died the other night?"

"No. Our paths never crossed. He only did a few shifts, and I was off a good part of December with my back."

"Sorry to hear that."

"Time off did me good and I'm on the mend. I'll get those drinks."

She left. Jayne and I picked up our menus. "The seafood curry is excellent," I said.

"How do you know that? First time I've seen it."

"I was lucky enough to have been given a sneak peek—or, I suppose I should say, sneak taste—when the chef himself was developing the recipe."

"Are you going to have it? You always have the stuffed sole."

"I believe I will. Live life on the edge, try new and unexpected things. Experiment with exciting flavors and textures. Shake things up."

Jayne snorted. "It might be good, but I'm not in the mood for spicy. I'll have the fettuccine."

"I gave Ashleigh a raise today," I said. "And I threw in an extra couple of days' annual vacation."

"Glad to hear it," Jayne said. "If I may be so bold, she does a lot for you, and you can't be the easiest boss to work for."

I contemplated that for a moment. "I think I'm easy."

"When you're there, yes. But you do have a tendency to not be entirely focused on business matters at all times."

I couldn't argue with that, so I didn't.

The waitress returned with our bottle of wine and two glasses. She set the cooler next to the table, opened the bottle, and poured a small serving for me. I tasted it, said it was excellent,

Before she could fill our glasses, the bottle was whisked out of her hands. She gave Andy a grin and left us.

"Madams." He tucked one arm behind his back, swooped low, and poured the wine. He was dressed in his chef's uniform of gray checked trousers and white jacket, with "Andy" printed across the breast pocket in script. His face was red with the residue of heat from the ovens, and his hair rumpled.

Jayne and I laughed. He leaned over and gave Jayne a peck on the cheek. Her smile in return was radiant.

As was his. I almost got up and left to give them a private moment.

Instead, Andy said, "Nice to see you two. Sorry I can't join you, but we have a full house tonight; one of the assistant cooks found another job when I was closed, not giving me enough time to find a replacement; and I'm trying to work around some major supply problems. No arugula in the salad tonight."

"Thanks for the warning," Jayne said. "You get back to it, then. Arugula or not, we're looking forward to our meal. Gemma's going to live life to the fullest and have the curry."

Andy grinned at me. "Only," I said, "because I already know it's good. Do you mind if I have a quiet word, Andy? Won't take long and I can come into the kitchen if you have to get back."

He glanced at Jayne who shrugged. "Okay," he said. "But not too long, please. It's a madhouse in there tonight and only going to get worse."

Madhouse, to a noncook, was right. Pots bubbled, flames flared, knives flashed, cooks yelled, waiters yelled back.

"What's up?" Andy asked as he picked up a deadly sharp knife. It reminded me of the one that killed Robbie, although this one was longer, thinner, and considerably sharper. Robbie had been stabbed with a chef's knife, the detectives said, but not expensive and not unusual. Not from a restaurant like this one, then.

"I'll take care of this," Andy said to Martin, his sous-chef. "See to that chowder."

"Yes, Chef." Martin gave me a look but said nothing as he went to the stove.

Andy's knife slashed and onions fell apart. "So, Gemma, what's up?"

"George Friedman. Did you know he's interested in opening a restaurant in West London?"

"George is always talking about opening a new place. Nothing comes of it. Years ago, he started three restaurants with money he inherited from an uncle, I think. Since then, nothing new, and only two remain."

"How are his places doing? Bunny went out with him the other night, and she said they were swanky."

"That's one word for it," Martin laughed.

"Dated is another word," Andy said. "Red banquettes, steak with bearnaise sauce, surf and turf. He does okay, but not much more than okay. Why do you ask?"

"He wants Bunny to invest."

"I didn't know Bunny had that kind of money."

"She doesn't. Which is why I'm asking around."

"I'm not going to comment on the guy's business plans, Gemma. I don't know enough." Andy shoved the chopped onions aside and reached for a bowl of fat red tomatoes.

"Fair enough." I was standing close to the stove. The contents of the soup pot simmered on one hob, onions were caramelizing on another, and my curry bubbled happily on another. Further down the line, flames leapt up from the grill as a thick steak was thrown onto it. I was getting very warm.

"Where's that bruschetta?" a waiter asked.

"On it." Andy chopped furiously. "Someone get me those herbs. Martin, that steak's on the verge of being overdone."

"It is not," Martin replied. "I know what I'm doing."

"Not so as I'd notice." Andy grabbed a handful of herbs. Behind his back, Martin threw him a furious glare before turning his attention to the steak. Andy mumbled something under his breath that might have been "He's gotta go." I assumed he was referring to Martin.

"I have one quick question before I get out of your way," I said. "Have you had any thoughts of taking George on as a partner in this place?"

Andy stopped chopping and looked up. "Why on earth would I do that? I told you I'm struggling, Gemma, but no more than's normal in this business. I hope you're not implying otherwise."

"I am not," I said. "Bunny said something about it."

He went back to his tomatoes and herbs. "And we know how reliable Bunny is about these things."

"This Bunny," Martin said to me. "Would that be Bunny Leigh, the pop star? My mom talks about her all the time. Is she a friend of yours? Looking for a good investment opportunity?"

"Always looking," I said as I made my retreat, almost colliding with a waiter picking up huge bowls of clam chowder.

I found Jayne tapping on her phone and sipping her wine. She looked up with a smile. "Mom, asking about the place cards. You did get them done, didn't you, Gemma?"

"Uh . . . yes. Let me confirm that."

I texted Ashleigh: *What's happening with J's place cards?*

Ashleigh responded right away: *On your desk. Told you that!*

"All done," I said to Jayne. "I'll give them to you tomorrow."

"Not me. Call Mom to come and pick them up. You didn't do them yourself, did you?"

"I outsourced the project like the efficient manager I am."

"Long as they get done on time and within budget. You did remember my budget, didn't you, Gemma?"

"I'll cover the extra costs of the outsourcing," I said.

Jayne shook her head. She sipped her wine. "So, what did you want to talk to Andy about not in my hearing?"

"I wouldn't say not in your hearing, but more I didn't want to interrupt his work. That kitchen environment is not conducive to a good conversation."

"All these years watching me work and you've only just realized that?"

"You don't have as much hot stuff on the go all at the same time. No open fires. And the way they wield those knives! I'm surprised chefs still have all their fingers."

"Years of training and practice, Gemma. So talk to me. What's bothering you? Robbie's death? I can't help but think about it all the time. I know you didn't like him, Gemma, and I'll admit that toward the end of our relationship, I didn't like him all that much either. But we did have some good times together; things just didn't work out for him the way he hoped, and it made him bitter. I've heard nothing more about Tina either, by which I assume the police haven't arrested anyone."

"No, they haven't. Not for either case."

"Do you think they're related?"

"I do. One way or another."

"Meaning?"

"I'm still not entirely convinced Tina's death was a murder. Robbie's obviously was. Has Andy ever said anything to you about possibly going into partnership with George Friedman?"

"Heavens, no. Andy's not looking for a partner. In other things in life, Andy's pretty laid back, easygoing. When it comes to this place, he's a control freak. He'd never take on a partner. Not willingly, anyway." She peered at me over the rim of her glass. "Unwillingly, is that what you're getting at, Gemma?"

"I don't know."

"Curry and the fettuccine." The waitress, a long pepper mill tucked under her arm, put the plates in front of us. My dish smelled absolutely fantastic. She pulled the pepper mill out and flourished it. Jayne said, "Please," but I refused; when I'd tried Andy's sample the other day, the curry had been perfectly seasoned. Tonight, it came served in a low, wide white bowl over rice. Green herbs were liberally sprinkled across the top, with thin slices of banana arranged on the side.

"What's the banana for?" Jayne asked.

"In England, curry often comes with plenty of accompaniments. Banana's one of the most common. Cuts the heat beautifully." We dug into our meals and didn't speak for several minutes.

"My working theory," I said through pleasantly burning lips, "is that Robbie knew who killed Tina, or thought he did, and attempted to blackmail that person. Said person then killed Robbie."

"You just said you don't think anyone killed Tina."

"I have to explore all options until I am fully confident of the facts."

"Fair enough. But blackmail? Would Robbie do something like that?"

I put down my fork and looked into her face. "I'm sorry to say it, but yes, Jayne, he would. On at least one occasion, when he was living in New York, he attempted to blackmail someone. I only know about it because she went to the police, so it's on record. Did he do the same with more success on other occasions? I can't say."

Jayne dipped her head. "Poor Robbie. Poor woman. Poor Tina. If that's the case, the origins of the crime are with Tina's death. Robbie's was just incidental. If you want to call it that."

I'd had about half of my curry and it was excellent, but I pushed my plate aside. "Finish up, Jayne. Chop chop. Good thing I didn't even have so much as a full glass of wine. I can drive."

"What? Now? Drive where?"

"I have questions, and it's time to get answers."

Chapter Twenty-Five

Jayne flagged down the waitress and asked her to pack up the rest of her fettuccine to go. The waitress nodded at my unfinished curry and Jayne said, "Might as well pack up that one too. And the bill, please."

"No charge. It's on Andy."

"I'll get the car," I said. "It's still at the shop. Meet me out front in a few minutes."

By the time I sprinted up the street and into the alley behind the Emporium, jumped into the car, joined the suddenly slow-moving traffic crawling east on Baker Street, and pulled up in front of the Blue Water Café, Jayne was waiting for me. She was wrapped in her coat and scarf and holding two takeaway containers in her mittened hands.

She got into the Miata, placed the food at her feet, and did up her seat belt. I drove away. Behind me, brakes squealed and the driver of an approaching car leaned on his horn. I ignored it. Not my fault if they weren't watching for incoming traffic.

"The dogs are going to be beyond excited next time they get into the car," I said as I attempted to stick, within reason, to the speed limit on Harbor Road. "Those scents will drive them nuts."

"My head is spinning. Gemma. Where are we going, and why are we in such a rush to get there?"

"Your wedding is the day after tomorrow, right?"

"I hope you're not needing to be reminded."

"I am not. Simply refreshing my memory. If I'm to arrive at a conclusion of this case, I have to do it now. I don't want any trace of it hanging over you and Andy."

"Why is it up to you, Gemma, to conclude this case or any other? I know you say you're curious and that's fine and well, but can't you let the police handle it?"

"A good point. Once I have answers to my questions, I'll hand everything over to the police and walk away. Here we are." I pulled into the lane leading to the Harbor Inn.

"Why are we here?" Jayne asked.

"Andy's cousin Audrey has been dancing around the reasons for her interest in Tina's death. Something happened the other night that caused Audrey to suddenly start—or resume—writing a book. Not to just get an idea for a book, but to pick up pen and paper even as the police were dusting for fingerprints and interviewing witnesses. Madison says she's so fully into it, she sent Madison to purchase the additional computer equipment she needs. I've allowed Audrey to brush me off more than once, believing anything to do with a Hollywood gossip book is of no relevance to events in West London. You reminded me tonight that everything to do with Tina's death is possibly relevant."

"I did? Glad to hear it."

"'The little things are infinitely the most important' or so said Sherlock Holmes. I wouldn't say always, but such can be the case."

"How do you know Audrey's in?"

"I don't. Only one way to find out." I opened my door and swung my legs out. "Come along, Jayne, don't dawdle."

This time, luck was not on my side. But it didn't much matter in the grand scheme of things because we found Madison sitting alone in the circle of chairs in front of the fireplace in the bar, a dirty martini and a book in front of her. *The Sherlock Files.* I was pleased to see she was reading the book she'd bought earlier in my own shop.

I led the way across the room and stopped in front of her. "Hi," I said cheerfully.

She started and looked up. "You again."

Not a terribly welcoming greeting, but I took it as an invitation and sat down. "Me again. And Jayne."

"Hi." Jayne perched uncomfortably on the edge of a chair. It was warm in the full blaze of the fireplace. Jayne unbuttoned her coat, unwrapped her scarf, and stuffed her mittens into her pockets.

"Will Audrey be joining you?" I asked Madison.

Madison glanced between me and Jayne, then she sighed and put down her book. She picked up her martini. Judging by the scent of tobacco clinging to her, she'd recently been on a cigarette break. "Audrey's gone to dinner with a bunch of the relatives. I was invited but—" She looked at Jayne. "Sorry, your fiancé's family's nice enough and all, but I've had enough of hanging around with the plus-sixty set."

"Understandable. Are you enjoying that book?"

"I am. The one nice thing about this incredibly boring vacation is I'm getting lots of reading done. I used to read more but . . . you know, things happen. Always something else that needs doing."

"I know," Jayne said. "I've bought so many books to take on my honeymoon, I don't know if I'll be able to fit them all into my suitcase. But I intend to give it a good try."

"Good idea," I said. "Not as though you have anything better to do on honeymoon at a gorgeous Caribbean resort."

Only when Jayne and Madison burst out laughing, did I realize what I'd said. I felt my cheeks burning, and I knew I was blushing. Goodness, that would never do.

Time to get the conversation back on track. "What do you know about this book Audrey's supposedly writing?"

"Nothing 'supposedly' about it. She is writing it. She's been at it for hours every day. She barely stops for meals and has lunch delivered by room service." Madison leaned over and touched her book. "Like I said, most boring vacation ever."

"Does she talk to you about it? Her writing, I mean."

"Yes. She used to talk over her columns with my grandma back in the day. Grandma helped her write some of her pieces, and Audrey freely admits it. My grandma's not entirely with it these days; she comes and goes. Audrey called her last week, and Grandma didn't know what she was talking about. She kept telling Audrey she didn't like the cabin they've given her on this cruise."

"Sad," Jayne said.

"So Audrey turned to me. She likes to talk things over as she's typing. More to herself than to a listener, but I provide the occasional feedback about words or phrasing. Why do you ask?"

"I'm interested in Tina Armstrong. What about Tina's death got Audrey writing so enthusiastically?"

"She told you that. The tragedy of a young woman's death makes the book marketable."

"There must be more to the story. Tina might have had promise in Hollywood, but the promise never came to anything. Her death wouldn't make the book a success. Barely even worth writing about. Audrey implied that the official account of Tina's accident wasn't the real one. Do you know the real story?"

Madison picked up her martini glass and leaned back against the couch, a soft smile playing across her face.

I saw the waiter approaching and waved him away. I crossed my ankles, laid my hands in my lap, and waited. Jayne shifted in her chair but said nothing.

"Yeah," Madison said at last. "She has a bombshell alright. And the sudden death of the failed actress who supposedly almost killed Julien Best has opened the door to it."

"I have no interest whatsoever in the lives of movie stars and failed wannabes. If Audrey's bombshell directly or indirectly led to Tina's death, I need to know about it."

"Why?"

"I can't see how it could have anything to do with what happened the night of the party. Not directly. None of the other people involved were at the restaurant. Just Tina. Alone and forgotten. But the minute Audrey heard Tina was dead, she decided the time was right to tell the story . . . if she was ever going to. You tell me Audrey's been dithering about this book for years. She can't just rehash all the old gossip from the old days; she needs something big, something shocking. Something that will get her on the TV shows and her book reviewed in the major papers."

"Let Audrey give it a try," Madison said. "She's totally committed to the project now. She thinks the consequences will be worth it if this book is as big as she hopes."

"Because Tina Armstrong didn't cause the accident Julien Best was in, did she? He was the one driving."

Madison's eyes flickered. "How do you know that?"

"You said *supposedly* Tina almost killed him, meaning she did not, but that's the story that was put out at the time. Likely to preserve his reputation. That's the only thing making it newsworthy a couple of years after the fact. Not only was he the one driving, but they'd been at a party. He was drunk, wasn't he?"

"Absolutely and totally plastered. It's no secret he's a heavy drinker, but as long as he shows up on set when he's required to and does his best to try to act, no one much cares."

"Unless he almost kills someone," Jayne said.

"Unless that. It's a shame really. He's a handsome man, but I can't see him aging attractively like Pitt or Clooney. Drink has a way of ravaging the looks, doesn't it? One of the cooks at Andy's restaurant looks a bit like Julien. I noticed that, even before Tina died. Do you believe in premonitions?"

"No. Julien paid off any witnesses, maybe even the police officer who was first on the scene," I said. "Did he pay off Audrey?"

"Not Julien, but his wife, Sandra McCaskill. She took care of the finer details. Julien is not only a drunk, he's stupid. He would never have had the sense to do what needed to be done. What Sandra thought needed to be done. She didn't pay off Audrey, not in money, but she made subtle enough threats. Audrey got the story from a valet at the restaurant. Julien Best was drunk when he left that night. Tina was supposed to drive him home, but as the valet went to hand her the keys, Julien snatched them, jumped in the car, and threw it into gear. Tina leapt in after him. He took out several plant pots and a section of the bushes on his way out of the parking lot. The valet was one of Audrey's best sources, and he called her right there and then. She knew about it before anyone got word of the crash. Audrey doesn't know if Tina even knew she wasn't the one driving. Short-term memories are often lost in that sort of trauma, and she was in the hospital for months."

"How would Sandra get away with pinning the accident on someone else?" Jayne asked.

"Hollywood, honey. Julien Best is famous. His wife is mega-rich. It was a single car accident—he drove into a tree and they flipped. Neither of them had their seat belts on. We don't know for sure why not, but the valet said Tina was arguing with Julien as they drove away, so she might not have remembered to put it on. As for Julien, he was too drunk to care. He was only slightly banged up in the crash, and he had the sense to call Sandra immediately. Audrey knows that for sure because a housekeeper at their house was an informant of Audrey's at the time."

"Really?" Jayne said.

"Some of the rich and famous don't know the importance of keeping their staff happy. High turnover, high dissatisfaction, no guilt about earning a few extra bucks dropping bits of gossip. The housekeeper couldn't say exactly what was said between Sandra and Julien, but Sandra flew into a rage. She screamed at Julien, telling him to stay put and say nothing to anyone. She then called her driver. The housekeeper heard no more, but the driver's the only member of the staff who's been with Sandra for years, even before she married Julien, and he's known to be a fixer."

"I'd love to have a fixer," Jayne said. "Whatever that is."

"So Audrey had the story. But when she tried to follow up, the valet suddenly wasn't sure Julien was driving; maybe it was Tina after all. The housekeeper quit abruptly and left town without a trace. Audrey was told she'd be sued for everything she had if she kept digging."

"I don't see how Tina's death would change what happened," Jayne asked. "Unless you think Julien Best came after her and killed her."

"If Julien Best came to West London, everyone would know about it," I said. "If he or his wife hired someone to kill Tina, how would that person have secured admittance to a private party?"

"You don't think . . . Robbie?" Jayne said.

"No, I do not. Would you trust Robbie with a contract killing? I wouldn't have hired him to take out my trash." I thought of Keith, with his mob connections. Keith might have known where to find a hit man, but why would he care? "Julien had no reason to get rid of Tina, and certainly not more than a year later. She was seriously injured. Even if she did eventually remember the events leading up to the crash and told someone, it would be easy enough to say she's confused and remembering wrong after all this time."

"Julien Best is still a big star," Madison said. "But his wife is in serious financial trouble, and that's no secret. She invested in a couple of big-budget movies that either flopped or went straight to the streaming services. Rumor has it the couple are on the verge of splitting. He's been seen a great deal in the company of his most recent costar. Audrey thinks Sandra will have more on her mind these days than trying to protect Julien from scandal and possible charges. If he's about to leave her for another woman, she might not even want to protect him. To be on the safe side, Audrey will finger the driver but not say Sandra instructed him as to what to do. That includes, not unincidentally, bribing a police officer to fabricate evidence and lie on his report. The cop, the one who was first on the accident scene, took early retirement about six months after. Bought himself a nice ranch in Montana."

"As retired L.A. cops can afford to do," I said.

"I told you Audrey has contacts." Madison grinned. "If this book is the hit she hopes, she's talking about her and me working together. She still has plenty of friends and some of her old network, while I have the social media savvy to get her heard again."

"Tina's death worked out well for both of you, then," I said.

Madison's smile was wicked. "I see where your mind is going, but don't look at me. I didn't know any of this until Audrey started writing about it. And that was after Tina's death. As for Audrey, she was popping out to the deck for a smoke all night long, but you can't possibly imagine her lifting up a far younger woman and tossing her over the railing, can you?"

"The gate was unlocked. Steps lead down to the dock below and the water below that."

Madison shook her head. "Not Audrey's style. I'm not saying the idea wouldn't have crossed her mind, but she would have tried to talk to Tina first. Find out if she remembered anything Audrey could use. If not," the grin widened, "then she'd consider bumping her off."

I stood up. Jayne scrambled to follow. "You've been surprisingly candid."

Madison toasted me with her empty martini glass. "When I get my name established as *the* online source for celebrity gossip, I could use someone like you. You know what questions to ask and you're able to find things out. The other night, the cops never even asked if Audrey and I had a previous connection to Tina."

"Thanks for the offer," I said. "But I'm not looking for a job."

As Jayne and I left the bar, she said, "Do you believe her?"

"About killing Tina? I believe Madison didn't do it, yes. Tina meant nothing to her until Audrey told her the story and what she could do with it. As for Audrey? Hard to see. It's possible she'd somehow been able to get Tina to stand at the top of the stairs and pushed her down, but that method of killing was hardly guaranteed to succeed. And that's what's been bothering me about this all along. A big risk. Not to mention killing Robbie. If the two cases are connected—and I refuse to believe they are not—I'm absolutely positive I did not chase Audrey Whitehall from Robbie's apartment."

"You could have chased Madison, though?"

"The possibility exists, yes. But my take on Audrey and Madison is they are not close enough to plan and execute a killing together. For Madison, this idea she has of becoming a gossip queen is still nothing but a daydream, a lark."

"What's next, then?"

"I have one thin line of inquiry remaining. If that leads nowhere, I'll let it go."

"Are you going to tell me what that thin line of inquiry is?"

"You know my methods, Jayne. I need to mull over my approach before confiding in anyone."

"Or as your sister once told me, you won't say in case you're wrong."

"That too."

Chapter Twenty-Six

As I drove Jayne home from the Harbor Inn, I asked her if she was planning to come to work the following morning.

She gave me a funny look and said, “Why wouldn’t I?”

“Maybe because it’s the day before your wedding? Do they call that Wedding Eve?”

“No, but it’s all the more reason for me to go in. We’re closed on Monday, as is the Emporium, and then I’m off on my honeymoon where I hope I’m not so totally bored I spend all my time reading. Never mind that now. I still have stuff to get done. I mean Mikey is good and all that, and I totally trust her to take care of my business while I’m away, but my scones are my scones. And my macarons are my macarons. I have to get enough of those things in the freezer to last a week. And then there’s—”

“I get the point, Jayne.”

“I told Mikey she’s not to contact me unless the place literally burns down.” Mikey was Jayne’s retired baker friend, who’d temporarily taken over other times Jayne had been away for more than a day or two.

“I’ll be on hand to handle any emergencies.”

"Yeah. That's what I'm afraid of."

* * *

Several lines of inquiry had opened for me today. When I got home, I made myself a pot of tea and settled in the den with my computer. Madison first. She called herself an influencer, so she was easy to find. Among other prominent social media sites, she had an Instagram page with a substantial number of followers, if not the hundred thousand she claimed at Jayne's party. Her most recent posts concerned her visit to West London in the company of her "beloved adoptive grandmother," and all were surprisingly positive. Nothing about what a "backwater" our town was. Instead, selfies of her shopping on Baker Street—even one of her posing outside my shop with the sign over the door prominently displayed; having drinks in the bar of the Harbor Inn; dinner at McGillivray's. In every picture, she wore something different, and she mentioned where she'd bought her clothes, shoes, and jewelry. A couple of references to Jayne's party (spelling Jayne's name as Jane) and the Blue Water Café, with pictures of Madison posing with the birthday girl or Andy. All of these had been taken inside. One photo showed the harbor as seen from the Café at night, looking across the dark water to the public pier and the fish market beyond. *Seals!* the text squealed. I enlarged the image and peered closer, but couldn't see anything, seals or otherwise, in the water. I continued flicking, but soon got bored. Nothing was said about Tina or her death. Probably not a good look when you're pushing clothes and jewelry.

I left Madison's public pages and dug deeper but came up with nothing of importance. She'd gone to law school but never graduated. Her mother was a lawyer, her father a bank executive. Madison had worked in some exclusive women's clothing shops but didn't appear to be gainfully employed at the moment.

I left Madison and turned my focus to Martin, Andy's sous-chef. Martin wasn't happy working for Andy, and Andy wasn't happy with Martin as an employee. I couldn't see how that could have anything to do with the death of Tina, but forewarned is forearmed, so I decided to see what I could find. I didn't have a last name for him, but food service people in West London are connected and Martin is not a common name among his age group.

Martin Eagerton was originally from the Cape Cod town of Sandwich. He'd gone to culinary school in New York City, then came back to the Cape where he moved from job to job before ending up at the Blue Water Café. He'd had a series of girlfriends over the years, but no one I recognized. I flicked idly through pictures on his social media pages. All dreadfully boring. I landed on a photograph of him with a large family group, likely at a wedding, and spent some time studying the faces. No one I recognized. Seated in pride of place at the front of the formal photo was an extravagantly bejeweled lady dressed much like Violet, Dowager Countess of Grantham. All silk and lace with ropes of pearls around her neck, bracelets up her arms, chunky rings with ostentatious gems on her fingers, most of which looked old enough to be family heirlooms. I didn't examine the jewelry too closely. The lady's jewelry collection didn't have any relevance to what Martin was up to these days.

I turned my attention to the next person of interest, and I learned some of what I wanted to know. But not enough. I needed to speak to him in person. I sent an email to the only contact info I could find. In the morning, if I didn't get a response, I'd try to track down the phone number. I closed my laptop and went to bed.

* * *

My phone rang as I was getting in from my early morning walk with the dogs. We'd gone to the beach. Cold, stark, empty, dark water rimmed with ice, sand firm and crispy beneath my feet. The dogs loved it, as did I.

While Violet and Peony ran for their water bowls and sniffed the floor around their empty food dishes, I answered the phone. "George, thanks for getting in touch. I wasn't sure if I could reach you through your restaurant."

"I might not cook and I might not show folks to their tables, but I'm totally involved in everything going on at my places. My staff know that, and they never hesitate to contact me. Day or night. What's up? Something to do with Bunny?"

"Bunny? Not directly, but I overheard her telling Ashleigh about your chain of restaurants, and she's very impressed." Two restaurants isn't exactly a chain, but I never mind feeding someone's ego if it suits my purposes.

"Nice of her to say so."

"I don't know if you're aware of this, but my Uncle Arthur is part-owner of Mrs. Hudson's Tea Room. Arthur has always been interested in the restaurant business. Big risk, big reward, he says. Particularly if you get in at the beginning before shovels are in the ground, so to speak. He wanted to invest with Andy, but Andy turned him down. I don't quite know why, but never mind. Anyway, at the moment one of Arthur's major restaurants in Mayfair, in London, is closing. It's been a huge success with a top-ranked celebrity chef at the helm, but the guy's having some health issues and he needs to get out. Meaning, Arthur will be in the position to start looking for another business to support from the ground up. Bunny told us you're looking for an opening in West London, and I've been thinking—"

I let my voice trail off. Every single word following Arthur being part-owner of Mrs. Hudson's was a total and complete lie.

George couldn't fall over himself fast enough to grab at the bait. "That might be something worth discussing, Gemma. Would Arthur be available to meet with me soon?"

"He's in London at the moment, taking care of other business affairs. He's my great-uncle, you understand, my father's uncle, so he's elderly and doesn't travel much these days." The biggest lie of them all. "However, I am authorized to act in his interests."

More than once, George had implied he'd like to get involved in Andy's restaurant, either as a co-owner or the actual owner. He was spreading rumors about Andy acting illegally when he originally started the Blue Water Café. He emphasized to Jayne how difficult family life would be for them because of their competing job schedules. He hinted to Bunny he'd like her help with a grand reopening of the Café. She was already planning on inviting Bruce Springsteen.

In my reading last night, I discovered that George's restaurants were barely clinging to life, financially speaking. They were clearly coming down in the world. Still struggling to be high-end steak and seafood places, but online reviews were increasingly critical. Several said they used to be a favorite restaurant for a "splurge" or an "indulgence," but the quality of the food and the service had slipped to the point it didn't justify the price, and the reviewers would not be going back.

George was running out of time if he hoped to save his business. He might already be out of time. Once a restaurant fell out of favor, it was mighty hard to get back in the game. Did he think taking control of the Blue Water Café would improve his prospects? Possibly. Much of the success of the Café was due to Andy's cooking. He was developing a good reputation throughout Cape Cod, and even beyond. But even more critical, perhaps, was the location. Deck over the water, by the harbor, fishing boats in port, the fish market a stone's throw away. Sailors hitching boats to the dock below and climbing up to the restaurant deck for a quick drink between ports.

Had George Friedman killed Tina Armstrong for no other reason than to cause trouble for Andy? The restaurant had to close for a few days for the police investigation. Had George hoped it would be longer? Had he hoped Andy, desperate to save his business, would invite George to be a partner?

I spent some time trolling through George's life. As far as I could tell, he'd never lived in New York City or Los Angeles or had any business interests in either city. He didn't have any contacts with anything or anyone to do with show business. His life didn't appear to overlap with Tina Armstrong's in any way. She lived in West London, while George lived in Hyannis. I thought back to the night I met Tina. She'd sat at our table but had shown no sign of recognizing George. Nor him of her.

To kill a total stranger in the vague hope their death would work out to benefit your business interests seemed a heck of a stretch, even to me. Nothing I could find tied George to Robbie either.

I was about to give up the search, dismiss George, and go to bed, when something I read leapt out at me.

I estimated George to be in his mid-fifties. He was of average height, slim, his face thin, the bones prominent. He walked easily and comfortably, no signs of stiff joints or back pain. I'd only ever seen him dressed in a suit jacket or a winter coat, so I had not been able to develop any concept of what sort of shape his muscle structure might be in.

George Friedman was a marathon runner. He'd run in the Boston Marathon as recently as last year, placing high in his age category. The picture I was looking at showed him at the finish line, punching the air in triumph, beaming from ear to ear. His racing gear revealed a fit, trim frame with powerful thighs and strong calves.

Despite his age, George Friedman could easily have vaulted over the patio wall and run from me the night Robbie died.

That he could have didn't mean he did. Because I could find no connection between him and Robbie didn't mean there wasn't one. George owned restaurants. Robbie was looking for work as a waiter. He might have had a gig at one of George's places, but despite what George said, I doubted very much he concerned himself with the casual staff.

It would be worth having a chat with George, I'd thought as I closed the lid on my laptop. And then, if nothing caught my attention, I'd hang up my deerstalker hat and allow myself to enjoy Jayne's wedding day.

"How about I pencil you in for next week," George said now. "We can talk things over."

"Next week?" I let the disappointed silence drag out. "I'm not too sure. Uncle Arthur's eyeing a place in Mayfair, not far from the one I've been talking about. Location matters, doesn't it? Once my uncle makes up his mind, he acts on it."

George hastened to make a new suggestion, one more to my liking. "Andy's getting married tomorrow to that delightful young lady. I'm honored to be attending, but we'll be too preoccupied to talk business. How about today? I have a spot free on my calendar for this afternoon."

"I can swing that."

"Great. That's why I like dealing with folks like you and your uncle, people who are already in the business. None of this 'but it's Sunday' nonsense. I have a couple of meetings around noon, so how about this afternoon. Say three? If you meet me at the bar at my restaurant in Hyannis, I can show you how we do things."

"That will work. Thanks."

"I'm looking forward to doing business with you, Gemma. Bunny says you're an astute businesswoman."

Not that Bunny Leigh has the slightest idea what an astute, or otherwise, businesswoman does. Nevertheless, I said, "That's good to hear."

* * *

"I need to go out about two," I said to Ashleigh. "Might not be back in time for my regular meeting with Jayne."

"I can't believe Jayne's come to work today. You'd think she'd have other things on her mind."

"Jayne's an astute businesswoman. She plans her time well."

"Unlike some, who randomly go out on Sunday afternoons with no plans to return."

I couldn't argue with that, so I didn't. "If I'm not back by closing, will you see to it, please? What are you planning to wear to the wedding?"

She gave me a broad wink. "That would be telling. Suffice it to say, I won't be in white. I thought it would be fun to go to my friend's wedding in a formal wedding dress I bought for a few bucks at a charity shop. Really get myself into the mood, you know."

"I gather that didn't work out too well."

"Nah. I didn't even get inside the church. Her mother ordered me to go home and change. I thought the iron chain I wore around my neck and the Doc Martens boots under the dress would show I was only having fun, but she didn't see it that way."

My curiosity was piqued, but I said no more. The Emporium and Mrs. Hudson's would be closed all day tomorrow so our staff could attend the wedding and the reception. The tearoom would only open for lunch the following day to give Mikey time to get back into the swing.

Customers browsed our shelves, and next door, people came and went, many carrying takeout cups and bags containing sandwiches or pastries. Jayne was not serving afternoon tea today, as that required more work than she wanted to do on her last day before the wedding and honeymoon.

"Has Bunny said anything more about George?" I asked.

"No. She had me around to her place last night for dinner, and all she could talk about was the over-the-top celebrity weddings she went to in her day."

In her day. "Did Bunny ever act?"

"She would have liked to, but when she was a pop star, touring and recording took all her time. Then when she was no longer a star, no one wanted her."

"Did she ever mention knowing Julien Best?"

Ashleigh's eyes opened wide, and she sucked in a breath. "The actor? Gosh, no. I wish she did. I'd love an intro. I read recently he's leaving his wife for an actress less than half his age, and his wife, who's, like, ten years older than him and paid for everything to do with building his career, is planning to make the divorce as drawn out and painful for him as she possibly can. Why do you ask?"

"No reason. Just fishing."

"Has Julien Best ever played Sherlock? There's an idea. Maybe you could have him in here one day to, like, promote the store."

"Excuse me," a customer said, "I'm looking for a gift for a twelve-year-old girl. Can you recommend something in the way of a suitable book?"

"I'd be happy to," I said.

* * *

Business in the Emporium was slow during the early afternoon, so I decided to leave early for my meeting with George and get some grocery shopping done. I vastly overestimated how long that would take, so I was half an hour early driving into Hyannis. I don't know the town well, so I followed the instructions from my GPS to locate the restaurant. I found it easily and slipped into a parking space across the street. George said he had meetings today, so I didn't want to go in early. Instead, I'd take advantage of the break and enjoy exploring the town. The day was sunny but sharply cold, and I bundled myself up in winter gear, including a hat with a bouncing pompom on the top. It made me look ridiculous, I thought, but it kept my ears warm.

I studied the restaurant. As Andy said, it gave off twentieth-century vibes and not in a good way. Instead of capturing the popular midcentury modern feel, it felt dated and behind the times. That might not matter if the food was top notch, but according to the reviews I'd read, it was not.

The door opened, and a man I recognized stepped out: Martin, who cooked for Andy. I wondered what he was doing here. Interviewing for a position? Possibly. He had to know Andy wasn't happy with him, and he didn't appear to be all that happy working for Andy either. Instead of trying to improve his attitude and work habits, he might be looking for another job. None of my business: as long as he wasn't planning to quit while Andy was away on his honeymoon, Martin could do as he liked.

He stopped in the doorway, took a packet of cigarettes out of his pocket and, using the shelter of his hands and the restaurant awning against the cold wind, lit it. He tossed the match to one side and walked away.

Did he look like Julien Best, as Madison said? Maybe a little bit. I thought no more about it.

* * *

I was back at the Emporium before four to find Ashleigh tidying the display on the merchandise table. "Looks like you sold several items," I said.

"Some puzzles and mugs. A few books. It's been slow. You're back early."

"Total and complete waste of my time. You might as well go home. I'll close up. See you tomorrow."

Ashleigh skipped up the stairs humming "Get Me to the Church on Time.'

I'd learned far more from George about the joys of the restaurant business than I ever wanted to know. His conversation had been nothing but upbeat. No mention of the high failure rate, of one of his own places recently closing down, of the other two struggling. I mumbled something about taking the idea to Uncle Arthur, and then I fled. I'd been offered a cup of tea, and it arrived as a mug of lukewarm water with a tea bag on the side.

If I had been interested in investing in his restaurant, the preparation of the tea alone would have been enough to put me off.

When he did talk about Andy and the Blue Water Café, it was more along the lines of helping a buddy out than trying to muscle in. I got the impression George knew his businesses were struggling, and he was trying to overcompensate, if only to himself.

I learned nothing about any connections George might have had with Tina or Robbie. I did learn George was not a good prospect for a business partner. I'd have to think carefully about how to warn Bunny off. The feeling I got when George talked about her was he was genuinely interested in her and enjoyed her company. That was good, but it wouldn't be wise for her to get involved in his business, certainly not at first and not with what limited financial resources she had these days.

I didn't intend to remove George completely from my list of suspects, but I did move him down to the bottom.

I've said before a negative can be as valuable as a positive, and I tried to remind myself of that as I made my escape from his restaurant.

Chapter Twenty-Seven

The wedding day dawned bright and sunny. The air was crisp, but the wind was light. A gentle snow had fallen overnight, not enough to impede traffic, but sufficient to make everything clean and white and fresh.

It was, I thought as I took the dogs for their early morning stroll, the perfect day for a winter wedding. Uncle Arthur texted me yesterday as I'd been on my way back from my meeting with George.

Sorry. Love to Jayne and Andy. Ran into old buddy at airport. He's off to Majorca where he keeps a boat. Invited me for a sail. Managed to get new ticket. I'll get nice gift in Majorca.

I can't say I'd been entirely surprised. Uncle Arthur is somewhat like the wind: he goes where he goes.

Walk over, dogs happy, I gathered muesli, yogurt, and blueberries, made a big pot of tea, placed everything on the table, and made a phone call.

"Rise and shine," I said.

"I rose long ago and am shining even as we speak," Jayne said. "I don't know if I can stand the excitement. I've been out for a run. When I got back, I had too much energy to come inside, so I ran my route again."

"Perish the thought. Do you need anything before we go to your mum's? A run to the shops? A taxi to speed you to the border?" We were due at Leslie's at eleven to get Jayne ready. The church service began at three.

"No, Gemma. I'm fine. I am . . ." Her voice trailed off.

"Yes?" I prompted.

"So happy I don't know if I can bear it."

A substantial lump formed in my throat. I swallowed. *Emotions! That would never do.* "See you soon."

I sniffed and wiped at my eyes. When I recovered, I placed another call. It rang a couple of times before being answered, and Ryan's sleepy voice said, "Gemma? What time is it?"

"It's after nine, a perfectly acceptable time to be calling. Don't you have something to do today?"

"Andy's wedding? I haven't forgotten, Gemma. Big day, but hours to go yet. Anyway, I'm only the best man. You don't have to check to make sure I'm not planning a run for the border."

"Good joke. I said the same to Jayne not five minutes ago."

He chuckled, and I imagined him sitting up and settling back against the pillows. We talked a bit about our plans for the day, and then I said, "Anything happening with the Armstrong and Ellis cases?"

"Regarding Tina Armstrong, not a single thing. We don't have even the slightest of trails to follow. No indication anyone meant her any harm. Even though her folks live in West London, I get the feeling they weren't all that close to her. They told us she recently broke up with a boyfriend, but they never met him and don't know if they ever got his name. The relationship was, according to them anyway, that casual."

"Might it not have been, from his POV, anyway? Nothing like a man scorned."

"Hard to say. The parents say Tina initiated the breakup, but she gave them no indication he was threatening toward her or she was worried about anything in that regard. She didn't have many close friends, as in girlfriends. Most of her high school crowd moved away or started families and made new friends over the years. The people she met at her realtor's courses and prospective job were a lot older than her. I'm starting to come around to your line of thinking, Gemma. Her death was either self-inflicted or an accident."

"My thoughts on that vary. Any results from her phone?"

"Haven't heard yet. The techies are backed up. It should be sufficiently dried out by now, so they can chance turning it on. They tell us they'll get to it when they get to it."

"Unlikely to be any clues to be found there in any event."

"Which is why we're not calling in favors to have it rushed. As for your pal Robbie—"

"Never a friend of mine."

"We have a few tenuous leads. He was involved in things he shouldn't have been, but all low-level stuff."

"What sort of low-level stuff?"

"The sort of stuff that's confidential until discussed in court. Even though the guy's dead, I won't share the details, but I can say he wasn't into the level of criminal activity that should have caused anyone to bump him off—not yet at any rate, although he was heading that way. His new friends, however, are the sort to get angry quickly and to act on that anger without thinking. We're following a couple of leads."

"I'm glad to hear it. You're confident it doesn't have anything to do with Andy or the Blue Water Café? Or even Tina's death?"

"I wouldn't say confident, but such would appear to be the case. Andy's alibi is rock solid, but he was never a viable option anyway. In my opinion, at least. You can enjoy yourself today without worrying."

"I wasn't worrying."

"No, but you were asking questions."

"As is my natural state."

He laughed. "Don't I know it. Louise knows I'm off all day today and tomorrow, so she won't call me except in an emergency."

Ryan and I planned to have an "us" day tomorrow. Tonight, we'd be up until the wee hours at Jayne and Andy's reception, and we intended to enjoy a long lie-in tomorrow and then spend the day doing not much of anything, but doing it together.

"See you at the church," I said.

"Love you," he said.

Chapter Twenty-Eight

Jayne and Andy's wedding was about as close to perfect as you could get. I'm not usually one for girly things, but I enjoyed Jayne's excitement as she had her hair and makeup done and fussing over arranging her dress "just so." Jayne's sister-in-law, Christy, came to help and also to fuss. Leslie served champagne before we left, and we toasted the blushing bride.

Jayne was beyond stunning in a high-necked, long-sleeved gown of unadorned white satin. The bodice was closely fitted, cinched with a white fabric belt, the skirt flaring to her feet and spreading out behind her. She matched the dress with a white fake-fur cropped jacket for traveling to and from the church and reception and for the outdoor photographs. Her long blond hair was loosely tied back and secured with a sparkling clip; her mother's diamond earrings were in her ears. The mother of the bride was in burgundy velvet, and I wore a knee-length pale blue dress with a matching jacket.

Leslie wept copiously as we drove to the church in the hired limo. I might have had a tear in my eye myself. Jayne said she wished her dad could be with her today, and Leslie wept some more.

The church was an old one by Cape Cod, if not English, standards: aging stone, scarred wooden beams and scratched pews, stained glass windows. Sparkling snow was draped over the pointed roof like a fuzzy warm blanket; melting ice glimmered from the eves and the branches of surrounding trees. The sidewalk had been shoveled and de-iced, presenting no obstacle to Jayne's delicate white ballet flats.

The coat rack by the main doors was full, and once inside, we added our own, including Jayne's jacket, to the mix. Christy and I arranged Jayne's skirts, and Leslie wrapped her daughter in an embrace so tight we had to arrange the skirts again. Then we gripped our flowers, the music sounded, and we began the stately procession.

Christy and I preceded Jayne up the aisle. The bride followed us, her mother walking on one side of her and her brother, Jeff, on the other. Andy stood at the front, wearing a dark gray suit with a cobalt blue tie, his dark blond hair combed back, his smile enormous. Next to him, Ryan looked amazingly handsome in a well-cut suit with a tie the same blue as Andy's. Slightly behind the two men stood Andy's three sisters. Two of them wore dresses in the color of Andy's tie, and one wore a black trouser suit over a blue blouse. They smiled that fond, indulgent smile older sisters have for younger brothers.

The service was longer than I might have liked, but I sat quietly between Ryan and Jeff and tried not to fidget too much. Jayne and Andy had both grown up in West London, and they and their families knew an enormous number of people. The church was almost full. I recognized many faces from Leslie's charitable and community groups as well as assorted friends and relatives who'd been at Jayne's party. Mrs. Ramsbatten, escorted by Irene Talbot. Audrey and Madison sitting together.

Keith, the mob accountant, with his wife. Donald, once again dressed in full Victorian men's wear, complete with his beloved frock coat, which I'd returned to him. Andy's parents, wiping tears from their eyes. A handful of small children, shifting with excitement in their best clothes. The staff from the tea-room, along with some of Andy's workers, and Ashleigh and Gale.

Bunny had come with George. As I'd walked slowly down the aisle toward them, George gave me a wink. I suspected he was already calculating how much he'd ask Uncle Arthur for. Whereas Jayne and I closed our businesses for the day, the Blue Water Café would remain open. Andy invited his longtime employees to his wedding, but not many of the people on staff had been with him since the beginning. Turnover in the restaurant business is high.

Which reminded me of seeing Martin leaving George's place yesterday. Martin had looked pleased with himself, so I assumed the interview had gone his way. I had a sudden thought and twisted in my seat to look behind me. I had no idea how much notice Martin was required to give if he did find another job. Less than a week? Was George planning to lure Martin from Andy's restaurant while Andy was away? Leaving no one to cook and thus another opportunity for George to try to get his foot in the door, if not take over the Café completely?

Jayne's tearoom is quite different from a full-service restaurant. Smaller, offering mostly takeout, a limited menu, almost all the food prepared ahead of time. The couple of times I'd been in the kitchen of the Café when it was open, several people had been cooking. If Andy wasn't available and Martin walked out, could the remaining staff keep the place open? You'd think they'd be okay for a week. Wouldn't they?

I had an image of Martin as he stood in the doorway under the awning yesterday, lighting his cigarette.

His cigarette.

The minister droned on. Ryan shifted with boredom and took my hand. He tickled my palm with his index finger, and I tried not to giggle. Someone coughed. A second person took it up and then a third. A child began kicking the back of the pew in front of him. His father shushed him. Andy and Jayne smiled at each other. Still, the minister droned on

So many people here, in this church today, come together to celebrate two people they knew and loved. So many connections. A web of connections.

Thoughts flew through my head, crashing into each other, every one of them clamoring for my attention. Tina, whose death was increasingly looking as though it had not been a murder. Robbie's, whose definitely was. The police, in the persons of Ryan and Louise, weren't sure if the two incidents were related. I kept insisting how could they not be. Robbie and Tina had known each other in the past, but more to the point, these days they were part of that complicated web of connections. Six degrees of separation. Sometimes, far less than six.

I became aware of people getting to their feet. Ryan stood up and held out his hand. "Gemma?"

"What?"

"It's time to go. Wedding party first."

I jumped up. "Right. Let's go."

Jayne and Andy led the way down the aisle. Their parents followed, then the couple's siblings with their partners, and finally Ryan and me. I twitched with such impatience, Ryan threw me a look and whispered, "Are you okay, Gemma?"

"Fine. Perfectly fine. I wish they'd hurry up."

At last, we gathered up our coats and burst through the wide doors of the church into the late afternoon winter sunshine. The plan was for the wedding party to go to the harbor for pictures while the rest of the guests got the party started at the yacht club. As it was January, the gardens typically used for wedding photographs were not in bloom, so the photographer suggested the open ocean as a nice background for the formal pictures.

Before we did that, Jayne and Andy and their families posed on the church steps while guests lifted cameras and phones, children ran in circles across the lawns, and a few people headed for their cars.

It was getting colder as evening approached, and the sun was touching the tops of the trees to the west, and I was glad of my good winter coat.

I studied the crowd. Ashleigh was standing with Bunny and George. Despite what she told me yesterday, I'd feared Ashleigh wouldn't be able to resist the temptation to get into the "mood" and would wear a bridal dress. She was sure to have something suitable somewhere in the depths of that vast closet of hers. Or, at the worst, she would go all Miss Haversham. Instead, she was surprisingly subdued in a navy-blue pantsuit with a white blouse, black ankle boots, and a single gold hoop in each ear. Bunny, on the other hand, was decked out in pink tulle and lace. Pink and gray feathers adorned the fascinator on her head. She even had lace gloves on her hands.

"Nice service," I said to them. "Did you enjoy it?"

"She did rather go on," George said, before hastily adding, "But nice, yeah."

"Bunny, can I have a quick word?" I said.

"What about?"

"Please."

"Okay. Be right back," she said to Ashleigh and George. George eyed me suspiciously.

"It's nice to see you and George getting on," I said to Bunny, once we were out of earshot.

She smiled. "I like him. Nothing too serious yet, but early days. I know what you want to talk to me about, Gemma, but you don't need to. Ashleigh already told me it would not be a good idea for me to get involved in George's business affairs, not this early in a potential relationship. I informed her I am not a total fool. I am also not completely broke, but I have no intention of lending him money." She tossed her head, the feathers on her fascinator bobbing, and she gave me a wink. "Although I might call in a few favors from the old days. Get some nice pictures of my friends and me dining at George's place."

"That's good. Glad to hear it. But that's not what I want to talk to you about. You were supposed to have dinner with George last Wednesday. On Thursday morning, I asked Ashleigh how it had gone, and she said he had to postpone."

Bunny blinked at me. "What on earth does that have to do with anything?"

"Humor me. It was postponed until . . . when?"

"Thursday. We had such a lovely time that night, we went out on Friday also. Do you think I'm rushing into this, Gemma? I'm not as young as I once was, nor is George, but if we—"

"What did you do on Thursday, and at what time?"

"I still don't—"

"Please?"

"We went to his restaurant in Hyannis. He picked me up around seven-thirty and we arrived shortly before eight. We had a lovely, long meal, lingered over liqueurs, and then he called a taxi because he'd been drinking, and we went to my place." Her face colored slightly. "What happened after that, Gemma, I am absolutely not going to tell you."

"Thank you," I said.

George had an alibi for the time of Robbie's death. Judging by the blush on Bunny's cheeks and the twinkle in her eye, he had not been fleeing from me at ten-thirty on Thursday night.

Bunny returned to Ashleigh and George. Audrey, well wrapped in a long wool coat with big shiny gold buttons, approached Bunny and they exchanged greetings. Madison hung back, standing alone. I had a question for her too and hurried to join her.

"Lovely wedding," I said.

"Yeah, it was." She cracked a smile. "I'm glad I came. Weddings always make me happy, and Jayne's so beautiful. Look at the expression on Andy's face." She sighed. "I took a bunch of pictures for my Insta page. I'm thinking of announcing that winter weddings are going to be the new in-thing. I should be able to get some sponsorship out of that, don't you think? The dresses, in particular, need to be different than—"

"Would you do me a quick favor and think back to Jayne's party? You told me something the other night I've been wondering about."

"What?"

I asked her the question I'd been pondering throughout the wedding service. Satisfied with her answer, I had one more question before I left her. "You went down to the dock during the party, didn't you? Where you took a photo for your Instagram page?"

"What about it?"

"Was the gate open?"

"No. It had a fiddly little latch, but I wanted a shot straight across the water, not from above, so I worked on it a bit. And then . . . ta-da . . . it opened." She looked pleased with herself.

"Did you refasten the latch when you came back up?"

"I might have not bothered. I know what you're going to say. Yeah, I heard the cops asking about that. But so much was going on and everyone was talking all at once, and some people were crying. Audrey was acting weird. I guess I sorta forgot. Then later, when I remembered, I decided it didn't matter. I didn't want to confuse things, right? I took some pictures of the cops out on the deck stringing up crime scene tape and the like, but I decided not to use them. It wouldn't suit the image I'm trying to create. Might frighten some of my potential sponsors away."

"Which is obviously far more important than getting to the cause of a young woman's death. Thanks for your time." I left her and sought out Andy.

Who was, to nobody's surprise, preoccupied.

"Gemma," Jayne called to me. "Get over here. I want you in the pictures."

I handed my coat to a woman I didn't know, plastered on a smile, climbed the church steps, and took my place.

Finally, finally, a laughing Andy held up his hand. "We're going down to the harbor for some formal photos. Anyone who doesn't want to come and wants to get a head start on the party, they're expecting us at the Cape Cod Yacht Club. Mention my dad's name and you'll get a good seat."

A round of cheers, led by Pete Whitehall himself, went up. People began heading for their cars.

I needed to talk to Andy, but he was surrounded by well-wishers. Before I had a chance, he and Jayne got into the limo, gave us all a big wave, and drove off.

"Ready, Gemma?" Ryan asked.

"Yup. Let's go."

"Aren't you cold? Where's your coat?"

"My what? Oh, my coat. It's around here somewhere."

A woman handed it to me and I mumbled my thanks.

"Is something on your mind?" Ryan said. "You seem distracted all of a sudden."

I hesitated. I don't like to share my theories, not with anyone, when they're in a formative stage. But Ryan was asking, and he was well acquainted with the details of the case.

The drive from the church to the parking lot at the harbor takes about a minute and a half. Before I could make up my mind whether or not to confide in Ryan, we arrived. He'd barely switched off the engine before one of Andy's sisters appeared. "Let's get this done, buddy," she said. "It's getting cold, and a beer's waiting for me."

We got out of the car. I glanced across the water at the Blue Water Café. The fairy lights draped around its deck were on, reflecting off the dark water below. Light streamed through the windows. A shape moved across the kitchen windows and was gone.

Chapter Twenty-Nine

It was coming up to five, and the winter sun was low in the west. To the east, the ocean was a sheet of black, the first stars appearing above. The background would look marvelous in the photos. As everyone mingled, not sure where they should stand, whether to leave coats on or take them off, I approached Andy. I touched his arm and led him aside.

"Your place looks great from here. You should take some shots of this view for advertising. Tourist brochures and the like."

He nodded and looked across the water. "Good idea."

"I don't want to spoil the mood or anything, but I thought you should know I was in Hyannis yesterday on . . . another matter . . . and I saw Martin at George's place."

Andy shrugged. "Don't worry about it, Gemma. If Martin wants to seek employment elsewhere, he's welcome to it. He's a good cook, he has the potential to be a great chef, but he needs to learn he's not at the top of the ladder yet."

"Meaning?"

"He's lazy. Cuts corners. He mouths off too much."

"You're leaving him in charge this week."

"Only nominally in charge of the cooking. Rachel, my head bartender, will be keeping everything else running, and as long as Martin doesn't have any grand ideas for putting new things on the menu, my other cooks can handle anything else, if needed."

"Andy!" Pete called. "What's keeping you? Let's get this show on the road."

"Be right there, Dad."

"One thing quickly, and then I'll let you go," I said. "Can you give me an example, a recent example, of Martin slacking off?"

Andy studied my face. Then he looked over my shoulder to where everyone, including his new wife, waited impatiently for him. "Why are you asking, Gemma?"

"Indulge me, please."

"We had words at Jayne's party. Obviously, it was an important night for me, and I was trying to be the host, not the chef. I relied on Martin and he let me down. To be fair, we all have rough nights and personal problems sometimes get in the way, but something was eating at him that night."

"You've no idea what?"

"No, I didn't ask."

"Martin smokes, right?"

"Yeah, he does. Lots of people in the food business still smoke. A way of letting off tension. Or so they tell me."

"Did he go out onto the deck for this smoke?"

Andy looked at me in surprise. "How do you know that?"

"Just a guess. So he did?"

"Rachel told me she saw him going out onto the deck and lighting up. That's strictly not allowed."

"Even to take a break?"

"Of course, they can take a break. But not out on the deck. That area's for guests only. Staff have their own space."

"Did you tell the police this?"

"Tell them what?"

"That Martin was on the deck?"

His face crinkled in thought. "I can't say. I don't know if I mentioned him in particular. A lot of people were in and out all night and I mentioned that. I didn't think my cook's dissatisfaction with his job was pertinent. Do you think—?"

And that is why I have the reputation for solving cases the police cannot. Even when they're asked not to, people make assumptions about what they should say to the police or not. They don't want to waste anyone's time. They don't want to seem as though they're making something out of nothing or inadvertently getting someone in trouble. They decide on the spur of the moment, often under stress, whether a fact is pertinent or not. So they don't say something that might be important or, on the other hand, they flood the police with so much irrelevant information, it conceals the main point. Time passes, memories fade, details are forgotten, and the police have more than one case on their plate at any one time.

Whereas no one ever worries about wasting my time, nor do they fear they'll get an innocent person in trouble by telling me secrets. On more than one occasion, they've told me what they consider mere gossip of the sort they'd never share with the authorities. And that gossip turns out to be the key to the entire case.

Jayne slipped her arm through Andy's. "What are you two looking so serious about?"

"Nothing," I said.

Jayne tugged at Andy's arm. "If you don't come right now, your dad's threatening to leave."

"Go," I said. "I'm only speculating here. Everything can wait."

"That means you too, Gemma. You need to be in the pictures." Jayne let go of Andy's arm and took mine. The wind stirred her fair hair and soft tendrils drifted across her face. She tucked them back with a laugh. "Come along, Gemma. Don't dawdle."

Chapter Thirty

More than once, the photographer had to order me to smile and to stop fidgeting.

Finally, the photographs were taken and everyone headed to the warmth of their cars.

I put my coat back on and lingered by the railing of the pier, watching lights flicker in the Blue Water Café as the first of the dinner guests arrived.

"Okay, something's up." Ryan stood beside me. "Spill."

I spilled.

"I can't act on that," he said. "Way too nebulous. Yes, I can haul this person down to the station, ask a few more direct questions. No guarantee it will lead to anything, and if not, we have nothing. Are you really wanting me to do that tonight?"

"No. Maybe I'll have a quick chat. If I'm a few minutes late arriving at the reception, no one will notice. You go ahead. I'll grab a cab."

"I am not going ahead, Gemma. Nor am I letting you do this alone." Ryan sighed. "If you don't get that curiosity of yours satisfied, you'll be restless all night. Let's do it. As this is not exactly an official visit, I'll stay in the background. Observe and listen only. If you do learn anything, promise me you'll hand it all to Louise."

"Promise," I said sweetly.

Ryan rolled his eyes and we headed for the lights and laughter of the Blue Water Café.

Chapter Thirty-One

It was early, and the restaurant was largely empty as it likely would be for most of a Monday night in January. The hostess greeted us with a confused look. "Gemma? What are you doing here? Aren't you supposed to be at Andy's wedding?"

"We're on our way," I said. "I want to talk to Martin about something first. Is he in?"

"Yeah. He's in the kitchen. Want me to call him?"

"No, thanks. I know the way. Ryan?"

"After you," he said. Clearly, Ryan was not at all pleased with this development, but he trusted my instincts. He sorta trusted my instincts. Someday, he's said to me on more than one occasion, I'll go too far. What he'll have to do then, he never says.

The kitchen was in full dinner preparation frenzy. Cooks dodged each other, fat spat from frying pans, water bubbled on the red-hot elements of the gas stove. Martin Eagerton was chopping onions, knife moving so fast it was a blur. He looked up when we came in, and he did not smile. "You again? Andy's not here."

"I know that. I've come to talk to you."

He went back to the onions. "Not a good time."

"I want to ask you about Tina Armstrong and what you said to her the night she died."

The knife stopped moving, but Martin did not put it down. "What business is that of yours?" He glanced behind me at Ryan. Ryan said nothing.

"None, except that, as I've been told many times, I'm the curious sort. And I am curious about that. Humor me."

"You brought the cops with you to satisfy your curiosity?"

"A coincidence. This is my date for Andy and Jayne's wedding, and he insisted on tagging along."

"In that case, get lost. I'm busy."

All around us the staff were obviously listening, while pretending to continue going about the business of getting food on the table. Tables.

"Okay. We'll talk here, then. The night of Jayne's party, you went out to the deck at least once, even though staff aren't allowed there when the restaurant's open. Tina was having a cigarette. You spoke to her. She died not long after that conversation. That's if she didn't die then and there."

"Is that true, Martin?" a waiter asked.

Martin threw down the knife. "Okay, you win. Let's get out of here. Mandy, get these onions caramelized. I'll be right back. Anyone thinks they can slack off tonight, you'll be looking for another job tomorrow."

He headed for the door. A wave of whispered conversation swept through the kitchen behind him.

"Why don't we go out onto the deck," I said. "No one's out there at the moment."

I didn't wait for Martin to agree or not, but I led the way. He followed me, and Ryan brought up the rear. As darkness arrived the temperature dropped rapidly. The wooden boards of the deck were beginning to take on a thin layer of ice. I placed my wedding-suitable, high heel clad feet with care.

Ryan and I were in our coats, but all Martin had on was his indoor clothes. I wouldn't be long, though, One or two quick questions, and I'd decide where to go from there.

I looked out over the calm ocean. The lights of the town twinkled in the distance. Below me, the dark, sleek shape of a seal bobbed in the water. I turned around. "You and Tina dated recently," I said. "Nothing too serious, not on her part anyway, and it didn't last long. Why didn't you tell the police that?"

Martin shrugged. He didn't appear to be particularly concerned at my question. "They didn't ask."

I didn't know, not for sure, that Martin had been the ex-boyfriend Tina's parents told the police about. But everything else I surmised flowed from that premise, and so I acted on it.

"They didn't ask me if I'd dated her either, but if I had I might have mentioned it," I pointed out.

"You were asked, along with all the other staff, if you'd seen anything out on the deck that night we needed to know," Ryan said.

"Yeah, well, I didn't see anything out on the deck you needed to know. I spoke to Tina, briefly, and then went back to work. She came in behind me. I didn't want to get involved in whatever happened after that. We see a heck of a lot of things in this line of work."

"She came inside after you? Are you sure about that?" I said.

"I'm sure. I shut the door in her face, not feeling much like being a gentleman. When I turned the corner to the kitchen, she was coming in."

"What time was this?"

"I can't say for sure. Nine-thirty maybe. Main courses had been served."

About half an hour before she died.

"Did you ask her to give the ring back?" I asked.

"How'd you—?" Martin snapped his mouth shut.

"The ring she was wearing that night looked to be an heirloom of some sort. Not particularly valuable as jewels go, but it might have had some sentimental importance to someone. As I said, I'm the curious sort, and I recently saw that ring in a picture on a social media account. An elderly lady wore it to your brother's wedding, which took place a few years ago. Your grandmother, I assume."

The ring had simply flashed past as I flipped through social media pictures, and I paid no particular attention to it at the time. I'd forgotten what I so recently told Jayne: the little things can be the most important. As they say, the devil can be found in the details. Only when Madison told me Martin resembled the actor Julien Best, did I start to wonder how Madison knew what Martin looked like. Yes, the kitchen staff took seats in the restaurant after the police had been called, but Madison specifically said she noticed the resemblance *before* Tina died. Guests didn't normally mingle with the kitchen staff at a restaurant. If Martin had left the kitchen and gone onto the deck for a smoke—as Andy told me he did—he would have walked past the bar and Madison saw him then.

Once I remembered that, down the rabbit hole of memory I went. The ring on Martin's grandmother's hand. What appeared to be the same ring on Tina's. An antique ring that suited the elderly lady but was totally out of place on Tina.

If Tina had Martin's grandmother's ring, he had to have given it to her. And the only reason he would give it to her would be if they dated at one time. The relationship hadn't lasted. According to her parents, she ended it.

He'd gone out on the deck, where he wasn't supposed to go, while Tina was still alive.

Martin dug in his breast pocket and pulled out a lighter and pack of cigarettes. He took one out and lit it. "Yeah," he said at last. "I gave Tina my grandma's ring. She refused to give it back when she dumped me. Frankly, I didn't much care that she dumped me—she wasn't worth the hassle—but I knew my mom would be out of her mind if she found out I'd given the ring away. Like you said, it wasn't worth a lot, but it's been in my grandma's family for a long time and she intended for me to give it to my wife someday."

"Tina refused to return it."

"Yeah, she did. She said she liked it. She said I'd given it to her, so it was hers now."

I studied Martin carefully as he spoke. He was alert, not entirely relaxed, obviously aware of Ryan standing behind him, but not frightened or worried at the direction my questions were taking. He took a drag on his cigarette and half turned his head, to avoid blowing smoke directly into my face. Thoughtful of him.

"What did you do then?" I asked, also aware of Ryan, tense, alert, ready to move.

"I still don't see how this is any of your business, but you'll follow me into the kitchen and start making accusations in front of everyone if I don't give you what you want. So let's get this over with. I started arguing with her. I'll admit I yelled at her. Told her she had no right to keep it. Told her what I thought of her. She laughed at me, made a crude joke, so I made a grab for her. She pulled away, and I could see I'd frightened her. I'm not proud of that, and I can honestly say I don't know what would have happened next, but a bunch of guys at the bar started laughing at some joke and I was reminded of where we were. I turned around and walked away. I went back to work. I promise, she was alive when I last saw her."

I studied his face. I saw no fear there, only wariness. He knew he hadn't killed her, so he wasn't afraid of being arrested for Tina's murder.

"Why didn't you tell us this?" Ryan asked.

For the first time, Martin turned to face Ryan. "Because I know how you bunch operate. You would have blown it up out of all proportion. You would have stopped trying to find out who killed her and started harassing me. Like you're doing now."

"Hardly harassing. Gemma is asking you to tell us what you did and saw that night."

"And now I have. Okay?" Martin's voice was steady. He was annoyed at being found out, irritated at having, as he saw it, his time wasted.

"What happened after you left Tina?" I asked.

"I went back to work and didn't think about her again. It was a busy night, right? You know that. You were here. I didn't leave the kitchen until someone said a guest had gone into the water and the cops had been called. Even then, I didn't know it was her. Not for a while longer." His face fell. "I was sorry, sorry she died. She didn't deserve that. I didn't kill her, and I don't know who did."

Ryan nodded. He was thinking along the same lines as me. It was possible Martin was a heck of a good actor and he was stringing us a story, but if that was the case, he'd break eventually.

"I need you to come down to the station and tell Detective Estrada everything you've told us," Ryan said. "You're working now, so it can wait until morning. If you don't . . ." He left the sentence hanging.

"Thanks. I'll do that. Promise." All the tension flooded out of Martin's body. The muscles in his neck relaxed, his shoulders sagged. He threw his cigarette over the railing and started to walk away.

"One more thing," I said.

He turned back to me, slightly wary, not too concerned yet.

"Did anyone observe this altercation between you and Tina?"

His eyes narrowed. He took a quick glance at Ryan. He wiped his hands on his trousers. "No. I mean I didn't see anyone else out here."

"You didn't see anyone at the time, but later you learned someone had been watching. This person saw the whole thing. Am I right?"

He shifted his feet. His eyes moved rapidly back and forth, subconsciously seeking escape.

"Robbie Ellis saw you arguing with Tina. He saw you grab her. You didn't kill her, but you didn't tell the police about your argument with her. Robbie didn't tell the police about it either. The only reason he wouldn't have done so was if he intended to use the information for his own benefit."

The blood drained from Martin's face. His eyes continued moving. He didn't look at me. He snorted. "Ellis? That loser?"

"That loser. The one with a prior record for blackmail. Detective Ashburton, you might want to ask Martin here where he was last Thursday around ten o'clock. Now that I'm facing him, I'm pretty sure he was the man I saw fleeing Robbie Ellis's apartment. Based on that evidence, you should be able to get a warrant to search his home. Compare any shoes you find there with the muddy treads left on Robbie's carpet." No shoe treads had been left in the apartment, but I glanced down, as though I was checking out Martin's shoe size.

That was a mistake.

He let out a roar and leapt toward me. I yelped and jumped backward. Ryan moved, but he was too fast, not taking care, and his foot skidded on a patch of ice. His legs shot out from under him and he fell. Hard. I yelled, but before I could move, my own feet left the deck.

No one had lifted Tina Armstrong up and thrown her over the railing. But Martin was strong enough to have done so, and I'd foolishly stood too close to the edge.

Next thing I knew, I was in the icy sea. I went under and freezing water rushed into my lungs. I was wrapped in a heavy wool coat, which began absorbing water immediately, pulling me further down. I tried to kick, to push myself up toward the light, but the weight dragged at me. Panic began to take control. If I let it, I'd be done for. Thankfully, the coat was not buttoned. I struggled to get my arms out. If anything, the water was colder than the last time I'd been in it, and I hadn't had time to clear my lungs and take in a fresh gulp of precious air. Over my head, the waters splashed and churned. Pieces of wood dropped next to me. Legs appeared. Legs kicking, arms flailing. Bodies struggling.

One arm out of the coat, then the second. It drifted down, and I kicked up. I was almost out of air and rapidly losing contact with my limbs. I scarcely knew which way was up, and I didn't know if my legs and arms would obey my commands. With one enormous push of effort, my head cleared the surface. I sucked in air, tried to blink salty water out of my eyes, and looked around me. Ryan was a few feet away, struggling with Martin. "Help, help!" I yelled. "Woman overboard! Man in the water!"

Faces appeared at the railing. An orange ring hit the water not far from me. I swam toward it, although by now I could hardly swim, just flail about in the icy ocean. I could vaguely hear voices calling encouragement to me.

I grabbed the life preserver and clung to it. I kicked hard, trying to turn around, trying to locate Ryan. It was hard enough keeping myself above water, never mind fighting for my life as he was. I spotted him and Martin, still grappling with each other. Martin put his hand on the top of Ryan's head and pushed. Ryan went under, but he managed to break free and swim a few strokes away. He came up not far from me, spitting and choking.

Martin's dark head was slowly heading for the shore. Tonight, the ocean was calm, with little in the way of undertow, but he was struggling as the cold and the shock took over.

"Over here! Over here! Gemma!" People had run down to the dock. They jumped up and down, trying to attract my attention.

I looked at Ryan. Lips blue, face white, treading water in front of me. "He won't get far," I said. Although the words might not have come out as I intended.

The scream of sirens. Doors slammed. Voices yelled.

Ryan nodded. He took the other side of my life preserver and together we kicked toward the outstretched hands.

* * *

Once again, I was in the ladies' room of the Blue Water Café, trying to dry off with the help of the weak heat of the hand dryer. My lovely dress had been stripped off me, and as soon as I was reasonably dry, I'd been stuffed into a waiter's uniform about two sizes too large. Medics attended to me and helped to warm me, but I refused a ride to the hospital.

"I have to get to a wedding." My coat had sunk to the bottom of the ocean, taking my phone along with it.

"I hope you're not the bride," the medic said.

"No. Just bridesmaid."

"That's okay, then," she said. "My colleague tells me Detective Ashburton's saying much the same. Not that he's a bridesmaid, though."

Finally, I was allowed out of the ladies' room. The hostess kept to one side of me, the medic to the other, but I didn't need the help. As I'd warmed up, feeling had flooded back into my legs and I was able to walk if I moved slowly and carefully.

Curious diners watched as I came into the main room. I gave them a jaunty wave. A waiter handed me a glass of brandy, which I gratefully accepted.

Outside, bright lights had been brought in and figures moved about on the deck. A section of the railing had been shattered.

Ryan came out of the men's room accompanied by a scowling Louise Estrada.

"Are you allowed in there?" I said to her.

She didn't bother to answer. A second glass appeared in Ryan's hand.

"Detective Ashburton told me what went down out there," Estrada said. "Seeing as to how all the drama, so to speak, took place outside, I've said the restaurant can remain open, although the cooks might have trouble concentrating on their duties. The guests have been informed service will be slow and minimal for the rest of the evening."

I didn't think anyone would mind. They looked quite pleased at being able to watch the drama while enjoying their drinks and dinner.

"We'll talk in my car," Estrada said. "And then, as Detective Ashburton has managed to convince me, against my better judgment, I will let you two go to the wedding."

"Martin?"

"He's been taken to the hospital with signs of hypothermia. And that's where you two should be."

"We have a wedding to get to," Ryan said.

"Unbelievable," she said.

Chapter Thirty-Two

Estrada offered to drive us to the yacht club, but first she had a few questions. We sat in her car, the heater going full blast, and related the story.

"I don't doubt what you're saying," Estrada said, "but was Martin truly that naive? If the photo Robbie took shows what you think it shows, it's nowhere near grounds for laying a murder charge. Why didn't he just tell Robbie what he could do with his picture?"

"More a matter, I think, of him deciding he'd had enough of Robbie." Before I could continue, she said, "Hold on. Call coming in."

Estrada got out of the car to take the call. When she came back, she gave me a sideways look.

"I don't know why we bother sometimes," she said at last. "Gemma was right, as she usually is. Much as I hate to say it."

"As you usually say," I said. "Thank you. Although I must confess, I'm forced to ask what I'm right about. I was not right about Martin. Not until the very last minute." I believed Martin when he said he hadn't killed Tina, but the moment he turned to leave us, his relief was so obvious, I wondered what he'd done he feared us finding out. And then I remembered Robbie. Poor dumb Robbie and his blackmail tendencies. Robbie had seen Martin arguing with Tina not long before she died. Robbie's phone had not been found, which almost certainly meant his killer had taken it. It was possible, likely even, he'd taken a picture of Martin and Tina arguing. Maybe even one of Martin lunging for her. Had he asked Martin for a few bucks or he'd show the pictures to the cops? Had Martin gone to Robbie's that night to pay him off and they argued? Or had Martin realized blackmail rarely ended with the first demand?

More likely, I thought, Martin simply didn't like to be taken advantage of, and not by someone he considered a loser. I'd seen the two of them sniping at each other at Jayne's party. The animosity between them was obvious. Knowing Robbie. I considered it entirely likely he'd goaded Martin with the threat of going to the police with his photo and his accusations. For Martin was that simply a step too far? Very possible.

As for the photo itself, it showed nothing incriminating, and the police would have realized that right away.

Martin had argued with Tina, yes, but she'd been seen alive after that. Any photos on Robbie's phone would have a time stamp on them. Robbie's blackmail attempt was useless.

His death had been useless.

What a mess.

Leaving me with the question as to who, if anyone, killed Tina. I tried not to give Estrada too smug a grin. I'd been right from the very beginning, but I'd allowed others to muddle my thinking. I'd try to avoid that in the future.

"That call confirmed Tina's death was an accident, didn't it?" I said.

"Yeah. Finally, someone got into her phone. They found an outgoing message that hadn't left her WhatsApp yet. The techies suspect she pressed Send, but it hadn't been transmitted before she hit the water, killing the signal." Estrada handed me the phone so I could read the photograph that had been sent to her. Ryan leaned in.

The text was a mess of bad grammar, misspelled words, autocorrect that didn't quite work, but parsing carefully I was able to understand the essence of it.

I should never have come. This is hideously embarrassing. Andy's obviously head over heels about that baker, and so be it. Let him go. Plenty more fish in the sea, right? I'll worry about that tomorrow. Now I'm going to do what I always do when I'm down and have a swim. Love me some cold water! Talk more tomorrow.

Ryan let out a long breath but said nothing.

"Tina was a keen swimmer according to her family and friends," Estrada said. "She dove competitively in school and took part in charity polar dips; she surfed in California. She'd had way too much to drink that night; she was humiliated and embarrassed. Not thinking clearly. That she had her phone on her seemed to indicate she hadn't gone in on purpose, but if she was acting out of drunken instinct—"

"She texted her friend, put her phone in her bag, and jumped over the railing," Ryan finished the sentence.

"It's only a few yards to shore," I said, "if she had experience swimming in cold water, she thought she could make it. She must have misjudged the distance in the dark, hit her head on the dock, rolled into the water, and from there, she didn't have a chance."

We sat quietly for a while. Finally, Estrada said, "I have to go to the hospital, check up on Martin. You still want me to drop you at the yacht club?"

"Yes, please," Ryan said.

* * *

We were slightly late arriving at Jayne's reception. And not exactly appropriately dressed. At least the chef's uniform Ryan wore fitted him reasonably well. Although I don't know who Marion is. Or was.

The flip-flops on my feet were appropriately named. They were too big and flopped like clown's shoes as I walked. I folded the waistband of my trousers over three times to try to get them to stop falling down. As we entered the Cape Cod Yacht Club, I attempted to avoid looking at myself in the mirror. In that I failed. My hair was a rat's nest of hastily dried and not styled curls. My eye makeup ran in streaks down my cheeks and my skin was as pale as . . . as pale as though I'd been dunked in freezing water.

I glanced at Ryan. Even without the makeup and the curls, he didn't look much better. I giggled.

He stopped walking and looked at me. He grinned.

I laughed. Ryan laughed.

And there, as we roared with laughter, an alternately furious and worried Jayne and Andy found us.

"You call this being delayed?" Jayne said.

Ryan's phone had gone with Estrada, who promised to dry it out. She lent him hers while he was warming up, so he could call Andy and do what he could to explain our tardiness. Andy had already heard from his bartender what was going on, and his staff promised to do the very best they could under the circumstances.

As we walked into the ballroom, everyone stared at us, open-mouthed.

"We fell in," I said. "No harm done."

"Didn't want to miss any more of the party," Ryan said. "So we didn't take the time to go home to change. Borrowed clothes."

"Dinner is about to be served," Andy said. "Everyone, please, take your seats."

"I demand an exclusive," Irene Talbot said. "I can't believe I came straight here instead of going down to the harbor for the photos and I missed it all."

"The department will be putting out a statement in the morning," Ryan said. "Perhaps Gemma will give you the finer details."

"She never speaks to the press," Irene said.

"Quite right," I said.

"Anyone else," Mrs. Ramsbatten said to me, "I'd ask why they went for an evening dip, but as it's you, I'll not bother. Arthur texted me a few minutes ago. Said he's been trying to contact you, but your phone is unavailable."

"It's swimming with the fishes, Mrs. R.," I said.

She rolled her eyes. "I'll reply to that effect. He wants you to extend his best wishes to the happy couple and his regrets that he's unable to attend."

"I'll mention that, thanks."

We found our seats. Ryan and I were at the head table. I looked out over the ballroom, beautifully decorated in shades of blue, Jayne's favorite color. More people were checking their phones than was perhaps polite at a formal dinner, but word of tonight's activity was spreading. Irene typed frantically. Even Mrs. Ramsbatten was checking her phone, likely filling Uncle Arthur in on the evening's events. Heads dipped toward others and excited whispers were exchanged.

I smiled serenely.

The meal was delicious, the wine excellent, the speeches short. I'd had to dispense with my sodden bra, and the cheap black shirt I'd been given was itchy. I tried to forget about it and not fidget too much. Ryan's and my attire might ruin some of the photos, but that couldn't be helped now.

When it was my turn, I stood to make my own speech. I hoisted my trousers before saying how happy I was that Jayne and Andy were in my life and I wished them many marvelous years ahead. I tried to make a joke about baking, but it fell rather flat. Jokes have never been my strong suit. I passed on Uncle Arthur's wishes, along with those of my sister, Pippa, and her husband, Grant Thompson. As I sat down, Ryan squeezed my hand. "Never mind," he whispered. "I thought it was funny."

* * *

Dinner over, speeches given, toasts made, the waiters cleared the tables and the room was prepared for dancing. The DJ played a great selection of music, something suitable for all age groups.

I'm as good a dancer as I am a comedian, so I stayed in my seat enjoying another glass of champagne while Ryan approached Mrs. Ramsbatten to ask for a dance.

When everyone was up and moving to the music, Jayne slipped into the seat beside me. Her face was flushed, her smile broad, her eyes glowing. "They're saying an arrest has been made for Robbie's murder."

"Yes."

"Can I assume that's why you were . . . delayed?"

"Yes."

"Tina's too?"

"No. Tina's death was an accident."

Some of the smile faded, and Jayne dipped her head.

I put my hand on her arm. "Let's not talk about that tonight. Tonight's about happiness and love and friendship, and all that good stuff."

She smiled at me. "You need to have a dance."

I lifted my leg. The flip-flop hung off my toe. "My shoes are not suitable."

She stood up and pulled me after her. "Too bad. Andy! Gemma needs a dance partner."

Andy left his mother and approached us. He gave me a deep bow, sweeping his right arm before him. "Madam."

"If I must," I said.

We sort of bobbed up and down for a few minutes, and then Andy led the way off the dance floor to a quiet corner. We stood together for a few moments, watching the dancers move, some with more style than others. "I'm guessing Martin won't be back at work any time soon," Andy said at last.

"Unlikely."

"On the bright side, they didn't close my place tonight and send all my customers out into the night."

"Be thankful for small mercies."

"What happened?" he asked. I filled him in.

"Poor Tina. I wish I'd realized—"

"Don't go there," I said. "Nothing that happened to either her or Robbie is your fault in any way. She showed up where she knew she wasn't welcome, and she finally realized that. Her text to her friend was mumbled but surprisingly upbeat. She knew she'd made a mistake; she saw how much you love Jayne and she was ready to turn the page. Unfortunately, before she could do that, she made a serious miscalculation."

"Sad."

"Yes. Yes, it is."

We watched Bunny and George dance past us. Bunny moved like the pop star she'd been. George moved like a marathon runner. The two styles did not complement each other, and Andy and I laughed.

"George has offered to lend me a cook for next week, an extra hand while I'm away,"

"Do you need one?"

"I might. Either all my customers will stay away permanently because of the police attention we've been attracting lately, or I'll be full every night because people want to offer their support. Martin was looking for a new job anyway. He must have realized he and I were not going to get along. He had an interview with George. Moot point now."

"I'm not too sure about George."

"George is okay, Gemma. Jayne told me he was in the tearoom the other day, being a downer about how hard the restaurant life is. That's just George. One of the world's biggest pessimists. Always look on the worst possible side, he says, and you won't be disappointed. I know he tells that story about me supposedly burning down the burger joint so I could have the space for my restaurant. There's not a shred of truth in the story, and he knows it. He thinks of himself as a great raconteur."

"It's not funny, Andy."

"No, I guess not. He knows he's running out of time. His creditors are circling. His places suffered in the pandemic, like everyone else's, but he can't seem to bring them back. He never had much business sense; he was able to get his start only because of money he inherited. He wants me to partner with him in setting up a new place."

"And?"

"I told him I'll think about it while I'm away. He needs help creating menus, finding good cooks with good reputations. I can do that."

"Do you want to?"

"Always up for a challenge." He watched Jayne, dancing with his father, laughing at something he said. "Whatever happens, I have Jayne by my side now. And that means I can do anything."

Despite my inclination not to dance, I found myself doing a substantial amount of it as the evening progressed. I enjoyed myself, but before long the events of the day began catching up to me.

When I was momentarily on my own, I went in search of Ryan. I found him at a table by the bar, enjoying a whiskey with Audrey and Mrs. Ramsbatten.

Ryan slipped his arm around my waist. "Ms. Whitehall has been telling me some stories."

"Every word of which is true," Audrey said. "I intend to change the focus of my book."

"Why and to what?" I asked.

"Somehow, Sandra McAllister got word of what I was writing." Audrey's lips tightened as she looked across the room to where Madison was sitting by herself, typing away on her phone. "She is threatening legal action if I try to imply that she, or people in her employ, paid off a police officer to cover a crime committed by her husband. I told her I have absolutely no idea why she'd think I'd do such a thing. Irrelevant, as I no longer fear Sandra. She has enough problems of her own. No, young Tina's death was sad and tragic. I'll let her rest in peace. A simple memoir of my life and times, the people I knew, should suffice. I have knowledge of plenty of old scandals I can revive. The sort of stuff people love to read but won't cause anyone any harm. Not anymore." She finished her drink and put the glass on the table. "It's time for me to be off. It was lovely meeting you, Gemma. If you ever find yourself in California, do look me up. I'm in need of a good research assistant." Another glance at Madison. "I will not be attempting to become an influencer."

"Tempted?" Ryan asked me after Audrey had taken her leave.

I kissed the top of his head. "I could be a good gossip columnist. Too bad I have absolutely no intention of going to California."

"I wonder if there's a need for an influencer for the over-eighties set," Mrs. Ramsbatten said. "The best places to get your hearing aid repaired, the most fashionable walker and cane shops."

"Give it a try," I said.

"I have the necessary computer equipment and technical skills, yes. Unfortunately, too many members of my intended audience do not. Perhaps an idea for another day." She held up her empty glass. "I do believe I'll have another, young man."

Ryan took the glass and stood up. When Mrs. Ramsbatten had been served, he said to me, "Feel like a dance?"

"I'd rather—" I wanted to suggest we slip quietly away, but before I could finish my sentence Ryan's eyes fell on something happening behind me and his eyes lit up. He rubbed his hands together. "Great. Looks like they're bringing out the dessert buffet. Sorry, Gemma, were you about to say something?"

"It'll keep. There's always time for dessert."

Acknowledgements

My good friend and much-loved mystery maven Cheryl Freedman always gives me the benefit of her keen editor's eye for early versions of my manuscripts, and I am grateful for her help and continuing support, not only to me but also to the wider Canadian crime-writing community.

Thanks also to Sandy Harding, who pointed out all my errors and omissions and general goofs. As well as to the good people at Crooked Lane Books and my marvellous agent, Kim Lionetti of Bookends.

Acknowledgements